UNNATURAL DEATH

Miss Agatha Dawson, an elderly spinster suffering from cancer, passes away in her bed. Her GP, surprised by the suddenness of her death and unsatisfied as to its cause, orders and performs a post-mortem — which reveals no sign of foul play. But a scandal arises nonetheless. The locals, seeing the doctor's actions as tantamount to accusing Miss Dawson's niece and nurse of murder, ostracise him to the point where he sells his practice and leaves . . . Lord Peter Wimsey, upon hearing the tale, is intrigued, and mounts his own investigation. Then one of the old woman's maids turns up dead . . .

Books by Dorothy L. Sayers
Published in Ulverscroft Collections:

WHOSE BODY?
CLOUDS OF WITNESS
THE UNPLEASANTNESS AT THE
BELLONA CLUB

DOROTHY L. SAYERS

UNNATURAL DEATH

A Lord Peter Wimsey Mystery

Complete and Unabridged

ULVERSCROFT
Leicester

First published in Great Britain in 1927 by
Ernest Benn
London

This Ulverscroft Edition
published 2018
by arrangement with
Hodder & Stoughton
An Hachette UK Company
London

A catalogue record for this book is available from the British Library.

ISBN 978–1–4448–3752–0

Published by
F. A. Thorpe (Publishing)
Anstey, Leicestershire

Set by Words & Graphics Ltd.
Anstey, Leicestershire
Printed and bound in Great Britain by
T. J. International Ltd., Padstow, Cornwall

This book is printed on acid-free paper

Contents

Part One

THE MEDICAL PROBLEM

*'But how I caught it, found it, or came by it,
What stuff 'tis made of, whereof it is born, I
am to learn.'*
THE MERCHANT OF VENICE

1

Overheard

'The death was certainly sudden, unexpected, and to me mysterious.'
Letter from Dr Paterson to the Registrar in the case of Reg. v Pritchard

'But if he thought the woman was being murdered — '

'My dear Charles,' said the young man with the monocle, 'it doesn't do for people, especially doctors, to go about 'thinking' things. They may get into frightful trouble. In Pritchard's case, I consider Dr Paterson did all he reasonably could by refusing a certificate for Mrs Taylor and sending that uncommonly disquieting letter to the registrar. He couldn't help the man's being a fool. If there had only been an inquest on Mrs Taylor, Pritchard would probably have been frightened off and left his wife alone. After all, Paterson hadn't a spark of real evidence. And suppose he'd been quite wrong — what a dustup there'd have been!'

'All the same,' urged the nondescript young man, dubiously extracting a bubbling-hot Helix Pomatia from its shell, and eyeing it nervously before putting it in his mouth, 'surely it's a clear case of public duty to voice one's suspicions.'

'Of *your* duty — yes,' said the other. 'By the way, it's not a public duty to eat snails if *you* don't like 'em. No, I thought you didn't. Why wrestle with a harsh fate any longer? Waiter, take the gentleman's snails away and bring oysters instead . . . No — as I was saying, it may be part of *your* duty to have suspicions and invite investigation and generally raise hell for everybody, and if you're mistaken nobody says much, beyond that you're a smart, painstaking officer though a little overzealous. But doctors, poor devils! are everlastingly walking a kind of social tight-rope. People don't fancy calling in a man who's liable to bring out accusations of murder on the smallest provocation.'

'Excuse me.'

The thin-faced young man sitting alone at the next table had turned round eagerly.

'It's frightfully rude of me to break in, but every word you say is absolutely true, and mine is a case in point. A doctor — you can't have any idea how dependent he is on the fancies and prejudices of his patients. They resent the most elementary precautions. If you dare to suggest a post-mortem, they're up in arms at the idea of 'cutting poor dear So-and-so up', and even if you only ask permission to investigate an obscure disease in the interest of research, they imagine you're hinting at something unpleasant. Of course, if you let things go, and it turns out afterwards there's been any jiggery-pokery, the coroner jumps down your throat and the newspapers make a butt of you, and, whichever way it is, you wish you'd never been born.'

'You speak with personal feeling,' said the man with the monocle, with an agreeable air of interest.

4

'I do,' said the thin-faced man, emphatically. 'If I had behaved like a man of the world instead of a zealous citizen, I shouldn't be hunting about for a new job today.'

The man with the monocle glanced round the little Soho restaurant with a faint smile. The fat man on the right was unctuously entertaining two ladies of the chorus; beyond him, two elderly habitués were showing their acquaintance with the fare at the 'Au Bon Bourgeois' by consuming a Tripes à la Mode de Caen (which they do very excellently there) and a bottle of Chablis Moutonne 1916; on the other side of the room a provincial and his wife were stupidly clamouring for a cut off the joint with lemonade for the lady and whisky and soda for the gentleman, while at the adjoining table, the handsome silver-haired proprietor, absorbed in fatiguing a salad for a family party, had for the moment no thoughts beyond the nice adjustment of the chopped herbs and garlic. The head waiter, presenting for inspection a plate of Blue River Trout, helped the monocled man and his companion and retired, leaving them in the privacy which unsophisticated people always seek in genteel teashops and never, never find there.

'I feel,' said the monocled man, 'exactly like Prince Florizel of Bohemia. I am confident that you, sir, have an interesting story to relate, and shall be greatly obliged if you will favour us with the recital. I perceive that you have finished your dinner, and it will therefore perhaps not be disagreeable to you to remove to this table and entertain us with your story while we eat. Pardon

5

my Stevensonian manner — my sympathy is none the less on that account.'

'Don't be an ass, Peter,' said the nondescript man. 'My friend is a much more rational person than you might suppose to hear him talk,' he added, turning to the stranger, 'and if there's anything you'd like to get off your chest, you may be perfectly certain it won't go any farther.'

The other smiled a little grimly.

'I'll tell you about it with pleasure if it won't bore you. It just happens to be a case in point, that's all.'

'On my side of the argument,' said the man called Peter, with triumph. 'Do carry on. Have something to drink. It's a poor heart that never rejoices. And begin right at the beginning, if you will, please. I have a very trivial mind. Detail delights me. Ramifications enchant me. Distance no object. No reasonable offer refused. Charles here will say the same.'

'Well,' said the stranger, 'to begin from the very beginning, I am a medical man, particularly interested in the subject of cancer. I had hoped, as so many people do, to specialise on the subject, but there wasn't money enough, when I'd done my exams, to allow me to settle down to research work. I had to take a country practice, but I kept in touch with the important men up here, hoping to be able to come back to it some day. I may say I have quite decent expectations from an uncle, and in the meanwhile they agreed it would be quite good for me to get some all-round experience as a GP. Keeps one from getting narrow and all that.

6

'Consequently, when I bought a nice little practice at — I'd better not mention any names, let's call it X, down Hampshire way, a little country town of about 5,000 people — I was greatly pleased to find a cancer case on my list of patients. The old lady — '

'How long ago was this?' interrupted Peter.

'Three years ago. There wasn't much to be done with the case. The old lady was seventy-two, and had already had one operation. She was a game old girl, though, and was making a good fight of it, with a very tough constitution to back her up. She was not, I should say, and had never been, a woman of very powerful intellect or strong character as far as her dealings with other people went, but she was extremely obstinate in certain ways and was possessed by a positive determination not to die. At this time she lived alone with her niece, a young woman of twenty-five or so. Previously to that, she had been living with another old lady, the girl's aunt on the other side of the family, who had been her devoted friend since their school days. When this other old aunt died, the girl, who was their only living relative, threw up her job as a nurse at the Royal Free Hospital to look after the survivor — my patient — and they had come and settled down at X about a year before I took over the practice. I hope I am making myself clear.'

'Perfectly. Was there another nurse?'

'Not at that time. The patient was able to get about, visit acquaintances, do light work about the house, flowers and knitting and reading and so on, and to drive about the place — in fact, most of the things that old ladies do occupy their time with. Of course, she had her bad days of pain from time to time, but the niece's training was quite sufficient to enable her to do all that was necessary.'

'What was the niece like?'

'Oh a very nice, well-educated, capable girl, with a great deal more brain than her aunt. Self-reliant, cool, all that sort of thing. Quite the modern type. The sort of woman one can trust to keep her head and not forget things. Of course, after a time, the wretched growth made its appearance again, as it always does if it isn't tackled at the very beginning, and another operation became necessary. That was when I had been in X about eight months. I took her up to London to my old chief, Sir Warburton Giles, and it was performed very successfully as far as the operation itself went, though it was then only too evident that a vital organ was being encroached upon, and that the end could only be a matter of time. I needn't go into details. Everything was done that could be done. I wanted the old lady to stay in town under Sir Warburton's eye, but she was vigorously opposed to this. She was accustomed to a country life and could not be happy except in her own home. So she went back to X, and I was able to keep her going with visits for treatment at the nearest large town, where there is an excellent hospital. She rallied amazingly after the operation and eventually was able to dismiss her nurse and go on in the old way under the care of the niece.'

'One moment, doctor,' put in the man called

Charles, 'you say you took her to Sir Warburton Giles, and so on. I gather she was pretty well off.'

'Oh, yes, she was quite a wealthy woman.'

'Do you happen to know whether she made a will?'

'No. I think I mentioned her extreme aversion to the idea of death. She had always refused to make any kind of will because it upset her to think about such things. I did once venture to speak of the subject in the most casual way I could, shortly before she underwent her operation, but the effect was to excite her very undesirably. Also she said, which was quite true, that it was quite unnecessary. 'You, my dear,' she said to the niece, 'are the only kith and kin I've got in the world, and all I've got will be yours some day, whatever happens. I know I can trust you to remember my servants and my little charities.' So, of course, I didn't insist.

'I remember, by the way — but that was a good deal later on and has nothing to do with the story — '

'*Please*,' said Peter, '*all* the details.'

'Well, I remember going there one day and finding my patient not so well as I could have wished and very much agitated. The niece told me that the trouble was caused by a visit from her solicitor — a family lawyer from her home town, not our local man. He had insisted on a private interview with the old lady, at the close of which she had appeared terribly excited and angry, declaring that everyone was in a conspiracy to kill her before her time. The solicitor, before leaving, had given no explanation to the niece, but had impressed upon her that if at any time her aunt expressed a wish to see him, she was to send for him at any hour of the day or night and he would come at once.'

'And was he ever sent for?'

'No. The old lady was deeply offended with him, and almost the last bit of business she did for herself was to take her affairs out of his hands and transfer them to the local solicitor. Shortly afterwards, a third operation became necessary, and after this she gradually became more and more of an invalid. Her head began to get weak, too, and she grew incapable of understanding anything complicated, and indeed she was in too much pain to be bothered about business. The niece had a power of attorney, and took over the management of her aunt's money entirely.'

'When was this?'

'In April, 1925. Mind you, though she was getting a bit 'gaga' — after all, she was getting on in years — her bodily strength was quite remarkable. I was investigating a new method of treatment and the results were extraordinarily interesting. That made it all the more annoying to me when the surprising thing happened.

'I should mention that by this time we were obliged to have an outside nurse for her, as the niece could not do both the day and night duty. The first nurse came in April. She was a most charming and capable young woman — the ideal nurse. I placed absolute dependence on her. She had been specially recommended to me by Sir Warburton Giles, and though she was not then more than twenty-eight, she had the discretion and judgement of a woman twice her age. I may as well tell you at once that I became deeply attached to this lady and she to me. We are engaged, and had hoped to be married this year — if it hadn't been for my damned conscientiousness and public spirit.'

The doctor grimaced wryly at Charles, who murmured rather lamely that it was very bad luck.

'My fiancée, like myself, took a keen interest in the case — partly because it was my case and partly because she was herself greatly interested in the disease. She looks forward to being of great assistance to me in my life work if I ever get the chance to do anything at it. But that's by the way.

'Things went on like this till September. Then, for some reason, the patient began to take one of those unaccountable dislikes that feeble-minded patients do take sometimes. She got it into her head that the nurse wanted to kill her — the same idea she'd had about the lawyer, you see — and earnestly assured her niece that she was being poisoned. No doubt she attributed her attacks of pain to this cause. Reasoning was useless — she cried out and refused to let the nurse come near her. When that happens, naturally, there's nothing for it but to get rid of the nurse, as she can do the patient no possible good. I sent my fiancée back to town and wired to Sir Warburton's Clinic to send me down another nurse.

'The new nurse arrived the next day. Naturally, after the other she was a second-best as far as I was concerned, but she seemed quite up to her work and the patient made no objection. However, now I began to have trouble with the niece. Poor girl, all this long-drawn-out business was getting on her nerves, I suppose. She took it into her head that her aunt was very much worse. I said that of course she must gradually get worse, but that she was putting up a wonderful fight and there was no cause for alarm. The girl wasn't satisfied, however, and on one occasion early in November sent for me hurriedly in the middle of the night because her aunt was dying.

'When I arrived, I found the patient in great pain, certainly, but in no immediate danger. I told the nurse to give her a morphia injection and administered a dose of bromide to the girl, telling her to go to bed and not to do any nursing for the next few days. The following day I overhauled the patient very carefully and found that she was doing even better than I supposed. Her heart was exceptionally strong and steady, she was taking nourishment remarkably well and the progress of the disease was temporarily arrested.

'The niece apologised for her agitation, and said she really thought her aunt was going. I said that, on the contrary, I could now affirm positively that she would live for another five or six months. As you know, in cases like hers, one can speak with very fair certainty.

''Yes,' she said, 'poor Auntie. I'm afraid I'm selfish, but she's the only relative I have left in the world.''

'Three days later, I was just sitting down to dinner when a telephone message came. Would I go over at once? The patient was dead.'

'Good gracious!' cried Charles, 'it's perfectly obvious — '

'Shut up, Sherlock,' said his friend, 'the doctor's story is not going to be obvious. Far from it, as the private said when he aimed at the bull's-eye and hit the gunnery instructor. But I observe the waiter hovering uneasily about us while his colleagues pile up chairs and carry away the cruets. Will you not come and finish the story in my flat? I can give you a glass of very decent port. You will? Good. Waiter, call a taxi . . . 110A, Piccadilly.'

2

Miching Mallecho

'By the pricking of my thumbs
Something evil this way comes.'
Macbeth

The April night was clear and chilly, and a brisk
wood fire burned in a welcoming manner on the
hearth. The bookcases which lined the walls were
filled with rich old calf-bindings, mellow and
glowing in the lamp-light. There was a grand
piano, open, a huge chesterfield piled deep with
cushions and two armchairs of the build that
invites one to wallow. The port was brought in by
an impressive manservant and placed on a very
beautiful little Chippendale table. Some big
bowls of scarlet and yellow parrot tulips
beckoned, bannerlike, from dark corners.

The doctor had just written his new
acquaintance down as an aesthete with a literary
turn, looking for the ingredients of a human
drama, when the man-servant re-entered.

'Inspector Sugg rang up, my lord, and left this
message, and said would you be good enough to
give him a call as soon as you came in.'

'Oh, did he? — well, just get him for me,
would you? This is the Worplesham business,
Charles. Sugg's mucked it up as usual. The baker
has an alibi — naturally — he would have. Oh,

14

thanks . . . Hullo! that you, Inspector? What did I tell you? — Oh, routine, be hanged. Now, look here. You get hold of that gamekeeper fellow, and find out from him what he saw in the sand-pit . . . No, I know, but I fancy if you ask him impressively enough he will come across with it. No, of course not — if you ask if he was there, he'll say no. Say you know he was there and what did he see — and, look here! if he hums and haws about it, say you're sending a gang down to have the stream diverted . . . All right. Not at all. Let me know if anything comes of it.'

He put the receiver down.

'Excuse me, Doctor. A little matter of business. Now go on with your story. The old lady was dead, eh? Died in her sleep, I suppose. Passed away in the most innocent manner possible. Everything all shipshape and Bristol fashion. No struggle, no wounds, haemorrhages, or obvious symptoms, naturally, what?'

'Exactly. She had taken some nourishment at 6 o'clock — a little broth and some milk pudding. At eight, the nurse gave her a morphine injection and then went straight out to put some bowls of flowers on the little table on the landing for the night. The maid came to speak to her about some arrangements for the next day, and while they were talking, Miss . . . that is, the niece — came up and went into her aunt's room. She had only been there a moment or two when she cried out, 'Nurse! Nurse!' The nurse rushed in, and found the patient dead.

'Of course, my first idea was that by some

accident a double dose of morphine had been administered — '

'Surely that wouldn't have acted so promptly.'

'No — but I thought that a deep coma might have been mistaken for death. However, the nurse assured me that this was not the case, and, as a matter of fact, the possibility was completely disproved, as we were able to count the ampullae of morphine and found them all satisfactorily accounted for. There were no signs of the patient having tried to move or strain herself, or of her having knocked against anything. The little night-table was pushed aside, but that had been done by the niece when she came in and was struck by her aunt's alarmingly lifeless appearance.'

'How about the broth and the milk-pudding?'

'That occurred to me also — not in any sinister way, but to wonder whether she'd been having too much — distended stomach — pressure on the heart, and that sort of thing. However, when I came to look into it, it seemed very unlikely. The quantity was so small, and on the face of it, two hours were sufficient for digestion — if it had been that, death would have taken place earlier. I was completely puzzled, and so was the nurse. Indeed, she was very much upset.'

'And the niece?'

'The niece could say nothing but, 'I told you so, I told you so — I knew she was worse than you thought.' Well, to cut a long story short, I was so bothered with my pet patient going off like that, that next morning, after I had thought

16

the matter over, I asked for a post-mortem.'

'Any difficulty?'

'Not the slightest. A little natural distaste, of course, but no sort of opposition. I explained that I felt sure there must be some obscure morbid condition which I had failed to diagnose and that I should feel more satisfied if I might make an investigation. The only thing which seemed to trouble the niece was the thought of an inquest. I said — rather unwisely, I suppose, according to general rule — that I didn't think an inquest would be necessary.'

'You mean you offered to perform the post-mortem yourself.'

'Yes — I made no doubt that I should find a sufficient cause of death to enable me to give a certificate. I had one bit of luck, and that was that the old lady had at some time or the other expressed in a general way an opinion in favour of cremation, and the niece wished this to be carried out. This meant getting a man with special qualifications to sign the certificate with me, so I persuaded this other doctor to come and help me to do the autopsy.'

'And did you find anything?'

'Not a thing. The other man, of course, said I was a fool to kick up a fuss. He thought that as the old lady was certainly dying in any case, it would be quite enough to put in, Cause of death, Cancer; immediate cause, Heart Failure, and leave it at that. But I was a damned conscientious ass, and said I wasn't satisfied. There was absolutely nothing about the body to explain the death naturally, and I insisted on an analysis.'

'Did you actually suspect — ?'

'Well, no, not exactly. But — well, I wasn't satisfied. By the way, it was very clear at the autopsy that the morphine had nothing to do with it. Death had occurred so soon after the injection that the drug had only partially dispersed from the arm. Now I think it over, I suppose it must have been shock, somehow.'

'Was the analysis privately made?'

'Yes, but of course the funeral was held up and things got round. The coroner heard about it and started to make inquiries, and the nurse, who got it into her head that I was accusing her of neglect or something, behaved in a very unprofessional way and created a lot of talk and trouble.'

'And nothing came of it?'

'Nothing. There was no trace of poison or anything of that sort, and the analysis left us exactly where we were. Naturally, I began to think I had made a ghastly exhibition of myself. Rather against my own professional judgement, I signed the certificate — heart failure following on shock, and my patient was finally got into her grave after a week of worry, without an inquest.'

'Grave?'

'Oh, yes. That was another scandal. The crematorium authorities, who are pretty particular, heard about the fuss and refused to act in the matter, so the body is filed in the churchyard for reference if necessary. There was a huge attendance at the funeral and a great deal of sympathy for the niece. The next day I got a note from one of my most influential patients, saying that my professional services would no longer be required. The day after that, I was avoided in the street by the Mayor's wife. Presently I found my practice dropping away from me, and discovered I was getting known as 'the man who practically accused that charming Miss So-and-so of murder'. Sometimes it was the niece I was supposed to be accusing. Sometimes it was 'that nice Nurse — not the flighty one who was dismissed, the other one, you know.' Another version was, that I had tried to get the nurse into trouble because I resented the dismissal of my fiancée. Finally, I heard a rumour that the patient had discovered me 'canoodling' — that was the beastly word — with my fiancée, instead of doing my job, and I had done away with the old lady myself out of revenge — though why, in that case, I should have refused a certificate, my scandalmongers didn't trouble to explain.

'I stuck it out for a year, but my position became intolerable. The practice dwindled to practically nothing, so I sold it, took a holiday to get the taste out of my mouth — and here I am, looking for another opening. So that's that — and the moral is, Don't be officious about public duties.'

The doctor gave an irritated laugh, and flung himself back in his chair.

'I don't care,' he added, combatantly, 'the cats! Confusion to 'em!' and he drained his glass.

'Hear, hear!' agreed his host. He sat for a few moments looking thoughtfully into the fire.

'Do you know,' he said, suddenly, 'I'm feeling rather interested by this case. I have a sensation of internal gloating which assures me that there is something to be investigated. That feeling has never failed me yet — I trust it never will. It warned me the other day to look into my income tax assessment, and I discovered that I had been paying about £900 too much for the last three years. It urged me only last week to ask a bloke who was preparing to drive me over the Horseshoe Pass whether he had any petrol in the tank, and he discovered he had just about a pint — enough to get us nicely half-way round. It's a very lonely spot. Of course, I knew the man, so it wasn't *all* intuition. Still, I always make it a rule to investigate anything I feel like investigating. I believe,' he added, in a reminiscent tone, 'I was a terror in my nursery days. Anyhow, curious cases are rather a hobby of mine. In fact, I'm not just being the perfect listener. I have deceived you. I have an ulterior motive, said he, throwing off his side-whiskers and disclosing the well-known hollow jaws of Mr Sherlock Holmes.'

'I was beginning to have my suspicions,' said the doctor, after a short pause. 'I think you must be Lord Peter Wimsey. I wondered why your face was so familiar, but of course it was in all the papers a few years ago when you disentangled the Riddlesdale Mystery.'

'Quite right. It's a silly kind of face, of course, but rather disarming, don't you think? I don't know that I'd have chosen it, but I do my best with it. I do hope it isn't contracting a sleuth-like expression, or anything unpleasant. This is the real sleuth — my friend Detective-Inspector Parker of Scotland Yard. He's the one who really does the work. I make imbecile suggestions and he does the work of elaborately disproving them. Then, by a process of elimination, we find the right explanation, and the world says, 'My god, what intuition that young man has!' Well, look here — if you don't mind, I'd like to have a go at this. If you'll entrust me with your own name and address and the names of the parties concerned, I'd like very much to have a shot at looking into it.'

The doctor considered for a moment, then shook his head.

'It's very good of you, but I think I'd rather not. I've got into enough bother already. Anyway, it isn't professional to talk, and if I stirred up any more fuss, I should probably have to chuck this country altogether and end up as one of those drunken ship's doctors in the South Seas or somewhere, who are always telling their life-history to people and delivering awful warnings. Better to let sleeping dogs lie. Thanks very much, all the same.'

'As you like,' said Wimsey. 'But I'll think it over, and if any useful suggestion occurs to me, I'll let you know.'

'It's very good of you,' replied the visitor, absently, taking his hat and stick from the man-servant, who had answered Wimsey's ring. 'Well, good-night, and many thanks for hearing me so patiently. By the way, though,' he added, turning suddenly at the door, 'how do you propose to let me know when you haven't got my name and address?'

Lord Peter laughed.

'I'm Hawkshaw, the detective,' he answered, 'and you shall hear from me anyhow before the end of the week.'

3

A Use for Spinsters

'There are two million more females than males in England and Wales: And this is an awe-inspiring circumstance.'

GILBERT FRANKAU

'What do you really think of that story?' inquired Parker. He had dropped in to breakfast with Wimsey the next morning, before departing in the Notting Dale direction, in quest of an elusive anonymous letter-writer. 'I thought it sounded rather as though our friend had been a bit too cocksure about his grand medical specialising. After all, the old girl might so easily have had some sort of heart attack. She was very old and ill.'

'So she might, though I believe as a matter of fact cancer patients very seldom pop off in that unexpected way. As a rule, they surprise everybody by the way they cling to life. Still, I wouldn't think much of that if it wasn't for the niece. She prepared the way for the death, you see, by describing her aunt as so much worse than she was.'

'I thought the same when the doctor was telling his tale. But what did the niece do? She can't have poisoned her aunt or even smothered her, I suppose, or they'd have found signs of it on the body, and the aunt *did* die — so perhaps the niece was right and the opinionated young medico wrong.'

'Just so. And of course, we've only got his version of the niece and the nurse — and he obviously was what the Scotch call ta'en a scunner at the nurse. We mustn't lose sight of her, by the way. She was the last person to be with the old lady before her death, and it was she who administered that injection.'

'Yes, yes — but the injection had nothing to do with it. If anything's clear, that is. I say, do you think the nurse can have said anything that agitated the old lady and gave her a shock that way. The patient was a bit gaga, but she may have had sense enough to understand something really startling. Possibly the nurse just said something stupid about dying — the old lady appears to have been very sensitive on the point.'

'Ah!' said Lord Peter, 'I was waiting for you to get on to that. Have you realised that there really is one rather sinister figure in the story, and that's the family lawyer?'

'The one who came down to say something about the will, you mean, and was so abruptly sent packing?'

'Yes. Suppose he'd wanted the patient to make a will in favour of somebody quite different — somebody outside the story as we know it. And when he found he couldn't get any attention paid to him, he sent the new nurse down as a sort of substitute.'

'It would be rather an elaborate plot,' said Parker, dubiously. 'He couldn't know that the doctor's fiancée was going to be sent away. Unless he was in league with the niece, of course, and induced her to engineer the change of nurses.'

'That cock won't fight, Charles. The niece wouldn't be in league with the lawyer to get herself disinherited.'

'No, I suppose not. Still, I think there's something in the idea that the old girl was either accidentally or deliberately startled to death.'

'Yes — and whichever way it was, it probably wasn't legal murder in that case. However, I think it's worth looking into. That reminds me.' He rang the bell. 'Bunter, just take a note to the post for me, will you?'

'Certainly, my lord.'

Lord Peter drew a writing pad towards him.

'What are you going to write?' asked Parker, looking over his shoulder with some amusement.

Lord Peter wrote:

'Isn't civilisation wonderful?'

He signed this simple message and slipped it into an envelope.

'If you want to be immune from silly letters, Charles,' he said, 'don't carry your monomark in your hat.'

'And what do you propose to do next?' asked Parker. 'Not, I hope, to send me round to Monomark House to get the name of a client. I couldn't do that without official authority, and they would probably kick up an awful shindy.'

'No,' replied his friend, 'I don't propose violating the secrets of the confessional. Not in that quarter at any rate. I think, if you can spare a moment from your mysterious correspondent, who probably does not intend to be found, I will ask you to come and pay a visit to a friend of mine. It won't take long. I think you'll be interested. I — in fact, you'll be the first person I've ever taken to see her. She will be very much touched and pleased.'

He laughed a little self-consciously.

'Oh,' said Parker, embarrassed. Although the men were great friends, Wimsey had always preserved a reticence about his personal affairs — not so much by concealing as by ignoring them. This revelation seemed to mark a new stage of intimacy, and Parker was not sure that he liked it. He conducted his own life with an earnest middle-class morality which he owed to his birth and upbringing, and, while theoretically recognising that Lord Peter's world acknowledged different standards, he had never contemplated being personally faced with any result of their application in practice.

' — rather an experiment,' Wimsey was saying a trifle shyly; 'anyway, she's quite comfortably fixed in a little flat in Pimlico. You can come, can't you, Charles? I really should like you two to meet.'

'Oh, yes, rather,' said Parker, hastily, 'I should like to very much. Er — how long — I mean — '

'Oh, the arrangement's only been going a few months,' said Wimsey, leading the way to the lift, 'but it really seems to be working out quite satisfactorily. Of course, it makes things much easier for me.'

'Just so,' said Parker.

'Of course, as you'll understand — I won't go

into it all till we get there, and then you'll see for yourself,' Wimsey chattered on, slamming the gates of the lift with unnecessary violence — 'but, as I was saying, you'll observe it's quite a new departure. I don't suppose there's ever been anything exactly like it before. Of course, there's nothing new under the sun, as Solomon said, but, after all, I daresay all those wives and porcupines, as the child said, must have soured his disposition a little, don't you know.'

'Quite,' said Parker. 'Poor fish,' he added to himself, 'they *always* seem to think it's different.'

'Outlet,' said Wimsey, energetically, 'hi! taxi! . . . outlet — everybody needs an outlet — 97A, St George's Square — and, after all, one can't really blame people if it's just that they need an outlet. I mean, why be bitter? They can't help it. I think it's much kinder to give them an outlet than to make fun of them in books — and, after all, it isn't very difficult to write books. Especially if you either write a rotten story in good English or a good story in rotten English, which is as far as most people seem to get nowadays. Don't you agree?'

Mr Parker agreed, and Lord Peter wandered away along the paths of literature, till the cab stopped before one of those tall, awkward mansions which, originally designed for a Victorian family with fatigue-proof servants, have lately been dissected each into half a dozen inconvenient bandboxes and let off in flats.

Lord Peter rang the top bell, which was marked 'CLIMPSON', and relaxed negligently against the porch.

27

'Six flights of stairs,' he explained; 'it takes her some time to answer the bell, because there's no lift you see. She wouldn't have a more expensive flat, though. She thought it wouldn't be suitable.'

Mr Parker was greatly relieved, if somewhat surprised, by the modesty of the lady's demands, and, placing his foot on the door-scraper in an easy attitude, prepared to wait with patience. Before many minutes, however, the door was opened by a thin, middle-aged woman, with a sharp, sallow face and very vivacious manner. She wore a neat, dark coat and skirt, a high-necked blouse and a long gold neck-chain with a variety of small ornaments dangling from it at intervals, and her iron-grey hair was dressed under a net, in the style fashionable in the reign of the late King Edward.

'Oh, Lord Peter! How *very* nice to see you. Rather an *early* visit, but I'm sure you will excuse the sitting-room being a trifle in disorder. *Do* come in. The lists are *quite* ready for you. I finished them last night. In fact, I was just about to put on my hat and bring them round to you. I do *hope* you don't think I have taken an *unconscionable* time, but there was a quite *surprising* number of entries. It is *too* good of you to trouble to call.'

'Not at all, Miss Climpson. This is my friend, Detective Inspector Parker, whom I have mentioned to you.'

'How do you do, Mr Parker — or ought I to say Inspector? Excuse me if I make mistakes — this is really the first time I have been in the hands of the police. I hope it's not rude of me to

28

say that. Please come up. A great many stairs, I am afraid, but I hope you do not mind. I do so like to be *high up.* The air is so much better, and you know, Mr Parker, thanks to Lord Peter's great kindness, I have such a *beautiful, airy* view, right over the houses. I think one can work so much *better* when one doesn't feel cribbed, cabined and confined, as Hamlet says. Dear me! Mrs Winbottle *will* leave the pail on the stairs, and always in that very dark corner. I am *continually* telling her about it. If you keep close to the banisters you will avoid it nicely. Only one more flight. Here we are. Please overlook the untidyness. I always think breakfast things look so *ugly* when one has finished with them — almost sordid, to use a nasty word for a nasty subject. What a pity that some of these clever people can't invent *self-cleaning* and *self-clearing plates*, is at not? But please *do* sit down; I won't keep you a moment. And I know, Lord Peter, that you will not hesitate to smoke. I do so enjoy the smell of your cigarettes — quite delicious — and you are so *very* good about extinguishing the ends.'

The little room was, as a matter of fact, most exquisitely neat, in spite of the crowded array of knick-knacks and photographs that adorned every available inch of space. The sole evidences of dissipation were an empty eggshell, a used cup and a crumby plate on a breakfast tray. Miss Climpson promptly subdued this riot by carrying the tray bodily on to the landing.

Mr Parker, a little bewildered, lowered himself cautiously into a small armchair, embellished with a hard, fat little cushion which made it impossible to lean back. Lord Peter wriggled into the window-seat, lit a Sobranie and clasped his hands about his knees. Miss Climpson, seated upright at the table, gazed at him with a gratified air which was positively touching.

'I have gone *very* carefully into all these cases,' she began, taking up a thick wad of type-script. 'I'm afraid, indeed, my notes are rather *copious*, but I trust the typist's bill will not be considered too heavy. My handwriting is very clear, so I don't think there can be any errors. Dear me! such *sad* stories some of these poor women had to tell me! But I have investigated most fully, with the kind assistance of the clergyman — a very nice man and so helpful — and I feel sure that in the majority of the cases your assistance will be *well bestowed*. If you would like to go through — '

'Not at the moment, Miss Climpson,' interrupted Lord Peter, hurriedly. 'It's all right, Charles — nothing whatever to do with Our Dumb Friends or supplying Flannel to Unmarried Mothers. I'll tell you about it later. Just now, Miss Climpson, we want your help on something quite different.'

Miss Climpson produced a businesslike notebook and sat at attention.

'The inquiry divides itself into two parts,' said Lord Peter. 'The first part, I'm afraid, is rather dull. I want you (if you will be so good) to go down to Somerset House and search, or get them to search, through all the death-certificates for Hampshire in the month of November, 1925.

I don't know the town and I don't know the name of the deceased. What you are looking for is the death-certificate of an old lady of 73; cause of death, cancer; immediate cause, heart-failure; and the certificate will have been signed by two doctors, one of whom will be either a Medical Officer of Health, Police Surgeon, Certifying Surgeon under the Factory and Workshops Act, Medical Referee under the Workmen's Compensation Act, Physician or Surgeon in the big General Hospital, or a man specially appointed by the Cremation authorities. If you want to give any excuse for the search, you can say that you are compiling statistics about cancer; but what you really want is the names of the people concerned and the name of the town.'

'Suppose there are more than one answering to the requirements?'

'Ah! that's where the second part comes in, and where your remarkable tact and shrewdness are going to be so helpful to us. When you have collected all the 'possibles', I shall ask you to go down to each of the towns concerned and make very, very skilful inquiries, to find out which is the case we want to get on to. Of course, you mustn't appear to be inquiring. You must find some good gossipy lady living in the neighbourhood and just get her to talk in a natural way. You must pretend to be gossipy yourself — it's not in your nature, I know, but I'm sure you can make a little pretence about it — and find out all you can. I fancy you'll find it pretty easy if you once strike the right town, because I know for a certainty that there was a terrible lot of ill-natured talk about this particular death, and it won't have been forgotten yet by a long chalk.'

'How shall I know when it's the right one?'

'Well, if you can spare the time, I want you to listen to a little story. Mind you, Miss Climpson, when you get to wherever it is, you are not supposed ever to have heard a word of this tale before. But I needn't tell you that. Now, Charles, you've got an official kind of way of puttin' these things clearly. Will you just weigh in and give Miss Climpson the gist of that rigmarole our friend served out to us last night?'

Pulling his wits into order, Mr Parker accordingly obliged with a digest of the doctor's story. Miss Climpson listened with great attention, making notes of the dates and details. Parker observed that she showed great acumen in seizing on the salient points, she asked a number of very shrewd questions, and her grey eyes were intelligent. When he had finished, she repeated the story, and he was able to congratulate her on a clear head and retentive memory.

'A dear old friend of mine used to say that I should have made a very good lawyer,' said Miss Climpson, complacently, 'but of course, when I was young, girls didn't have the education or the *opportunities* they get nowadays, Mr Parker. I should have liked a good education, but my dear father didn't believe in it for women. Very old-fashioned, you young people would think him.'

'Never mind, Miss Climpson,' said Wimsey, 'you've got just exactly the qualifications we

32

want, and they're rather rare, so we're in luck. Now we want this matter pushed forward as fast as possible.'

'I'll go down to Somerset House at once,' replied the lady, with great energy, 'and let you know the minute I'm ready to start for Hampshire.'

'That's right,' said his lordship, rising. 'And now we'll just make a noise like a hoop and roll away. Oh! and while I think of it, I'd better give you something in hand for travelling expenses and so on. I think you had better be just a retired lady in easy circumstances looking for a nice little place to settle down in. I don't think you'd better be wealthy — wealthy people don't inspire confidence. Perhaps you would oblige me by living at the rate of about £800 a year — your own excellent taste and experience will suggest the correct accessories and so on for creating that impression. If you will allow me, I will give you a cheque for £50 now, and when you start on your wanderings you will let me know what you require.'

'Dear me,' said Miss Climpson, 'I don't — '

'This is a pure matter of business, of course,' said Wimsey, rather rapidly, 'and you will let me have a note of the expenses in your usual businesslike way.'

'Of course.' Miss Climpson was dignified. 'And I will give you a proper receipt immediately.'

'Dear, dear,' she added, hunting through her purse, 'I do not appear to have any penny stamps. How extremely remiss of me. It is most *unusual* for me not to have my little book of stamps — so handy I always think they are — but only last night Mrs Williams borrowed my last stamp to send a very urgent letter to her son in Japan. If you will excuse me a moment — '

'I think I have some,' interposed Parker.

'Oh, thank you very much, Mr Parker. Here is the two-pence. I never allow myself to be without pennies — on account of the bathroom geyser, you know. Such a very *sensible* invention, most *convenient*, and prevents *all* dispute about hot water among the tenants. Thank you so much. And now I sign my name *across* the stamps. That's right, isn't it? My dear father would be surprised to find his daughter so businesslike. He always said a woman should never *need* to know anything about money matters, but times have changed so greatly, have they not?'

Miss Climpson ushered them down all six flights of stairs, volubly protesting at their protests, and the door closed behind them.

'May I ask — ?' began Parker.

'It is not what you think,' said his lordship, earnestly.

'Of course not,' agreed Parker.

'There, I knew you had a nasty mind. Even the closest of one's friends turn out to be secret thinkers. They think in private thoughts which they publicly repudiate.'

'Don't be a fool. Who *is* Miss Climpson?'

'Miss Climpson,' said Lord Peter, 'is a manifestation of the wasteful way in which this country is run. Look at electricity. Look at water-power. Look at the tides. Look at the sun.

34

Millions of power units being given off into space every minute. Thousands of old maids, simply bursting with useful energy, forced by our stupid social system into hydros and hotels and communities and hostels and posts as companions, where their magnificent gossip-powers and units of inquisitiveness are allowed to dissipate themselves or even become harmful to the community, while ratepayers' money is spent on getting work for which these women are providentially fitted, inefficiently carried out by ill-equipped policemen like you. My god! it's enough to make a man write to *John Bull*. And then bright young men write nasty little patronising books called *Elderly Women*, and *On the Edge of the Explosion* — and the drunkards make songs about 'em, poor things.'

'Quite, quite,' said Parker. 'You mean that Miss Climpson is a kind of inquiry agent for you.'

'She is my ears and tongue,' said Lord Peter, dramatically, 'and especially my nose. She asks questions which a young man could not put without a blush. She is the angel that rushes in where fools get a clump on the head. She can smell a rat in the dark. In fact, she is the cat's whiskers.'

'That's not a bad idea,' said Parker.

'Naturally — it is mine, therefore brilliant. Just think. People want questions asked. Whom do they send? A man with large flat feet and a notebook — the sort of man whose private life is conducted in a series of inarticulate grunts. I send a lady with a long, woolly jumper on knitting-needles and jingly things round her neck. Of course she asks questions — everyone expects it. Nobody is surprised. Nobody is alarmed. And so-called superfluity is agreeable and usefully disposed of. One of these days they will put up a statue to me, with an inscription:

> ''To the Man who Made
> Thousands of Superfluous Women
> Happy
> without Injury to their Modesty
> or Exertion to Himself.''

'I wish you wouldn't talk so much,' complained his friend. 'And how about all those typewritten reports? Are you turning philanthropist in your old age?'

'No — no,' said Wimsey, rather hurriedly hailing a taxi. 'Tell you about that later. Little private pogrom of my own — Insurance against the Socialist Revolution — when it comes. 'What did you do with your great wealth, comrade?' 'I bought First Editions.' 'Aristocrat! à la lanterne!' 'Stay, spare me! I took proceedings against 500 moneylenders who oppressed the workers.' 'Citizen, you have done well. We will spare your life. You shall be promoted to cleaning out the sewers.' Voilà! We must move with the times. Citizen taxi-driver, take me to the British Museum. Can I drop you anywhere? No? So long. I am going to collate a 12th-century manuscript of Tristan, while the old order lasts.'

Mr Parker thoughtfully boarded a westward-bound bus and was rolled away to do some routine questioning, on his own account, among the female population of Notting Dale. It did not appear to him to be a milieu in which the talents of Miss Climpson could be usefully employed.

4

A Bit Mental

'A babbled of green fields.'
King Henry V

*Letter from Miss Alexandra Katherine Climpson
to Lord Peter Wimsey.*

'C/o Mrs Hamilton Budge,
'Fairview, Nelson Avenue,
'Leahampton, Hants.
'April 29th, 1927.

'MY DEAR LORD PETER,
'You will be happy to hear, after my *two
previous* bad shots (!), that I have found the *right*
place at last. The Agatha Dawson certificate is
the *correct* one, and the dreadful *scandal* about
Dr Carr is still very much alive, I am sorry to say
for the sake of *human nature*. I have been
fortunate enough to secure rooms in the *very
next street* to Wellington Avenue, where Miss
Dawson used to live. My landlady seems a very
nice woman, though a *terrible gossip!* — which
is *all to the good!!* Her charge for a very pleasant
bedroom and sitting-room with *full board* is 3½
guineas weekly. I trust you will not think this *too
extravagant*, as the situation is *just* what you
wished me to look for. I enclose a careful

statement of my expenses up-to-date. You will *excuse* the mention of *underwear*, which is, I fear, a *somewhat large* item! but wool is so expensive nowadays, and it is necessary that every detail of my equipment should be suitable to my (supposed!) position in life. I have been careful to *wash* the garments though, so that they do not look *too new*, as this might have a *suspicious* appearance!!

'But you will be anxious for me to (if I may use a vulgar expression) 'cut the cackle, and come to the horses' (!!). On the day after my arrival, I informed Mrs Budge that I was a great sufferer from *rheumatism* (which is quite true, as I have a sad legacy of that kind left me by, alas! my *port-drinking* ancestors!) — and inquired what *doctors* there were in the neighbourhood. This at once brought forth a *long catalogue*, together with a *grand panegyric* of the sandy soil and healthy situation of the town. I said I should prefer an *elderly* doctor, as the *young men*, in my opinion, were *not to be depended on*. Mrs Budge heartily agreed with me, and a little discreet questioning brought out the *whole story* of Miss Dawson's illness and the 'carrying-ons' (as she termed them) of Dr Carr and *the nurse*! 'I never did trust that first nurse,' said Mrs Budge, 'for all she had her training at Guy's and ought to have been trustworthy. A sly, redheaded *baggage*, and it's my belief that all Dr Carr's fussing over Miss Dawson and his visits all day and every day were just to get love-making with Nurse Philliter. No wonder poor Miss Whittaker couldn't stand it any longer and gave the girl the sack — none too soon, in my opinion. Not quite so attentive after that, Dr Carr wasn't — why, up to the last minute, he was pretending the old lady was quite all right, when Miss Whittaker had only said the day before that she felt sure she was going to be taken from us.'

'I asked if Mrs Budge knew Miss Whittaker personally. Miss Whittaker is the *niece*, you know.

'Not personally, she said, though she had met her in a social way at the Vicarage working-parties. But she knew all about it, because her maid was own sister to the maid at Miss Dawson's. Now is not that a fortunate *coincidence*, for you know how these girls *talk*!

'I also made careful inquiries about the *Vicar*, Mr Tredgold, and was much gratified to find that he teaches *sound Catholic* doctrine, so that I shall be able to attend the Church (S. Onesimus) without doing *violence* to my religious beliefs — a thing I could *not* undertake to do, *even in your interests*. I am sure you will *understand* this. As it happens, *all is well*, and I have written to my *very good friend*, the Vicar of S. Edfrith's, Holborn, to ask for an *introduction* to Mr Tredgold. By this means, I feel sure of meeting *Miss Whittaker* before long, as I hear she is quite a 'pillar of the church'! I do hope it is not *wrong* to make use of the Church of God to a *worldly* end; but after all, you are only seeking to establish *Truth* and *Justice*! — and in so good a cause we may perhaps permit ourselves to be a little bit *JESUITICAL*!!!

'This is all I have been able to do *as yet*, but I

40

shall not be *idle*, and will write to you again as soon as I have *anything to report*. By the way, the *pillar-box* is *most conveniently placed* just at the corner of Wellington Avenue, so that I can easily *run out* and post my letters to you *myself* (away from *prying eyes*!!) — and just take a little peep at Miss *Dawson's* — now *Miss Whittaker's* — house, 'The Grove', at the same time.

  'Believe me,
   'Sincerely yours,
  'ALEXANDRA KATHERINE CLIMPSON.'

The little red-headed nurse gave her visitor a quick, slightly hostile look-over.

'It's quite all right,' he said, apologetically, 'I haven't come to sell you soap or gramophones, or to borrow money or enrol you in the Ancient Froth-blowers or anything charitable. I really am Lord Peter Wimsey — I mean, that really is my title, don't you know, not a Christian name like Sanger's Circus or Earl Derr Biggers. I've come to ask you some questions and I've no real excuse, I'm afraid, for butting in on you — do you ever read the *News of the World*?'

Nurse Philliter decided that she was to be asked to go to a mental case and that the patient had come to fetch her in person.

'Sometimes,' she said, guardedly.

'Oh — well, you may have noticed my name croppin' up in a few murders and things lately. I sleuth, you know. For a hobby. Harmless outlet for natural inquisitiveness, don't you see, which might otherwise strike inward and produce introspection an' suicide. Very natural, healthy

41

pursuit — not too strenuous, not too sedentary; trains and invigorates the mind.'

'I know who you are now,' said Nurse Philliter, slowly. 'You — you gave evidence against Sir Julian Freke. In fact, you traced the murder to him, didn't you?'

'I did — it was rather unpleasant,' said Lord Peter, simply, 'and I've got another little job of the same kind in hand now, and I want your help.'

'Won't you sit down?' said Nurse Philliter, setting the example. 'How am I concerned in the matter?'

'You know Dr Edward Carr, I think — late of Leahampton — conscientious but a little lackin' in worldly wisdom — not serpentine at all, as the Bible advises, but far otherwise.'

'What!' she cried, 'do *you* believe it was murder, then?'

Lord Peter looked at her for a few seconds. Her face was eager, her eyes gleaming curiously under her thick, level brows. She had expressive hands, rather large and with strong, flat joints. He noticed how they gripped the arms of her chair.

'Haven't the faintest,' he replied, nonchalantly, 'but I wanted your opinion.'

'Mine?' — she checked herself. 'You know, I am not supposed to give opinions about my cases.'

'You have given it me already,' said his lordship, grinning. 'Though possibly I ought to allow for a little prejudice in favour of Dr Carr's diagnosis.'

'Well, yes — but it's not merely personal, I mean, my being engaged to Dr Carr wouldn't affect my judgement of a cancer case. I have worked with him on a great many of them, and I know that his opinion is really trustworthy — just as I know that, as a motorist, he's exactly the opposite.'

'Right. I take it that if he says the death was inexplicable, it really was so. That's one point gained. Now about the old lady herself. I gather she was a little queer towards the end — a bit mental, I think you people call it?'

'I don't know that I'd say that either. Of course, when she was under morphia, she would be unconscious, or only semiconscious, for hours together. But up to the time when I left, I should say she was quite — well, quite all there. She was obstinate, you know, and what they call a character, at the best of times.'

'But Dr Carr told me she got odd fancies — about people poisoning her?'

The red-haired nurse rubbed her fingers slowly along the arm of the chair, and hesitated.

'If it will make you feel any less unprofessional,' said Lord Peter, guessing what was in her mind, 'I may say that my friend Detective-Inspector Parker is looking into this matter with me, which gives me a sort of right to ask questions.'

'In that case — yes — in that case I think I can speak freely. I never understood about that poisoning idea. I never saw anything of it — no aversion, I mean, or fear of me. As a rule, a patient will show it, if she's got any queer ideas

43

about the nurse. Poor Miss Dawson was always most kind and affectionate. She kissed me when I went away and gave me a little present, and said she was sorry to lose me.'

'She didn't show any sort of nervousness about taking food from you?'

'Well, I wasn't allowed to give her any food that last week. Miss Whittaker said her aunt had taken this funny notion, and gave her all her meals herself.'

'Oh! that's very interestin'. Was it Miss Whittaker, then, who first mentioned this little eccentricity to you?'

'Yes. And she begged me not to say anything about it to Miss Dawson, for fear of agitating her.'

'And did you?'

'I did not. I wouldn't mention it in any case to a patient. It does no good.'

'Did Miss Dawson ever speak about it to anyone else? Dr Carr, for instance?'

'No. According to Miss Whittaker, her aunt was frightened of the doctor too, because she imagined he was in league with me. Of course, that story rather lent colour to the unkind things that were said afterwards. I suppose it's just possible that she saw us glancing at one another or speaking aside, and got the idea that we were plotting something.'

'How about the maids?'

'There were new maids about that time. She probably wouldn't talk about it to them, and, anyhow, I wouldn't be discussing my patient with her servants.'

44

'Of course not. Why did the other maids leave? How many were there? Did they all go at once?'

'Two of them went. They were sisters. One was a terrible crockery-smasher, and Miss Whittaker gave her notice, so the other left with her.'

'Ah, well! one can have too much of seeing the Crown Derby rollin' round the floor. Quite. Then it had nothing to do with — it wasn't on account of any little — '

'It wasn't because they couldn't get along with the nurse, if you mean that,' said Nurse Philliter, with a smile. 'They were very obliging girls, but not very bright.'

'Quite. Well, now, is there any little odd, out-of-the-way incident you can think of that might throw light on the thing. There was a visit from a lawyer, I believe, that agitated your patient quite a lot. Was that in your time?'

'No, I only heard about it from Dr Carr. And he never heard the name of the lawyer, what he came about, or anything.'

'A pity,' said his lordship. 'I have been hoping great things of the lawyer. There's such a sinister charm, don't you think, about lawyers who appear unexpectedly with little bags, and alarm people with mysterious conferences, and then go away leaving urgent messages that if anything happens they are to be sent for. If it hadn't been for the lawyer, I probably shouldn't have treated Dr Carr's medical problem with the respect it deserves. He never came again, or wrote, I suppose?'

'I don't know. Wait a minute. I do remember one thing. I remember Miss Dawson having another hysterical attack of the same sort, and saying just what she said then — 'that they were trying to kill her before her time'.'

'When was that?'

'Oh, a couple of weeks before I left. Miss Whittaker had been up to her with the post, I think, and there were some papers of some kind to sign, and it seems to have upset her. I came in from my walk and found her in a dreadful state. The maids could have told you more about it than I could, really, for they were doing some dusting on the landing at the time and heard her going on, and they ran down and fetched me up to her. I didn't ask them about what happened myself, naturally — it doesn't do for nurses to gossip with the maids behind their employers' backs. Miss Whittaker said that her aunt had had an annoying communication from a solicitor.'

'Yes, it sounds as though there might be something there. Do you remember what the maids were called?'

'What was the name now? A funny one, or I shouldn't remember it — Gotobed, that was it — Bertha and Evelyn Gotobed. I don't know where they went, but I daresay you could find out.'

'Now one last question, and I want you to forget all about Christian kindliness and the law of slander when you answer it. What is Miss Whittaker like?'

An indefinable expression crossed the nurse's face.

'Tall, handsome, very decided in manner,' she said, with an air of doing strict justice against her will, 'an extremely competent nurse — she was at the Royal Free, you know, till she went to live with her aunt. I think she would have made a perfectly wonderful theatre nurse. She did not like me, nor I her, you know, Lord Peter — and it's better I should be telling you so at once, the way you can take everything I say about her with a grain of charity added — but we both knew good hospital work when we saw it, and respected one another.'

'Why in the world didn't she like you, Miss Philliter? I really don't know when I've seen a more likeable kind of person, if you'll 'scuse me mentionin' it.'

'I don't know.' The nurse seemed a little embarrassed. 'The dislike seemed to grow on her. You — perhaps you heard the kind of things people said in the town? when I left? — that Dr Carr and I — Oh! it really was damnable, and I had the most dreadful interview with Matron when I got back here. She *must* have spread those stories. Who else could have done it?'

'Well — you *did* become engaged to Dr Carr, didn't you?' said his lordship, gently. 'Mind you, I'm not sayin' it wasn't a very agreeable occurrence and all that, but — '

'But she said I neglected the patient. I *never* did. I wouldn't think of such a thing.'

'Of course not. No. But, do you suppose that possibly getting engaged was an offence in itself? Is Miss Whittaker engaged to anyone, by the way?'

'No. You mean, was she jealous? I'm sure Dr Carr never gave the slightest, not the *slightest* — '

'Oh, *please*,' cried Lord Peter, 'please don't be

ruffled. Such a nice word, ruffled — like a kitten, I always think — so furry and nice. But even without the least what-d'ye-call-it on Dr Carr's side, he's a very prepossessin' person and all that. Don't you think there *might* be something in it?'

'I did think so once,' admitted Miss Philliter, 'but afterwards, when she got him into such awful trouble over the post-mortem, I gave up the idea.'

'But she didn't object to the post-mortem?'

'She did not. But there's such a thing as putting yourself in the right in the eyes of your neighbours, Lord Peter, and then going off to tell people all about it at Vicarage tea-parties. I wasn't there, but you ask someone who was. I know those tea-parties.'

'Well, it's not impossible. People can be very spiteful if they think they've been slighted.'

'Perhaps you're right,' said Nurse Philliter, thoughtfully. 'But,' she added suddenly, 'that's no motive for murdering a perfectly innocent old lady.'

'That's the second time you've used that word,' said Wimsey, gravely. 'There's no proof yet that it was murder.'

'I know that.'

'But you think it was?'

'I do.'

'And you think she did it?'

'Yes.'

Lord Peter walked across to the aspidistra in the bow-window and stroked its leaves thoughtfully. The silence was broken by a buxom nurse who, entering precipitately first and knocking afterwards, announced with a giggle:

'Excuse me, I'm sure, but you're in request this afternoon, Philliter. Here's Dr Carr come for you.'

Dr Carr followed hard upon his name. The sight of Wimsey struck him speechless.

'I told you I'd be turning up again before long,' said Lord Peter, cheerfully. 'Sherlock is my name and Holmes is my nature. I'm delighted to see you, Dr Carr. Your little matter is well in hand, and seein' I'm not required any longer I'll make a noise like a bee and buzz off.'

'How did *he* get here?' demanded Dr Carr, not altogether pleased.

'Didn't you send him? I think he's very nice,' said Nurse Philliter.

'He's mad,' said Dr Carr.

'He's clever,' said the red-haired nurse.

5

Gossip

'With vollies of eternal babble.'
BUTLER: *Hudibras*

'So you are thinking of coming to live in Leahampton,' said Miss Murgatroyd. 'How *very* nice. I do hope you will be settling down in the parish. We are *not* too well off for weekday congregations — there is so much indifference and so much *Protestantism* about. There! I have dropped a stitch. Provoking! Perhaps it was meant as a little reminder to me not to think uncharitably about Protestants. All is well — I have retrieved it. Were you thinking of taking a house, Miss Climpson?'

'I am not quite sure,' replied Miss Climpson. 'Rents are so very high nowadays, and I fear that to buy a house would be almost beyond my means. I must look round very carefully, and view the question from *all sides*. I should certainly *prefer* to be in this parish — and close to the Church, if possible. Perhaps the Vicar would know whether there is likely to be anything suitable.'

'Oh, yes, he would doubtless be able to suggest something. It is such a very nice, residential neighbourhood. I am sure you would like it. Let me see — you are staying in Nelson

50

Avenue, I think Mrs Tredgold said?'

'Yes — with Mrs Budge at Fairview.'

'I am sure she makes you comfortable. Such a nice woman, though I'm afraid she never stops talking. Hasn't she got any ideas on the subject? I'm sure if there's any news going about, Mrs Budge never fails to get hold of it.'

'Well,' said Miss Climpson, seizing the opening with a swiftness which would have done credit to Napoleon, 'she did say something about a house in Wellington Avenue which she thought might be to let before long.'

'Wellington Avenue? You surprise me! I thought I knew almost everybody there. Could it be the Parfitts — really moving at last! They have been talking about it for at least seven years, and I really had begun to think it was *all talk*. Mrs Peasgood, do you hear that? Miss Climpson says the Parfitts are really leaving that house at last!'

'Bless me,' cried Mrs Peasgood, raising her rather prominent eyes from a piece of plain needlework and focusing them on Miss Climpson like a pair of opera-glasses. 'Well, that *is* news. It must be that brother of hers who was staying with them last week. Possibly he is going to live with them permanently, and that would clinch the matter, of course, for they couldn't get on without another bedroom when the girls come home from school. A very sensible arrangement, I should think. I believe he is quite well off, you know, and it will be a very good thing for those children. I wonder where they will go. I expect it will be one of the new houses out on the Winchester Road, though of course

51

that would mean keeping a car. Still, I expect he would want them to do that in any case. Most likely he will have it himself, and let them have the use of it.'

'I don't think Parfitt was the name,' broke in Miss Climpson hurriedly; 'I'm sure it wasn't. It was a Miss somebody — a Miss Whittaker, I think, Mrs Budge mentioned.'

'Miss Whittaker?' cried both the ladies in chorus. 'Oh, no! *surely* not?'

'I'm sure Miss Whittaker would have told me if she thought of giving up her house,' pursued Miss Murgatroyd. 'We are such great friends. I think Mrs Budge must have run away with a wrong idea. People do build up such amazing stories out of nothing at all.'

'I wouldn't go so far as that,' put in Mrs Peasgood, rebukingly. 'There *may* be something in it. I know dear Miss Whittaker has sometimes spoken to me about wishing to take up chicken-farming. I daresay she has not mentioned the matter *generally*, but then she always confides in *me*. Depend upon it, that is what she intends to do.'

'Mrs Budge didn't actually say Miss Whittaker was moving,' interposed Miss Climpson. 'She said, I think, that Miss Whittaker had been left alone by some relation's death, and she wouldn't be surprised if she found the house lonely.'

'Ah! that's Mrs Budge all over!' said Mrs Peasgood, nodding ominously. 'A most excellent woman, but she sometimes gets hold of the wrong end of the stick. Not but what I've often thought the same thing myself. I said to poor

Mary Whittaker only the other day, 'Don't you find it very lonely in that house, my dear, now that your poor dear Aunt is no more?' I'm sure it would be a very good thing if she did move, or got someone to live with her. It's not a natural life for a young woman, all alone like that, and so I told her. I'm one of those that believe in speaking their mind, you know, Miss Climpson.'

'Well, now, so am I, Mrs Peasgood,' rejoined Miss Climpson promptly, 'that is what I said to Mrs Budge at the time. I said, 'Do I understand that there was anything *odd* about the old lady's death?' — because she had spoken of the *peculiar circumstances* of the case, and, you know, I should not *at all like* to live in a house which could be called in any way *notorious*. I should really feel quite *uncomfortable* about it.' In saying which, Miss Climpson no doubt spoke with perfect sincerity.

'But not at all — not at all,' cried Miss Murgatroyd, so eagerly that Mrs Peasgood, who had paused to purse up her face and assume an expression of portentous secrecy before replying, was completely crowded out and left at the post. 'There never was a more wicked story. The death was natural — perfectly natural, and a most happy release, poor soul, I'm sure her sufferings at the last were truly terrible. It was all a scandalous story put about by that young Dr Carr (whom I'm sure I never liked) simply to aggrandise himself. As though any doctor would pronounce so definitely upon what exact date it would please God to call a poor sufferer to Himself! Human pride and vanity make a most shocking exhibition, Miss Climpson, when they lead us to cast suspicion on innocent people, simply because we are wedded to our own presumptuous opinions. Poor Miss Whittaker! She went through a most terrible time. But it was proved — absolutely *proved*, that there was nothing in the story at all, and I hoped that young man was properly ashamed of himself.'

'There may be two opinions about that, Miss Murgatroyd,' said Mrs Peasgood. 'I say what I think, Miss Climpson, and in my opinion there should have been an inquest. I try to be up-to-date, and I believe Dr Carr to have been a very able young man, though, of course, he was not the kind of old-fashioned family doctor that appeals to elderly people. It was a great pity that nice Nurse Philliter was sent away — that woman Forbes was no more use than a headache — to use my brother's rather vigorous expression. I don't think she knew her job, and that's a fact.'

'Nurse Forbes was a charming person,' snapped Miss Murgatroyd, pink with indignation at being called elderly.

'That may be,' retorted Mrs Peasgood, 'but you can't get over the fact that she nearly killed herself one day by taking nine grains of calomel by mistake for three. She told me that herself, and what she did in one case she might do in another.'

'But Miss Dawson wasn't given anything,' said Miss Murgatroyd, 'and, at any rate, Nurse Forbes's mind was on her patient, and not on flirting with the doctor. I've always thought that

Dr Carr felt a spite against her for taking his young woman's place, and nothing would have pleased him better than to get her into trouble.'

'You don't mean,' said Miss Climpson, 'that he would refuse a certificate and cause all that trouble, just to annoy the nurse. *Surely* no doctor would dare do that.'

'Of course not,' said Mrs Peasgood, 'and nobody with a grain of sense would suppose it for a moment.'

'Thank you very much, Mrs Peasgood,' cried Miss Murgatroyd, 'thank you very much. I'm sure — '

'I say what I think,' said Mrs Peasgood.

'Then I'm glad I haven't such uncharitable thoughts,' said Miss Murgatroyd.

'I don't think your own observations are so remarkable for their charity,' retorted Mrs Peasgood.

Fortunately, at this moment Miss Murgatroyd, in her agitation, gave a vicious tweak to the wrong needle and dropped twenty-nine stitches at once. The Vicar's wife, scenting battle from afar, hurried over with a plate of scones, and helped to bring about a diversion. To her, Miss Climpson, doggedly sticking to her mission in life, broached the subject of the house in Wellington Avenue.

'Well, I don't know, I'm sure,' replied Mrs Tredgold, 'but there's Miss Whittaker just arrived. Come over to my corner and I'll introduce her to you, and you can have a nice chat about it. You will like each other so much, she is such a keen worker. Oh! and Mrs Peasgood, my husband is so anxious to have a word with you about the choirboys' social. He is discussing it now with Mrs Findlater. I wonder if you'd be so very good as to come and give him your opinion? He values it so much.'

Thus tactfully the good lady parted the disputants and, having deposited Mrs Peasgood safely under the clerical wing, towed Miss Climpson away to an armchair near the teatable.

'Dear Miss Whittaker, I so want you to know Miss Climpson. She is a near neighbour of yours — in Nelson Avenue, and I hope we shall persuade her to make her home among us.'

'That will be delightful,' said Miss Whittaker.

The first impression which Miss Climpson got of Mary Whittaker was that she was totally out of place among the teatables of St Onesimus. With her handsome, strongly-marked features and quiet air of authority, she was of the type that 'does well' in City offices. She had a pleasant and self-possessed manner, and was beautifully tailored — not mannishly, and yet with a severe fineness of outline that negatived the appeal of a beautiful figure. With her long and melancholy experience of frustrated womanhood, observed in a dreary succession of cheap boarding-houses, Miss Climpson was able to dismiss one theory which had vaguely formed itself in her mind. This was no passionate nature, cramped by association with an old woman and eager to be free to mate before youth should depart. *That* look she knew well — she could diagnose it with dreadful accuracy at the first glance in the tone of a voice saying, 'How do you do?' But meeting

Mary Whittaker's clear, light eyes under their well-shaped brows, she was struck by a sudden sense of familiarity. She had seen that look before, though the where and the when escaped her. Chatting volubly about her arrival in Leahampton, her introduction to the Vicar and her approval of the Hampshire air and sand soil, Miss Climpson racked her shrewd brain for a clue. But the memory remained obstinately somewhere at the back of her head. 'It will come to me in the night,' thought Miss Climpson confidently, 'and meanwhile I won't say anything about the house; it would seem so pushing on a first acquaintance.'

Whereupon, fate instantly intervened to overthrow this prudent resolve, and very nearly ruined the whole effect of Miss Climpson's diplomacy at one fell swoop.

The form which the avenging Errinyes assumed was that of the youngest Miss Findlater — the gushing one — who came romping over to them, her hands filled with baby-linen, and plumped down on the end of the sofa beside Miss Whittaker.

'Mary my *dear*! Why didn't you tell me? You really are going to start your chicken-farming scheme at once. I'd no *idea* you'd got on so far with your plans. How *could* you let me hear it first from somebody else? You promised to tell me before anybody.'

'But, I didn't know it myself,' replied Miss Whittaker, coolly. 'Who told you this wonderful story?'

'Why, Mrs Peasgood said that she heard it

from ... ' Here Miss Findlater was in a difficulty. She had not yet been introduced to Miss Climpson and hardly knew how to refer to her before her face. 'This lady' was what a shopgirl would say; 'Miss Climpson' would hardly do, as she had, so to speak, no official cognisance of the name; 'Mrs Budge's new lodger' was obviously impossible in the circumstances. She hesitated — then beamed a bright appeal to Miss Climpson, and said: 'Our new helper — may I introduce myself? I do so detest formality, don't you, and to belong to the Vicarage work-party is a sort of introduction in itself, don't you think? Miss Climpson, I believe? How do you do? It is true, isn't it, Mary? — that you are letting your house to Miss Climpson, and starting a poultry farm at Alford.'

'Certainly not that I know of. Miss Climpson and I have only just met one another.' The tone of Miss Whittaker's voice suggested that the first meeting might very willingly be the last as far as she was concerned.

'Oh dear!' cried the youngest Miss Findlater, who was fair and bobbed and rather coltish, 'I believe I've dropped a brick. I'm *sure* Mrs Peasgood understood that it was all settled.' She appealed to Miss Climpson again.

'*Quite* a mistake!' said that lady, energetically, 'what *must* you be thinking of me, Miss Whittaker? *Of course*, I could not *possibly* have said such a thing. I only happened to mention — in the most *casual* way, that I was looking — that is, *thinking* of looking about — for a house in the neighbourhood of the Church — so convenient,

you know, for *Early Services* and *Saints' Days*
— and it was suggested — just *suggested*, I really
forget by *whom*, that you *might*, just *possibly*, at
some time, consider letting your house. I assure
you, that was all.' In saying which, Miss Climpson was not wholly accurate or disingenuous but
excused herself to her conscience on the rather
Jesuitical grounds that where so much responsibility was floating about it was best to pin it
down in the quarter which made for peace. 'Miss
Murgatroyd,' she added, 'put me right at once,
for she said you were *certainly* not thinking of
any such thing, or you would have told her
before anybody else.'

Miss Whittaker laughed.

'But I shouldn't,' she said, 'I should have told
my house agent. It's quite true, I did have it in
mind, but I certainly haven't taken any steps.'

'You really are thinking of doing it, then?'
cried Miss Findlater. 'I do hope so — because, if
you do, I mean to apply for a job on the farm!
I'm simply longing to get away from all these
silly tennis parties and things, and live close to
the earth and the fundamental crudities. Do you
read Sheila Kaye-Smith?'

Miss Climpson said no, but she was very fond
of Thomas Hardy.

'It really is terrible, living in a little town like
this,' went on Miss Findlater, 'so full of
aspidistras, you know, and small gossip. You've
no idea what a dreadfully gossipy place
Leahampton is, Miss Climpson. I'm sure, Mary
dear, you must have had more than enough of it,
with that tiresome Dr Carr and the things people

said. I don't wonder you're thinking of getting rid of that house. I shouldn't think you could ever feel comfortable in it again.'

'Why on earth not?' said Miss Whittaker, lightly. Too lightly? Miss Climpson was startled to recognise in eye and voice the curious quick defensiveness of the neglected spinster who cries out that she has no use for men.

'Oh, well,' said Miss Findlater, 'I always think it's a little sad, living where people have died, you know. Dear Miss Dawson — though of course it really was merciful that she should be released — all the same — '

Evidently, thought Miss Climpson, she was turning the matter off. The atmosphere of suspicion surrounding the death had been in her mind, but she shied at referring to it.

'There are very few houses in which somebody hasn't died sometime or other,' said Miss Whittaker. 'I really can't see why people should worry about it. I suppose it's just a question of not realising. We are not sensitive to the past lives of people we don't know. Just as we are much less upset about epidemics and accidents that happen a long way off. Do you really suppose, by the way, Miss Climpson, that this Chinese business is coming to anything? Everybody seems to take it very casually. If all this rioting and Bolshevism was happening in Hyde Park, there'd be a lot more fuss made about it.'

Miss Climpson made a suitable reply. That night she wrote to Lord Peter:

'Miss Whittaker has asked me to tea. She tells me that, *much as she would enjoy* an active,

60

country life, with something definite to do, she has a *deep affection* for the house in Wellington Avenue, and *cannot tear herself away.* She seems *very anxious* to give this impression. Would it be *fair* for me to say 'The lady doth protest *too much*, methinks'? The *Prince of Denmark* might even add: 'Let the galled jade wince' — if one can use that expression of a *lady*. How wonderful Shakespeare is! One can *always* find a phrase in his works for *any* situation!'

6

Found Dead

'Blood, though it sleep a time, yet never dies.'
CHAPMAN: *The Widow's Tears*

'You know, Wimsey, I think you've found a mare's nest,' objected Mr Parker. 'I don't believe there's the slightest reason for supposing that there was anything odd about the Dawson woman's death. You've nothing to go on but a conceited young doctor's opinion and a lot of silly gossip.'

'You've got an official mind, Charles,' replied his friend. 'Your official passion for evidence is gradually sapping your brilliant intellect and smothering your instincts. You're overcivilised, that's your trouble. Compared with you, I am a child of nature. I dwell among the untrodden ways beside the springs of Dove, a maid whom there are (I am shocked to say) few to praise, likewise very few to love, which is perhaps just as well. I *know* there is something wrong about this case.'

'How?'

'How? — well, just as I know there is something wrong about that case of reputed Lafite '76 which that infernal fellow Pettigrew-Robinson had the nerve to try out on me the other night. It has a nasty flavour.'

'Flavour be damned. There's no indication of violence or poison. There's no motive for doing away with the old girl. And there's no possibility of proving anything against anybody.'

Lord Peter selected a Villar y Villa from his case, and lighted it with artistic care.

'Look here,' he said, 'will you take a bet about it? I'll lay you ten to one that Agatha Dawson was murdered, twenty to one that Mary Whittaker did it, and fifty to one that I bring it home to her within the year. Are you on?'

Parker laughed. 'I'm a poor man, your Majesty,' he temporised.

'There you are,' said Lord Peter, triumphantly, 'you're not comfortable about it yourself. If you were, you'd have said, 'It's taking your money, old chap,' and closed like a shot, in the happy assurance of a certainty.'

'I've seen enough to know that nothing is a certainty,' retorted the detective, 'but I'll take you — in half-crowns,' he added, cautiously.

'Had you said ponies,' replied Lord Peter, 'I would have taken your alleged poverty into consideration and spared you, but seven-and-sixpence will neither make nor break you. Consequently, I shall proceed to make my statements good.'

'And what step do you propose taking?' inquired Parker, sarcastically. 'Shall you apply for an exhumation order and search for poison, regardless of the analyst's report? Or kidnap Miss Whittaker and apply the third-degree in the Gallic manner?'

'Not at all. I am more modern. I shall use

up-to-date psychological methods. Like the people in the Psalms, I lay traps; I catch men. I shall let the alleged criminal convict herself.'

'Go on! You are a one, aren't you?' said Parker, jeeringly.

'I am indeed. It is a well-established psychological fact that criminals cannot let well alone. They — '

'Revisit the place of the crime?'

'Don't interrupt, blast you. They take unnecessary steps to cover the traces which they haven't left, and so invite, seriatim, Suspicion, Inquiry, Proof, Conviction and the Gallows. Eminent legal writers — no, pax! don't chuck that St Augustine about, it's valuable. Anyhow, not to cast the jewels of my eloquence into the pig-bucket, I propose to insert this advertisement in all the morning papers. Miss Whittaker must read *some* product of our brilliant journalistic age, I suppose. By this means, we shall kill two birds with one stone.'

'Start two hares at once, you mean,' grumbled Parker. 'Hand it over.'

'BERTHA AND EVELYN GOTOBED formerly in the service of Miss Agatha Dawson, of 'The Grove,' Wellington Avenue, Leahampton, are requested to communicate with J. Murbles, solicitor, of Staple Inn, when they will hear of SOMETHING TO THEIR ADVANTAGE.'

'Rather good, I think, don't you?' said Wimsey. 'Calculated to rouse suspicion in the most innocent mind. I bet you Mary Whittaker will fall for that.'

'In what way?'

'I don't know. That's what's so interesting. I hope nothing unpleasant will happen to dear old Murbles. I should hate to lose him. He's such a perfect type of the family solicitor. Still, a man in his profession must be prepared to take risks.'

'Oh, bosh!' said Parker. 'But I agree that it might be as well to get hold of the girls, if you really want to find out about the Dawson household. Servants always know everything.'

'It isn't only that. Don't you remember that Nurse Philliter said the girls were sacked shortly before she left herself? Now, passing over the odd circumstances of the nurse's own dismissal — the story about Miss Dawson's refusing to take food from her hands, which wasn't at all borne out by the old lady's attitude to her nurse — isn't it worth considerin' that these girls should have been pushed off on some excuse just about three weeks after one of those hysterical attacks of Miss Dawson's? Doesn't it rather look as though everybody who was likely to remember anything about that particular episode had been got out of the way?'

'Well, there was a good reason for getting rid of the girls.'

'Crockery? — well, nowadays it's not so easy to get good servants. Mistresses put up with a deal more carelessness than they did in the dear dead days beyond recall. Then, about that attack. Why did Miss Whittaker choose just the very moment when the highly-intelligent Nurse

Philliter had gone for her walk, to bother Miss Dawson about signin' some tiresome old lease or other? If business was liable to upset the old girl, why not have a capable person at hand to calm her down?'

'Oh, but Miss Whittaker is a trained nurse. She was surely capable enough to see to her aunt herself.'

'I'm perfectly sure she was a very capable woman indeed,' said Wimsey, with emphasis.

'Oh, all right. You're prejudiced. But stick the ad in by all means. It can't do any harm.'

Lord Peter paused, in the very act of ringing the bell. His jaw slackened, giving his long, narrow face a faintly foolish and hesitant look, reminiscent of the heroes of Mr P. G. Wodehouse.

'You don't think — ' he began. 'Oh! rats!' He pressed the button. 'It *can't* do any harm, as you say. Bunter, see that this advertisement appears in the personal columns of all this list of papers, every day until further notice.'

★ ★ ★

The advertisement made its first appearance on the Tuesday morning. Nothing of any note happened during the weeks, except that Miss Climpson wrote in some distress to say that the youngest Miss Findlater had at length succeeded in persuading Miss Whittaker to take definite steps about the poultry farm. They had gone away together to look at a business which they had seen advertised in the *Poultry News*, and

66

proposed to be away for some weeks. Miss Climpson feared that under the circumstances she would not be able to carry on any investigations of sufficient importance to justify her *far too generous* salary. She had, however, become friendly with Miss Findlater, who had promised to tell her *all about* their doings. Lord Peter replied in reassuring terms.

On the Tuesday following, Mr Parker was just wrestling in prayer with his charlady, who had a tiresome habit of boiling his breakfast kippers till they resembled heavily pickled loofahs, when the telephone whirred aggressively.

'Is that you, Charles?' asked Lord Peter's voice. 'I say, Murbles has had a letter about that girl, Bertha Gotobed. She disappeared from her lodgings last Thursday, and her landlady, getting anxious, and having seen the advertisement, is coming to tell us all she knows. Can you come round to Staple Inn at eleven?'

'Dunno,' said Parker, a little irritably. 'I've got a job to see to. Surely you can tackle it by yourself.'

'Oh, yes!' The voice was peevish. 'But I thought you'd like to have some of the fun. What an ungrateful devil you are. You aren't taking the faintest interest in this case.'

'Well — I don't believe in it, you know. All right — don't use language like that — you'll frighten the girl at the Exchange. I'll see what I can do. Eleven? — right! — Oh, I say!'

'Cluck!' said the telephone.

'Rung off,' said Parker, bitterly. 'Bertha Gotobed. H'm! I could have sworn — '

He reached across to the breakfast table for the *Daily Yell*, which was propped against the marmalade jar, and read with pursed lips a paragraph whose heavily leaded headlines had caught his eye, just before the interruption of the kipper episode.

'NIPPY' FOUND DEAD
IN EPPING FOREST

£5 Note in Handbag

He took up the receiver and asked for Wimsey's number. The manservant answered him.

'His lordship is in his bath, sir. Shall I put you through?'

'Please,' said Parker.

The telephone clucked again. Presently Lord Peter's voice came faintly, 'Hullo!'

'Did the landlady mention where Bertha Gotobed was employed?'

'Yes — she was a waitress at the Corner House. Why this interest all of a sudden? You snub me in my bed, but you woo me in my bath. It sounds like a music-hall song of the less refined. Why, oh why?'

'Haven't you seen the papers?'

'No. I leave these follies till breakfast time. What's up? Are we ordered to Shanghai? or have they taken sixpence off the income tax?'

'Shut up, you fool, it's serious. You're too late.'

'What for?'

'Bertha Gotobed was found dead in Epping Forest this morning.'

'Good God! Dead? How? What of?'

'No idea. Poison or something. Or heart failure. No violence. No robbery. No clue. I'm going down to the Yard about it now.'

'God forgive me, Charles. D'you know, I had a sort of awful feeling when you said that ad could do no harm. Dead. Poor girl! Charles, I feel like a murderer. Oh, damn! and I'm all wet. It does make one feel so helpless. Look here, you spin down to the Yard and tell 'em what you know and I'll join you there in half a tick. Anyway, there's no doubt about it now.'

'Oh, but look here. It may be something quite different. Nothing to do with your ad.'

'Pigs *may* fly. Use your common sense. Oh! and Charles, does it mention the sister?'

'Yes. There was a letter from her on the body, by which they identified it. She got married last month and went to Canada.'

'That's saved her life. She'll be in absolutely horrible danger, if she comes back. We must get hold of her and warn her. And find out what she knows. Good-bye. I *must* get some clothes on. Oh, hell!'

Cluck! the line went dead again, and Mr Parker, abandoning the kippers without regret, ran feverishly out of the house and down Lamb's Conduit Street to catch a diver tram to Westminster.

The Chief of Scotland Yard, Sir Andrew Mackenzie, was a very old friend of Lord Peter's. He received that agitated young man kindly and listened with attention to his slightly involved story of cancer, wills, mysterious solicitor and advertisement in the agony column.

'It's a curious coincidence,' he said, indulgently, 'and I can understand your feeling upset about it. But you may set your mind at rest. I have the police-surgeon's report, and he is quite convinced that the death was perfectly natural. No signs whatever of any assault. They will make an examination, of course, but I don't think there is the slightest reason to suspect foul play.'

'But what was she doing in Epping Forest?'

Sir Andrew shrugged gently.

'That must be inquired into, of course. Still — young people *do* wander about, you know. There's a fiancée somewhere. Something to do with the railway, I believe. Collins has gone down to interview him. Or she may have been with some other friend.'

'But if the death was natural, no one would leave a sick or dying girl like that?'

'*You* wouldn't. But say there had been some running about — some horse-play — and the girl fell dead, as these heart cases sometimes do. The companion may well have taken fright and cleared out. It's not unheard of.'

Lord Peter looked unconvinced.

'How long has she been dead?'

'About five or six days, our man thinks. It was quite by accident that she was found then at all; it's quite an unfrequented part of the Forest. A party of young people were exploring with a couple of terriers, and one of the dogs nosed out the body.'

'Was it out in the open?'

'Not exactly. It lay among some bushes — the sort of place where a frolicsome young couple might go to play hide-and-seek.'

'Or where a murderer might go to play hide and let the police seek,' said Wimsey.

'Well, well. Have it your own way,' said Sir Andrew, smiling. 'If it was murder, it must have been a poisoning job, for, as I say, there was not the slightest sign of a wound or a struggle. I'll let you have the report on the autopsy. In the meanwhile, if you'd like to run down there with Inspector Parker, you can of course have any facilities you want. And if you discover anything, let me know.'

Wimsey thanked him, and, collecting Parker from an adjacent office, rushed him briskly down the corridor.

'I don't like it,' he said, 'that is, of course, it's very gratifying to know that our first steps in psychology have led to action, so to speak, but I wish to God it hadn't been quite such decisive action. We'd better trot down to Epping straight away, and see the landlady later. I've got a new car, by the way, which you'll like.'

Mr Parker took one look at the slim black monster, with its long rakish body and polished-copper twin exhaust, and decided there and then that the only hope of getting down to Epping without interference was to look as official as possible and wave his police authority under the eyes of every man in blue along the route. He shoe-horned himself into his seat without protest, and was more unnerved than relieved to find himself shoot suddenly ahead of the traffic — not with the bellowing roar of the ordinary racing engine, but in a smooth, uncanny silence.

'The new Daimler Twin-Six,' said Lord Peter, skimming dexterously round a lorry without appearing to look at it. 'With a racing body. Specially built . . . useful . . . gadgets . . . no row — hate row . . . like Edmund Sparkler . . . very anxious there should be no row . . . Little Dorrit . . . remember . . . call her Mrs Merdle . . . for that reason . . . presently we'll see what she can do.'

The promise was fulfilled before their arrival at the spot where the body had been found. Their arrival made a considerable sensation among the little crowd which business or curiosity had drawn to the spot. Lord Peter was instantly pounced upon by four reporters and a synod of Press photographers, whom his presence encouraged in the hope that the mystery might turn out to be a three-column splash after all. Parker, to his annoyance, was photographed in the undignified act of extricating himself from 'Mrs Merdle'. Superintendent Walmisley came politely to his assistance, rebuked the onlookers, and led him to the scene of action.

The body had been already removed to the mortuary, but a depression in the moist ground showed clearly enough where it had lain. Lord Peter groaned faintly as he saw it.

'Damn this nasty warm spring weather,' he said, with feeling. 'April showers — sun and water — couldn't be worse. Body much altered, Superintendent?'

'Well, yes, rather, my lord, especially in the exposed parts. But there's no doubt about the identity.'

'I didn't suppose there was. How was it lying?'

'On the back, quite quiet and natural-like. No disarrangement of clothing, of anything. She must have sat down when she felt herself bad and fallen back.'

'M'm. The rain has spoilt any footprints or signs on the ground. And it's grassy. Beastly stuff, grass, eh, Charles?'

'Yes. These twigs don't seem to have been broken at all, Superintendent.'

'Oh, no,' said the officer, 'no signs of a struggle, as I pointed out in my report.'

'No — but if she'd sat down here and fallen back as you suggest, don't you think her weight would have snapped some of these young shoots?'

The Superintendent glanced sharply at the Scotland Yard man.

'You don't suppose she was brought and put here, do you, sir?'

'I don't suppose anything,' retorted Parker. 'I merely drew attention to a point which I think you should consider. What are these wheel-marks?'

'That's our car, sir. We backed it up here and took her up that way.'

'And all this trampling is your men too, I suppose?'

'Partly that, sir, and partly the party as found her.'

'You noticed no other person's tracks, I suppose?'

'No, sir. But it's rained considerably this last week. Besides, the rabbits have been all over the place, as you can see, and other creatures too, I fancy. Weasels, or something of that sort.'

'Oh! Well, I think you'd better take a look round. There might be traces of some kind a bit farther away. Make a circle, and report anything you see. And you oughtn't to have let all that bunch of people get so near. Put a cordon round and tell 'em to move on. Have you seen all you want, Peter?'

Wimsey had been poking his stick aimlessly into the bole of an oak-tree at a few yards' distance. Now he stooped and lifted out a package which had been stuffed into a cleft. The two policemen hurried forward with eager interest, which evaporated somewhat at the sight of the find — a ham sandwich and an empty Bass bottle, roughly wrapped up in a greasy newspaper.

'Picnickers,' said Walmisley, with a snort. 'Nothing to do with the body, I daresay.'

'I think you're mistaken,' said Wimsey placidly. 'When did the girl disappear, exactly?'

'Well, she went off duty at the Corner House at five, a week ago tomorrow, that's Wednesday, 27th,' said Parker.

'And this is the *Evening Views* of Wednesday, 27th,' said Wimsey. 'Late Final edition. Now that edition isn't on the streets till about 6 o'clock. So unless somebody brought it down and had supper here, it was probably brought by the girl

74

herself or her companion. It's hardly likely anyone would come and picnic here afterwards, not with the body there. Not that bodies need necessarily interfere with one's enjoyment of one's food. A la guerre comme à la guerre. But for the moment there isn't a war on.'

'That's true, sir. But you're assuming the death took place on the Wednesday or Thursday. She may have been somewhere else — living with someone in town or anywhere.'

'Crushed again,' said Wimsey. 'Still, it's a curious coincidence.'

'It is, my lord, and I'm very glad you found the things. Will you take charge of 'em, Mr Parker, or shall I?'

'Better take them along and put them with the other things,' said Parker, extending his hand to take them from Wimsey, whom they seemed to interest quite disproportionately. 'I fancy his lordship's right and that the parcel came here along with the girl. And that certainly looks as if she didn't come alone. Possibly that young man of hers was with her. Looks like the old, old story. Take care of that bottle, old man, it may have fingerprints on it.'

'You can have the bottle,' said Wimsey. 'May we ne'er lack a friend or a bottle to give him, as Dick Swiveller says. But I earnestly beg that before you caution your respectable young railway clerk that anything he says may be taken down and used against him, you will cast your eye, and your nose, upon this ham sandwich.'

'What's wrong with it?' inquired Parker.

'Nothing. It appears to be in astonishingly

75

good preservation, thanks to this admirable oak-tree. The stalwart oak — for so many centuries Britain's bulwark against the invader! Heart of oak are our ships — not hearts, by the way, as it is usually misquoted. But I am puzzled by the incongruity between the sandwich and the rest of the outfit.'

'It's an ordinary ham sandwich, isn't it?'

'Oh, gods of the wine-flask and the board, how long? how long? — it is a ham sandwich, Goth, but not an ordinary one. Never did it see Lyons's kitchen, or the counter of the multiple store or the delicatessen shop in the back street. The pig that was sacrificed to make this dainty tit-bit fattened in no dull style, never knew the daily ration of pig wash or the not unmixed rapture of the domestic garbage-pail. Observe the hard texture, the deep brownish tint of the lean; the rich fat, yellow as a Chinaman's cheek; the dark spot where the black treacle cure has soaked in, to make a dish fit to lure Zeus from Olympus. And tell me, man of no discrimination and worthy to be fed on boiled cod all the year round, tell me how it comes that your little waitress and her railway clerk came down to Epping Forest to regale themselves on sand-wiches made from coal-black, treacle-cured Bradenham ham, which long ago ran as a young wild boar about the woodlands, till death trans-lated it to an incorruptible and more glorious body? I may add that it costs about 3s. a pound uncooked — an argument which you will allow to be weighty.'

'That's odd, certainly,' said Parker. 'I imagine

that only rich people — '

'Only rich people or people who understand eating as a fine art,' said Wimsey. 'The two classes are by no means identical, though they occasionally overlap.'

'It may be very important,' said Parker, wrapping the exhibits up carefully. 'We'd better go along now and see the body.'

The examination was not a very pleasant one, for the weather had been damp and warm and there had certainly been weasels. In fact, after a brief glance, Wimsey left the two policemen to carry on alone, and devoted his attention to the dead girl's handbag. He glanced through the letter from Evelyn Gotobed — (now Evelyn Cropper) — and noted down the Canadian address. He turned the cutting of his own advertisement out of an inner compartment, and remained for some time in consideration of the £5 note which lay, folded up, side by side with a 10s. Treasury note, 7s. 8d. in silver and copper, a latchkey and a powder compact.

'You're having this note traced, Walmisley, I suppose?'

'Oh, yes, my lord, certainly.'

'And the latch-key, I imagine, belongs to the girl's lodgings.'

'No doubt it does. We have asked her landlady to come and identify the body. Not that there's any doubt about it, but just as a matter of routine. She may give us some help. Ah!' — the Superintendent peered out of the mortuary door — 'I think this must be the lady.'

The stout and motherly woman who emerged

from a taxi in charge of a youthful policeman, identified the body without difficulty, and amid many sobs, as that of Bertha Gotobed. 'Such a nice young lady,' she mourned. 'What a terrible thing, oh dear! who would go to do a thing like that? I've been in such a state of worriment ever since she didn't come home last Wednesday. I'm sure many's the time I've said to myself I wished I'd had my tongue cut out before I ever showed her that wicked advertisement. Ah, I see you've got it there, sir. A dreadful thing it is that people should be luring young girls with stories about something to their advantage. A sinful old devil — calling himself a lawyer, too! When she didn't come back and didn't come back I wrote to the wretch, telling him I was on his track and was coming round to have the law on him as sure as my name's Dorcas Gulliver. He wouldn't have got round me — not that I'd be the bird he was looking for, being sixty-one come Mid-Summer Day — and so I told him.'

Lord Peter's gravity was somewhat upset by the diatribe against the highly respectable Mr Murbles of Staple Inn, whose own version of Mrs Gulliver's communication had been decently expurgated. 'How shocked the old boy must have been,' he murmured to Parker. 'I'm for it next time I see him.'

Mrs Gulliver's voice moaned on and on.

'Such respectable girls, both of them, and Miss Evelyn married to that nice young man from Canada. Deary me, it will be a terrible upset for her. And there's poor John Ironsides, was to have married Miss Bertha, the poor lamb, this very Whitsuntide as ever is. A very steady, respectable man — a clurk on the Southern, which he always used to say, joking like, 'Slow but safe, like the Southern — that's me, Mrs G.' T'ch, t'ch — who'd a believed it? And it's not as if she was one of the flighty sort. I give her a latch-key gladly, for she's sometimes be on late duty, but never any staying out after her time. That's why it worried me so, her not coming back. There's many nowadays as would wash one's hands and glad to be rid of them, knowing what they might be up to. No. When the time passed and she didn't come back, I said, 'Mark my words, I said, she's been kidnapped, I said, by that Murbles.''

'Had she been long with you, Mrs Gulliver?' asked Parker.

'Not above fifteen months or so, she hadn't, but bless you, I don't have to know a young lady fifteen days to know if she's a good girl or not. You gets to know by the look of 'em almost, when you've 'ad my experience.'

'Did she and her sister come to you together?'

'They did. They come to me when they was lookin' for work in London. And they could a' fallen into a deal worse hands I can tell you, two young things from the country, and them that fresh and pretty looking.'

'They were uncommonly lucky, I'm sure, Mrs Gulliver,' said Lord Peter, 'and they must have found it a great comfort to be able to confide in you and get your advice.'

'Well, I think they did,' said Mrs Gulliver; 'not that young people nowadays seems to want much guidance from them as is older. Train up a child and away she go, as the Good Book says. But Miss Evelyn, that's now Mrs Cropper — she's had this London idea put into her head, and up they comes with the idea of bein' made ladies of, havin' only been in service before, though what's the difference between serving in one of them tea-shops at the beck of all the nasty tagrag and bobtail and serving in a lady's home, I *don't* see, except that you works harder and don't get your meals so comfortable. Still, Miss Evelyn, she was always the go-ahead one of the two, and she did very well for herself, I will say, meetin' Mr Cropper as used to take his breakfast regular at the Corner House every morning and took a liking to the girl in the most honourable way.'

'That was very fortunate. Have you any idea what gave them the notion of coming to town?'

'Well, now, sir, it's funny you should ask that, because it was a thing I never could understand. The lady as they used to be in service with, down in the country, she put it into Miss Evelyn's head. Now, sir, wouldn't you think that with good service 'ard to come by, she'd have done all she could to keep them with her? But no! There was a bit of trouble one day, it seems, over Bertha — this poor girl here, poor lamb — it do break one's 'eart to see her like that, don't it, sir? — over Bertha 'avin' broke an old teapot — a very valuable one by all accounts, and the lady told 'er she couldn't put up with 'avin' her things broke no more. So she says: 'You'll 'ave to go,' she says, 'but,' she says, 'I'll

80

give you a very good character and you'll soon get a good place. And I'll expect Evelyn'll want to go with you,' she says, 'so I'll have to find someone else to do for me,' she says. 'But,' she says, 'why not go to London? You'll do better there and have a much more interesting life than what you would at home,' she says. And the end of it was, she filled 'em up so with stories of how fine a place London was and how grand situations was to be had for the asking, that they was mad to go, and she give them a present of money and behaved very handsome take it all round.'

'H'm,' said Wimsey, 'she seems to have been very particular about her teapot. Was Bertha a great crockery-breaker?'

'Well, sir, she never broke nothing of mine. But this Miss Whittaker — that was the name — she was one of these opiniated ladies, as will 'ave their own way in everythink. A fine temper she 'ad, or so poor Bertha said, though Miss Evelyn — her as is now Mrs Cropper — *she* always 'ad an idea as there was somethink at the back of it. Miss Evelyn was always the sharp one, as you might say. But there, sir, we all 'as our peculiarities, don't we? It's my own belief as the lady had somebody of her own choice as she wanted to put in the place of Bertha — that's this one — and Evelyn — as is now Mrs Cropper, you understand me — and she jest trampled up an excuse, as they say, to get rid of 'em.'

'Very possibly,' said Wimsey. 'I suppose, Inspector, Evelyn Gotobed — '

81

'Now Mrs Cropper,' put in Mrs Gulliver with a sob.

'Mrs Cropper, I should say — has been communicated with?'

'Oh, yes, my lord. We cabled her at once.'

'Good. I wish you'd let me know when you hear from her.'

'We shall be in touch with Inspector Parker, my lord, of course.'

'Of course. Well, Charles, I'm going to leave you to it. I've got a telegram to send. Or will you come with me?'

'Thanks, no,' said Parker. 'To be frank, I don't like your methods of driving. Being in the Force, I prefer to keep on the windy side of the law.'

'Windy is the word for you,' said Peter. 'I'll see you in Town, then.'

7

Ham and Brandy

'Tell me what you eat and I will tell you what you are.'

BRILLAT-SAVARIN

'Well,' said Wimsey, as Parker was ushered in that same evening by Bunter, 'have you got anything fresh?'

'Yes, I've got a new theory of the crime, which knocks yours into a cocked hat. I've got evidence to support it, too.'

'Which crime, by the way?'

'Oh, the Epping Forest business. I don't believe the old Dawson person was murdered at all. That's just an idea of yours.'

'I see. And you're now going to tell me that Bertha Gotobed was got hold of by the White Slave people.'

'How did you know?' asked Parker, a little peevishly.

'Because Scotland Yard have two maggots which crop up whenever anything happens to a young woman. Either it's White Slavery or Dope Dens — sometimes both. You are going to say it's both.'

'Well, I was, as a matter of fact. It so often is, you know. We've traced the £5 note.'

'That's important, anyhow.'

'Yes. It seems to me to be the clue to the whole thing. It is one of a series paid out to a Mrs Forrest, living in South Audley Street. I've been round to make some inquiries.'

'Did you see the lady?'

'No, she was out. She usually is, I'm told. In fact, her habits seem to be expensive, irregular and mysterious. She has an elegantly furnished flat over a flower-shop.'

'A service flat?'

'No. One of the quiet kind, with a lift you work yourself. She only turns up occasionally, mostly in the evenings, spends a night or two and departs. Food ordered in from Fortnum & Mason's. Bills paid promptly by note or cheque. Cleaning done by an elderly female who comes in about eleven, by which time Mrs Forrest has usually gone out.'

'Doesn't anybody ever see her?'

'Oh dear, yes! The people in the flat below and the girl at the flower-shop were able to give me quite a good description of her. Tall, overdressed, musquash and those abbreviated sort of shoes with jewelled heels and hardly any uppers — you know the sort of thing. Heavily peroxided; strong aroma of origan wafted out upon the passer-by; powder too white for the fashion and mouth heavily obscured with sealing-wax red; eyebrows painted black to startle, not deceive; fingernails a monument to Kraska — the pink variety.'

'I'd no idea you studied the Woman's Page to such good purpose, Charles.'

'Drives a Renault Four-seater, dark green with tapestry doings. Garages just around the corner.

84

I've seen the man, and he says the car was out on the night of the 27th. Went out at 1.30. Returned about 8 the next morning.'

'How much petrol had been used?'

'We worked that out. Just about enough for a run to Epping and back. What's more, the charwoman says that there had been supper for two in the flat that night, and three bottles of champagne drunk. Also, there is a ham in the flat.'

'A Bradenham ham?'

'How do you expect the charwoman to know that? But I think it probably is, as I find from Fortnum & Mason's that a Bradenham ham was delivered to Mrs Forrest's address about a fortnight ago.'

'That sounds conclusive. I take it you think Bertha Gotobed was inveigled there for some undesirable purpose by Mrs Forrest, and had supper with her — '

'No; I should think there was a man.'

'Yes, of course. Mrs F. brings the parties together and leaves them to it. The poor girl is made thoroughly drunk — and then something untoward happens.'

'Yes — shock, perhaps, or a shot of dope.'

'And they bustle her off and get rid of her. It's quite possible. The post-mortem may tell us something about it. Yes, Bunter, what is it?'

'The telephone, my lord, for Mr Parker.'

'Excuse me,' said Parker, 'I asked the people at the flower-shop to ring me up here, if Mrs Forrest came in. If she's there, would you like to come round with me?'

'Very much.'

Parker returned from the telephone with an air of subdued triumph.

'She's just gone up to her flat. Come along. We'll take a taxi — not that death-rattle of yours. Hurry up, I don't want to miss her.'

The door of the flat in South Audley Street was opened by Mrs Forrest in person. Wimsey recognised her instantly from the description. On seeing Parker's card, she made no objection whatever to letting them in, and led the way into a pink and mauve sitting-room, obviously furnished by contract from a Regent Street establishment.

'Please sit down. Will you smoke? And your friend?'

'My colleague, Mr Templeton,' said Parker, promptly.

Mrs Forrest's rather hard eyes appeared to sum up in a practised manner the difference between Parker's seven-guinea 'fashionable lounge suiting, tailored in our own workrooms, fits like a made-to-measure suit', and his 'colleague's' Savile Row outlines, but beyond a slight additional defensiveness of manner she showed no disturbance. Parker noted the glance. 'She's summing us up professionally,' was his mental comment, 'and she's not quite sure whether Wimsey's an outraged brother or husband or what. Never mind. Let her wonder. We may get her rattled.'

'We are engaged, Madam,' he began, with formal severity, 'on an inquiry relative to certain events connected with the 26th of last month. I think you were in town at that time?'

Mrs Forrest frowned slightly in the effort to

86

recollect. Wimsey made a mental note that she was not as young as her bouffant apple-green frock made her appear. She was certainly nearing the thirties, and her eyes were mature and aware.

'Yes, I think I was. Yes, certainly. I was in town for several days about that time. How can I help you?'

'It is a question of a certain bank-note which has been traced to your possession,' said Parker, 'a £5 note numbered x/y58929. It was issued to you by Lloyd's Bank in payment of a cheque on the 19th.'

'Very likely. I can't say I remember the number, but I think I cashed a cheque about that time. I can tell in a moment by my cheque-book.'

'I don't think it's necessary. But it would help us very much if you can recollect to whom you paid it.'

'Oh, I see. Well, that's rather difficult. I paid my dressmakers about that time — no, that was by cheque. I paid cash to the garage, I know, and I think there was a £5 note in that. Then I dined at Verry's with a woman friend — that took the second £5 note, I remember, but there was a third. I drew out £25 — three fives and ten ones. Where did the third note go? Oh, of course, how stupid of me! I put it on a horse.'

'Through a Commission Agent?'

'No. I had nothing much to do one day, so I went down to Newmarket. I put the £5 on some creature called Brighteye or Attaboy or some name like that, at 50 to 1. Of course the wretched animal didn't win, they never do. A man in the train gave me the tip and wrote the name down for me. I handed it to the nearest bookie I saw — a funny little grey-haired man with a hoarse voice — and that was the last I saw of it.'

'Could you remember which day it was?'

'I think it was Saturday. Yes, I'm sure it was.'

'Thank you very much, Mrs Forrest. It will be a great help if we can trace those notes. One of them has turned up since in — other circumstances.'

'May I know what the circumstances are, or is it an official secret?'

Parker hesitated. He rather wished, now, that he had demanded point-blank at the start how Mrs Forrest's £5 note had come to be found on the dead body of the waitress at Epping. Taken by surprise, the woman might have got flustered. Now, he had let her entrench herself securely behind this horse story. Impossible to follow up the history of a bank-note handed to an unknown bookie at a race meeting. Before he could speak, Wimsey broke in for the first time, in a high, petulant voice which quite took his friend aback.

'You're not getting anywhere with all this,' he complained. 'I don't care a continental curse about the beastly note, and I'm sure Sylvia doesn't.'

'Who is Sylvia?' demanded Mrs Forrest with considerable amazement.

'Who is Sylvia? What is she?' gabbled Wimsey, irrepressibly. 'Shakespeare always has the right word, hasn't he? But, God bless my soul, it's no laughing matter. It's very serious and you've no business to laugh at it. Sylvia is very much upset, and the doctor is afraid it may have an effect on her heart. You may not know it, Mrs Forrest, but Sylvia Lyndhurst is my cousin. And what she wants to know, and what we all want to know — don't interrupt me, Inspector, all this shilly-shallying doesn't get us anywhere — I want to know, Mrs Forrest, who was it dining here with you on the night of April 26th. Who was it? Who was it? Can you tell me that?'

This time, Mrs Forrest was visibly taken aback. Even under the thick coat of powder they could see the red flush up into her cheeks and ebb away, while her eyes took on an expression of something more than alarm — a kind of vicious fury, such as one may see in those of a cornered cat.

'On the 26th?' she faltered. 'I can't — '

'I knew it!' cried Wimsey. 'And that girl Evelyn was sure of it too. Who was it, Mrs Forrest? Answer me that!'

'There — there was no one,' said Mrs Forrest, with a thick gasp.

'Oh, come, Mrs Forrest, think again,' said Parker, taking his cue promptly, 'you aren't going to tell us that you accounted by yourself for three bottles of Veuve Clicquot and two people's dinners.'

'Not forgetting the ham,' put in Wimsey, with fussy self-importance; 'the Bradenham ham specially cooked and sent up by Fortnum & Mason. Now, Mrs Forrest — '

'Wait a moment. Just a moment. I'll tell you everything.'

The woman's hands clutched at the pink silk

cushions, making little hot, tight creases. 'I — would you mind getting me something to drink? In the dining-room, through there — on the sideboard.'

Wimsey got up quickly and disappeared into the next room. He took rather a long time, Parker thought. Mrs Forrest was lying back in a collapsed attitude, but her breathing was more controlled, and she was, he thought, recovering her wits. 'Making up a story,' he muttered savagely to himself. However, he could not, without brutality, press her at the moment.

Lord Peter, behind the folding doors, was making a good deal of noise, chinking the glasses and fumbling about. However, before very long, he was back.

' 'Scuse my taking such a time,' he apologised, handing Mrs Forrest a glass of brandy and soda. 'Couldn't find the syphon. Always was a bit wool-gathering, y'know. All my friends say so. Starin' me in the face all the time, what? And then I sloshed a lot of soda on the sideboard. Hand shakin'. Nerves all to pieces and so on. Feelin' better? That's right. Put it down. That's the stuff to pull you together. How about another little one, what? Oh, rot, it can't hurt you. Mind if I have one myself? I'm feelin' a bit flustered. Upsettin', delicate business and all that. Just another spot. That's the idea.'

He trotted out again, glass in hand, while Parker fidgeted. The presence of amateur detectives was sometimes an embarrassment. Wimsey clattered in again, this time with more common sense, bringing decanter, syphon and

90

three glasses, bodily, on a tray.

'Now, now,' said Wimsey, 'now we're feeling better, do you think you can answer our question, Mrs Forrest?'

'May I know, first of all, what right you have to ask it?'

Parker shot an exasperated glance at his friend. This came of giving people time to think.

'Right?' burst in Wimsey. 'Right? Of course, we've a right. The police have a right to ask questions when anything's the matter! Here's murder the matter! Right, indeed?'

'Murder?'

A curious intent look came into her eyes. Parker could not place it, but Wimsey recognised it instantly. He had seen it last on the face of a great financier as he took up his pen to sign a contract. Wimsey had been called to witness the signature, and had refused. It was a contract that ruined thousands of people. Incidentally, the financier had been murdered soon after, and Wimsey had declined to investigate the matter, with a sentence from Dumas: 'Let pass the justice of God.'

'I'm afraid,' Mrs Forrest was saying, 'that in that case I can't help you. I *did* have a friend with me on the 26th, but he has not, so far as I know, been murdered, nor has he murdered anybody.'

'It was a man, then?' said Parker.

Mrs Forrest bowed her head with a kind of mocking ruefulness. 'I live apart from my husband,' she murmured.

'I am sorry,' said Parker, 'to have to press for

91

this gentleman's name and address.'

'Isn't that asking rather much? Perhaps if you would give me further details — ?'

'Well, you see,' cut in Wimsey again, 'if we could just know for certain it wasn't Lyndhurst. My cousin is so frightfully upset, as I said, and that Evelyn girl is making trouble. In fact — of course one doesn't want it to go any further — but actually Sylvia lost her head very completely. She made a savage attack on poor old Lyndhurst — with a revolver, in fact, only fortunately she is a shocking bad shot. It went over his shoulder and broke a vase — most distressin' thing — a Famille Rose jar, worth thousands — and of course it was smashed to atoms. Sylvia is really hardly responsible when she's in a temper. And, we thought, as Lyndhurst was actually traced to this block of flats — if you could give us definite proof it wasn't him, it might calm her down and prevent murder being done, don't you know. Because, though they might call it Guilty but Insane, still, it would be awfully awkward havin' one's cousin in Broadmoor — a first cousin, and really a very nice woman, when she's not irritated.'

Mrs Forrest gradually softened into a faint smile.

'I think I understand the position, Mr Templeton,' she said, 'and if I give you a name, it will be in strict confidence, I presume?'

'Of course, of course,' said Wimsey. 'Dear me, I'm sure it's uncommonly kind of you.'

'You'll swear you aren't spies of my husband's?' she said, quickly. 'I am trying to divorce him. How do I know this isn't a trap?'

'Madam,' said Wimsey, with intense gravity, 'I swear to you on my honour as a gentleman that I have not the slightest connection with your husband. I have never even heard of him before.'

Mrs Forrest shook her head.

'I don't think, after all,' she said, 'it would be much good my giving you the name. In any case, if you asked him whether he'd been here, he would say no, wouldn't he? And if you've been sent by my husband, you've got all the evidence you want already. But I give you my solemn assurance, Mr Templeton, that I know nothing about your friend, Mr Lyndhurst — '

'Major Lyndhurst,' put in Wimsey, plaintively.

'And if Mrs Lyndhurst is not satisfied, and likes to come round and see me, I will do my best to satisfy her of the fact. Will that do?'

'Thank you very much,' said Wimsey. 'I'm sure it's as much as anyone could expect. You'll forgive my abruptness, won't you? I'm rather — er — nervously constituted, and the whole business is exceedingly upsetting. *Good* afternoon. Come on, Inspector, it's quite all right — you see it's quite all right. I'm really very much obliged — uncommonly so. Please don't trouble to see us out.'

He teetered nervously down the narrow hallway, in his imbecile and well-bred way, Parker following with a policeman-like stiffness. No sooner, however, had the flat-door closed behind them than Wimsey seized his friend by the arm and bundled him helter-skelter into the lift.

'I thought we should never get away,' he panted. 'Now, quick — how do we get round to the back of these flats?'

'What do you want with the back?' demanded Parker, annoyed. 'And I wish you wouldn't stampede me like this. I've no business to let you come with me on a job at all, and if I do, you might have the decency to keep quiet.'

'Right you are,' said Wimsey, cheerfully, 'just let's do this little bit and you can get all the virtuous indignation off your chest later on. Round here, I fancy, up this back alley. Step lively and mind the dustbin. One, two, three, four — here we are! Just keep a look-out for the passing stranger, will you?'

Selecting a back window which he judged to belong to Mrs Forrest's flat, Wimsey promptly grasped a drain-pipe and began to swarm up it with the agility of a cat-burglar. About fifteen feet from the ground he paused, reached up, appeared to detach something with a quick jerk, and then slid gingerly to the ground again, holding his right hand at a cautious distance from his body, as though it were breakable.

And indeed, to his amazement, Parker observed that Wimsey now held a long-stemmed glass in his fingers, similar to those from which they had drunk in Mrs Forrest's sitting-room.

'What on earth — ?' said Parker.

'Hush! I'm Hawkshaw the detective — gathering fingerprints. Here we come a-wassailing and gathering prints in May. That's why I took the glass back. I brought a different one in the second time. Sorry I had to do this athletic stunt, but the only cotton-reel I could find hadn't much on it. When I changed the glass, I tip-toed into the bathroom and hung it out of the window. Hope she hasn't been in there since. Just brush my bags down, will you, old man? Gently — don't touch the glass.'

'What the devil do you want fingerprints for?'

'You're a grateful sort of person. Why, for all you know, Mrs Forrest is someone the Yard has been looking for for years. And anyway, you could compare the prints with those on the Bass bottle, if any. Besides, you never know when fingerprints mayn't come in handy. They're excellent things to have about the house. Coast clear? Right. Hail a taxi, will you? I can't wave my hand with this glass in it. Look so silly, don't you know. I say!'

'Well?'

'I saw something else. The first time I went out for the drinks, I had a peep into her bedroom.'

'Yes?'

'What do you think I found in the wash-stand drawer?'

'What?'

'A hypodermic syringe!'

'Really?'

'Oh, yes, and an innocent little box of ampullae, with a doctor's prescription headed 'The injection, Mrs Forrest. One to be injected when the pain is very severe.' What do you think of that?'

'Tell you when we've got the results of that post-mortem,' said Parker, really impressed. 'You didn't bring the prescription, I suppose?'

'No, and I didn't inform the lady who we were or what we were after or ask her permission to carry away the family crystal. But I made a note of the chemist's address.'

'Did you?' ejaculated Parker. 'Occasionally, my lad, you have some glimmering of sound detective sense.'

8

Concerning Crime

'Society is at the mercy of a murderer who is remorseless, who takes no accomplices and who keeps his head.'

EDMUND PEARSON:
Murder at Smutty Nose

Letter from Miss Alexandra Katherine Climpson to Lord Peter Wimsey.

'"Fair View',
'Nelson Avenue,
'Leahampton.
'12 May, 1927.

'MY DEAR LORD PETER,
'I have not *yet* been able to get ALL the information you ask for, as Miss Whittaker has been away for some weeks, inspecting *chicken-farms*!! With a view to purchase, I mean, of course, and not in any *sanitary capacity* (!). I *really think* she means to set up farming *with Miss Findlater*, though what Miss Whittaker can see in that very gushing and really *silly* young woman I cannot think . . . However, Miss Findlater has evidently quite a 'pash' (as we used to call it at school) for Miss Whittaker, and I am afraid none of us are above being *flattered* by

97

such outspoken admiration. I must say, I think it rather *unhealthy* — you may remember Miss Clemence Dane's *very clever book* on the subject? — I have seen so much of that kind of thing in my rather WOMAN-RIDDEN existence! It has such a bad effect, as a rule, upon the *weaker character* of the two — But I must not take up your time with my TWADDLE!!

'Miss Murgatroyd, who was quite a friend of old *Miss Dawson*, however, has been able to tell me a *little* about her past life.

'It seems that, until five years ago, Miss Dawson lived in Warwickshire with her cousin, a Miss Clara Whittaker, Mary Whittaker's great-aunt on the *father's* side. This Miss Clara was evidently rather a 'character', as my dear father used to call it. In her day she was considered very 'advanced' and *not quite nice (!)* because she refused several *good offers*, cut her hair SHORT *(!!)* and set up in business for herself as a HORSE-BREEDER!!! Of course, *nowadays*, nobody would think anything of it, but *then* the old lady — or *young* lady as she was when she embarked on this *revolutionary* proceeding — was quite a PIONEER.

'Agatha Dawson was a school-fellow of hers, and *deeply attached* to her. And as a result of this friendship, Agatha's *sister*, HARRIET, married Clara Whittaker's *brother* JAMES! But *Agatha* did not care about marriage, any more than *Clara*, and the two ladies lived together in a big house, with immense stables, in a village in Warwickshire — Crofton, I think the name was. Clara Whittaker turned out to be a remarkable *good business woman*, and worked up a big 'connection' among the *hunting folk* in those parts. Her hunters became quite *famous*, and from a capital of a few thousand pounds with which she started she made quite a *fortune*, and was a *very rich woman* before her death! Agatha Dawson never had anything to do with the *horsey* part of the business. She was the 'domestic' partner, and looked after the *house* and the *servants*.

'When Clara Whittaker died, she left *all her money* to AGATHA, passing over her *own family*, with whom she was *not on very good terms* — owing to the narrow-minded attitude they had taken up about her horse-dealing!! Her nephew, Charles Whittaker, who was a clergyman, and the father of *our* Miss Whittaker, resented very much not getting the money, though, as he had kept up the feud in a very *un-Christian* manner, he had really *no right* to complain, especially as Clara had built up her fortune *entirely* by her own exertions. But, of course, he inherited the *bad, old-fashioned* idea that women *ought not* to be their own mistresses, or make money for themselves, or do what they liked with their own!

'He and his family were the only surviving Whittaker relations, and when *he and his wife* were killed in a motor-car accident, Miss Dawson asked Mary to leave her work as a nurse and make her home with her. So that, you see, Clara Whittaker's money was destined to *come back* to James Whittaker's daughter in the end!! Miss Dawson made it *quite* CLEAR that this was her intention, provided Mary would come and *cheer the declining days* of a lonely old lady!

'Mary accepted, and as her aunt — or, to speak more *exactly*, her great-aunt — had given up the big old Warwickshire house after Clara's death, they lived in London for a short time and then moved to Leahampton. As you know, poor old Miss Dawson was then already suffering from the *terrible disease* of which she died, so that Mary did not have to wait long for Clara Whittaker's money!!

'I hope this information will be of some *use* to you. Miss Murgatroyd did not, of course, know anything about the rest of the family, but she always understood that there were *no other* surviving relatives, either on the Whittaker or the Dawson side.

'When Miss Whittaker returns, I hope to *see* more of her. I enclose my *account* for expenses up to date. I do *trust* you will not consider it *extravagant*. How are your money-lenders progressing? I was sorry not to see more of those *poor women* whose cases I investigated — their stories were *so* PATHETIC!

'I am,
'Very sincerely yours,
'ALEXANDRA K. CLIMPSON.'

'P.S. — I *forgot* to say that Miss Whittaker has a little motor-car. I do not, of course, know anything about these matters, but Mrs Budge's maid tells me that Miss Whittaker's maid says it is an Austin 7 (is this right?). It is grey, and the number is XX9917.'

Mr Parker was announced, just as Lord Peter finished reading this document, and sank rather wearily in a corner of the chesterfield.

'What luck?' inquired his lordship, tossing the letter over to him. 'Do you know, I'm beginning to think you were right about the Bertha Gotobed business, and I'm rather relieved. I don't believe one word of Mrs Forrest's story, for reasons of my own, and I'm now hoping that the wiping out of Bertha was a pure coincidence and nothing to do with my advertisement.'

'Are you?' said Parker, bitterly, helping himself to whisky and soda. 'Well, I hope you'll be cheered to learn that the analysis of the body has been made, and that there is not the slightest sign of foul play. There is no trace of violence or of poisoning. There was a heart weakness of fairly long standing, and the verdict is syncope after a heavy meal.'

'That doesn't worry me,' said Wimsey. 'We suggested shock, you know. Amiable gentleman met at flat of friendly lady suddenly turns funny after dinner and makes undesirable overtures. Virtuous young woman is horribly shocked. Weak heart gives way. Collapse. Exit. Agitation of amiable gentleman and friendly lady, left with corpse on their hands. Happy thought: motorcar; Epping Forest; *exeunt omnes*, singing and washing their hands. Where's the difficulty?'

'Proving it is the difficulty, that's all. By the way, there were no fingermarks on the bottle — only smears.'

'Gloves, I suppose. Which looks like camouflage, anyhow. An ordinary picnicking couple wouldn't put on gloves to handle a bottle of Bass.'

'I know. But we can't arrest all the people who wear gloves.'

'I weep for you, the Walrus said, I deeply sympathise. I see the difficulty, but it's early days yet. How about those injections?'

'Perfectly O.K. We've interrogated the chemist and interviewed the doctor. Mrs Forrest suffers from violent neuralgic pains, and the injections were duly prescribed. Nothing wrong there, and no history of doping or anything. The prescription is a very mild one, and couldn't possibly be fatal to anybody. Besides, haven't I told you that there was no trace of morphia or any other kind of poison in the body?'

'Oh, well!' said Wimsey. He sat a few minutes looking thoughtfully at the fire.

'I see the case has more or less died out of the papers,' he resumed, suddenly.

'Yes. The analysis has been sent to them, and there will be a paragraph tomorrow and a verdict of natural death, and that will be the end of it.'

'Good. The less fuss there is about it the better. Has anything been heard of the sister in Canada?'

'Oh, I forgot. Yes. We had a cable three days ago. She's coming over.'

'Is she? By Jove! What boat?'

'The *Star of Quebec* — due in next Friday.'

'H'm! We'll have to get hold of her. Are you meeting the boat?'

'Good heavens, no! Why should I?'

'I think someone ought to. I'm reassured

102

— but not altogether happy. I think I'll go myself, if you don't mind. I want to get that Dawson story — and this time I want to make sure the young woman doesn't have a heart attack before I interview her.'

'I really think you're exaggerating, Peter.'

'Better safe than sorry,' said his lordship. 'Have another peg, won't you? Meanwhile, what do you think of Miss Climpson's latest?'

'I don't see much in it.'

'No?'

'It's a bit confusing, but it all seems quite straightforward.'

'Yes. The only thing we know now is that Mary Whittaker's father was annoyed about Miss Dawson's getting his aunt's money and thought it ought to have come to him.'

'Well, you don't suspect *him* of having murdered Miss Dawson, do you? He died before her, and the daughter's got the money, anyhow.'

'Yes, I know. But suppose Miss Dawson had changed her mind? She might have quarrelled with Mary Whittaker and wanted to leave her money elsewhere.'

'Oh, I see — and been put out of the way before she could make a will?'

'Isn't it possible?'

'Yes, certainly. Except that all the evidence we have goes to show that will-making was about the last job anybody could persuade her to do.'

'True — while she was on good terms with Mary. But how about that morning Nurse Philliter mentioned, when she said people were trying to kill her before her time? Mary may really have been impatient with her for being such an unconscionable time a-dying. If Miss Dawson became aware of that, she would certainly have resented it and may very well have expressed an intention of making her will in someone else's favour — as a kind of insurance against premature decease!'

'Then why didn't she send for her solicitor?'

'She may have tried to. But after all, she was bedridden and helpless. Mary may have prevented the message from being sent.'

'That sounds quite plausible.'

'Doesn't it? That's why I want Evelyn Cropper's evidence. I'm perfectly certain those girls were packed off because they had heard more than they should. Or why such enthusiasm over sending them to London?'

'Yes. I thought that part of Mrs Gulliver's story was a bit odd. I say, how about the other nurse?'

'Nurse Forbes? That's a good idea. I was forgetting her. Think you can trace her?'

'Of course, if you really think it important.'

'I do. I think it's damned important. Look here, Charles, you don't seem very enthusiastic about this case.'

'Well, you know, I'm not so certain it is a case at all. What makes you so fearfully keen about it? You seem dead set on making it a murder, with practically nothing to go upon. Why?'

Lord Peter got up and paced the room. The light from the solitary reading-lamp threw his lean shadow, diffused and monstrously elongated, up to the ceiling. He walked over to a book-shelf, and the shadow shrank, blackened, settled down. He stretched his hand, and the hand's shadow flew with it, hovering over the gilded titles of the books and blotting them out one by one.

'Why?' repeated Wimsey. 'Because I believe this is the case I have always been looking for. The case of cases. The murder without discernible means, or motives or clue. The norm. All these' — he swept his extended hand across the book-shelf, and the shadow outlined a vaster and more menacing gesture — 'all these books on this side of the room are books about crimes. But they only deal with the abnormal crimes.'

'What do you mean by abnormal crimes?'

'The failures. The crimes that have been found out. What proportion do you suppose they bear to the successful crimes — the ones we hear nothing about?'

'In this country,' said Parker, rather stiffly, 'we manage to trace and convict the majority of criminals — '

'My good man, I know that where a crime is known to have been committed, you people manage to catch the perpetrator in at least sixty per cent of the cases. But the moment a crime is even suspected, it falls, *ipso facto*, into the category of failures. After that, the thing is merely a question of greater or less efficiency on the part of the police. But how about the crimes which are never even suspected?'

Parker shrugged his shoulders.

'How can anybody answer that?'

'Well — one may guess. Read any newspaper

105

today. Read the *News of the World*. Or, now that the Press has been muzzled, read the divorce court lists. Wouldn't they give you the idea that marriage is a failure? Isn't the sillier sort of journalism packed with articles to the same effect? And yet, looking round among the marriages you know of personally, aren't the majority of them a success, in a humdrum, undemonstrative sort of way? Only you don't hear of them. People don't bother to come into court and explain that they dodder along very comfortably on the whole, thank you. Similarly, if you read all the books on this shelf, you'd come to the conclusion that murder was a failure. But bless you, it's always the failures that make the noise. Successful murderers don't write to the papers about it. They don't even join in imbecile symposia to tell an inquisitive world 'What Murder means to me', or 'How I became a Successful Poisoner'. Happy murderers, like happy wives, keep quiet tongues. And they probably bear just about the same proportion to the failures as the divorced couples do to the happily mated.'

'Aren't you putting it rather high?'

'I don't know. Nor does anybody. That's the devil of it. But you ask any doctor, when you've got him in an unbuttoned, well-lubricated frame of mind, if he hadn't often had grisly suspicions which he could not and dared not take steps to verify. You see by our friend Carr what happens when one doctor is a trifle more courageous than the rest.'

'Well, he couldn't prove anything.'

106

'I know. But that doesn't mean there's nothing to be proved. Look at the scores and scores of murders that have gone unproved and unsuspected till the fool of a murderer went too far and did something silly which blew up the whole show. Palmer, for instance. His wife and brother and mother-in-law and various illegitimate children, all peacefully put away — till he made the mistake of polishing Cook off in that spectacular manner. Look at George Joseph Smith. Nobody'd have thought of bothering any more about those first two wives he drowned. It was only when he did it the third time that he aroused suspicion. Armstrong, too, is supposed to have got away with many more crimes than he was tried for — it was being clumsy over Martin and the chocolates that stirred up the hornet's nest in the end. Burke and Hare were convicted of murdering an old woman, and then brightly confessed that they'd put away sixteen people in two months and no one a penny the wiser.'

'But they *were* caught.'

'Because they were fools. If you murder someone in a brutal, messy way, or poison someone who has previously enjoyed rollicking health, or choose the very day after a will's been made in your favour to extinguish the testator, or go on killing everyone you meet till people begin to think you're first cousin to a upas tree, naturally you're found out in the end. But choose somebody old and ill, in circumstances where the benefit to yourself isn't too apparent, and use a sensible method that looks like natural death or accident, and don't repeat your effects too often, and you're safe. I swear all the heart-diseases and gastric enteritis and influenzas that get certified are not nature's unaided work. Murder's so easy, Charles, so damned easy — even without special training.'

Parker looked troubled.

'There's something in what you say. I've heard some funny tales myself. We all do, I suppose. But Miss Dawson — '

'Miss Dawson fascinates me, Charles. Such a beautiful subject. So old and ill. So likely to die soon. Bound to die before long. No near relations to make inquiries. No connections or old friends in the neighbourhood. And so rich. Upon my soul, Charles, I lie in bed licking my lips over ways and means of murdering Miss Dawson.'

'Well, anyhow, till you can think of one that defies analysis and doesn't seem to need a motive, you haven't found the right one,' said Parker, practically, rather revolted by this ghoulish conversation.

'I admit that,' replied Lord Peter, 'but that only shows that as yet I'm merely a third-rate murderer. Wait till I've perfected my method and then I'll show you — perhaps. Some wise old buffer has said that each of us holds the life of one other person between his hands — but only one, Charles, only one.'

9

The Will

'Our wills are ours, to make them thine.'
TENNYSON: *In Memoriam*

'Hullo! hullo — ullo! oh, operator, shall I call
thee bird or but a wandering voice? . . . Not at
all, I had no intention of being rude, my child,
that was a quotation from the poetry of Mr
Wordsworth . . . well, ring him again . . . thank
you, is that Dr Carr? . . . Lord Peter Wimsey
speaking . . . oh, yes . . . yes . . . aha! . . . not a
bit of it . . . We are about to vindicate you and
lead you home, decorated with triumphal
wreaths of cinnamon and senna-pods . . . No,
really . . . we've come to the conclusion that the
thing is serious . . . Yes . . . I want Nurse
Forbes's address . . . Right, I'll hold on . . . Luton?
. . . oh, Tooting, yes, I've got that . . . Certainly,
I've no doubt she's a tartar, but I'm the Grand
Panjandrum with the little round button a-top
. . . Thanks awfully . . . cheer-frightfully-ho!
— oh! I say! — hullo! — I say, she doesn't do
Maternity work, does she? Maternity work? — M
for Mother-in-law — Maternity? — No — You're
sure? . . . It would be simply awful if she did and
came along . . . I couldn't possibly produce a
baby for her . . . As long as you're quite sure
. . . Right — right — yes — not for the world

— nothing to do with you at all. Good-bye, old thing, good-bye.'

Lord Peter hung up, whistling cheerfully, and called for Bunter.

'My lord?'

'What is the proper suit to put on, Bunter, when one is an expectant father?'

'I regret, my lord, to have seen no recent fashions in paternity wear. I should say, my lord, whichever suit your lordship fancies will induce a calm and cheerful frame of mind in the lady.'

'Unfortunately I don't know the lady. She is, in fact, only the figment of an over-teeming brain. But I think the garments should express bright hope, self-congratulation, and a tinge of tender anxiety.'

'A newly married situation, my lord, I take it. Then I would suggest the lounge suit in pale grey — the willow-pussy cloth, my lord — with a dull amethyst tie and socks and a soft hat. I would not recommend a bowler, my lord. The anxiety expressed in a bowler hat would be rather of the financial kind.'

'No doubt you are right, Bunter. And I will wear those gloves that got so unfortunately soiled yesterday at Charing Cross. I am too agitated to worry about a clean pair.'

'Very good, my lord.'

'No stick, perhaps.'

'Subject to your lordship's better judgement, I should suggest that a stick may be suitably handled to express emotion.'

'You are always right, Bunter. Call me a taxi, and tell the man to drive to Tooting.'

Nurse Forbes regretted very much. She would have liked to oblige Mr Simms-Gaythorpe, but she never undertook maternity work. She wondered who could have misled Mr Simms-Gaythorpe by giving him her name.

'Well, y'know, I can't say I was misled,' said Mr Simms-Gaythorpe, dropping his walking-stick and retrieving it with an ingenuous laugh. 'Miss Murgatroyd — you know Miss Murgatroyd of Leahampton, I think — yes — she — that is, I heard about you through her' (this was a fact), 'and she said what a charming person — excuse my repeatin' these personal remarks, won't you? — what a charmin' person you were and all that, and how nice it would be if we could persuade you to come, don't you see. But she said she was afraid perhaps you didn't do maternity work. Still, y'know, I thought it was worth tryin', what? Bein' so anxious, what? — about my wife, that is, you see. So necessary to have someone young and cheery at these — er — critical times, don't you know. Maternity nurses often such ancient and ponderous sort of people — if you don't mind my sayin' so. My wife's highly nervous — naturally — first effort and all that — doesn't like middle-aged people tramplin' round — you see the idea?'

Nurse Forbes, who was a bony woman of about forty, saw the point perfectly, and was very sorry she really could not see her way to undertaking the work.

'It was very kind of Miss Murgatroyd,' she

111

said. 'Do you know her well? Such a delightful woman, is she not?'

The expectant father agreed.

'Miss Murgatroyd was so very much impressed by your sympathetic way — don't you know — of nursin' that poor old lady, Miss Dawson, y'know. Distant connection of my own, as a matter of fact — er, yes — somehow about fifteenth cousin twelve times removed. So nervous, wasn't she? A little bit eccentric like the rest of the family, but a charming old lady, don't you think?'

'I became very much attached to her,' said Nurse Forbes. 'When she was in full possession of her faculties, she was a most pleasant and thoughtful patient. Of course, she was in great pain, and we had to keep her under morphia a great part of the time.'

'Ah, yes! poor old soul! I sometimes think, Nurse, it's a great pity we aren't allowed just to help people off, y'know, when they're so far gone. After all, they're practically dead already, as you might say. What's the point of keepin' them sufferin' on like that?'

Nurse Forbes looked rather sharply at him.

'I'm afraid that wouldn't do,' she said, 'though one understands the lay person's point of view, of course. Dr Carr was not of your opinion,' she added, a little acidly.

'I think all that fuss was simply shockin',' said the gentleman warmly. 'Poor old soul! I said to my wife at the time, why couldn't they let the poor old thing rest. Fancy cuttin' her about, when obviously she'd just mercifully gone off in a natural way! My wife quite agreed with me.

She was quite upset about it, don't you know.'

'It was very disturbing to everybody concerned,' said Nurse Forbes, 'and of course, it put me in a very awkward position. I ought not to talk about it, but as you are one of the family, you will quite understand.'

'Just so. Did it ever occur to you, Nurse' — Mr Simms-Gaythorpe leaned forward, crushing his soft hat between his hands in a nervous manner — 'that there might be something behind all that?'

Nurse Forbes primmed up her lips.

'You know,' said Mr Simms-Gaythorpe, 'there *have* been cases of doctors tryin' to get rich old ladies to make wills in their favour. You don't think — eh?'

Nurse Forbes intimated that it was not her business to think things.

'No, of course not, certainly not. But as man to man — I mean, between you and me, what? — wasn't there a little — er — friction, perhaps, about sending for the solicitor-johnnie, don't you know? Of course, my Cousin Mary — I call her cousin, so to speak, but it's no relation at all, really — of course, I mean, she's an awfully nice girl and all that sort of thing, but I'd got a sort of idea perhaps she wasn't altogether keen on having the will-making wallah sent for, what?'

'Oh, Mr Simms-Gaythorpe, I'm sure you're quite wrong there. Miss Whittaker was most anxious that her aunt should have every facility in that way. In fact — I don't think I'm betraying any confidence in telling you this — she said to me, 'If at any time Miss Dawson should express a wish to see a lawyer, be sure you send for him at once.' And so, of course, I did.'

'You did? And didn't he come, then?'

'Certainly he came. There was no difficulty about it at all.'

'There! That just shows, doesn't it? how wrong some of these gossipy females can be! Excuse me, but y'know, I'd got absolutely the wrong impression about the thing. I'm quite *sure* Mrs Peasgood said that no lawyer had been sent for.'

'I don't know what Mrs Peasgood could have known about it,' said Nurse Forbes with a sniff; 'her permission was not asked in the matter.'

'Certainly not — but you know how these ideas get about. But, I say — if there was a will, why wasn't it produced?'

'I didn't say that, Mr Simms-Gaythorpe. There was no will. The lawyer came to draw up a power of attorney, so that Miss Whittaker could sign cheques and so on for her aunt. That was very necessary, you know, on account of the old lady's failing powers.'

'Yes — I suppose she was pretty woolly towards the end.'

'Well, she was quite sensible when I took over from Nurse Philliter in September, except, of course, for that fancy she had about poisoning.'

'She really was afraid of that?'

'She said once or twice, 'I'm not going to die to please anybody, Nurse.' She had great confidence in me. She got on better with me than with Miss Whittaker, to tell you the truth, Mr Simms-Gaythorpe. But during October, her mind began to give way altogether, and she

114

rambled a lot. She used to wake up sometimes all in a fright and say, 'Have they passed it yet, Nurse?' — just like that. I'd say, 'No, they haven't got that far yet,' and that would quiet her. Thinking of her hunting days, I expect she was. They often go back like that, you know, when they're being kept under drugs. Dreaming, like, they are, half the time.'

'Then in the last month or so, I suppose she could hardly have made a will, even if she wanted to.'

'No, I don't think she could have managed it then.'

'But earlier on, when the lawyer was there, she could have done so if she had liked?'

'Certainly she could.'

'But she didn't?'

'Oh no. I was there with her all the time, at her particular request.'

'I see. Just you and Miss Whittaker.'

'Not even Miss Whittaker most of the time. I see what you mean, Mr Simms-Gaythorpe, but indeed you should clear your mind of any unkind suspicions of Miss Whittaker. The lawyer and Miss Dawson and myself were alone together for nearly an hour, while the clerk drew up the necessary papers in the next room. It was all done then, you see, because we thought that a second visit would be too much for Miss Dawson. Miss Whittaker only came in quite at the end. If Miss Dawson had wished to make a will, she had ample opportunity to do so.'

'Well, I'm glad to hear that,' said Mr Simms-Gaythorpe, rising to go. 'These little doubts are so apt to make unpleasantness in families, don't you know. Well, I must be toddlin' now. I'm frightfully sorry you can't come to us, Nurse — my wife will be so disappointed. I must try to find somebody else equally charmin' if possible. Good-bye.'

Lord Peter removed his hat in the taxi and scratched his head thoughtfully.

'Another good theory gone wrong,' he murmured. 'Well, there's another string to the jolly old bow yet. Cropper first and then Crofton — that's the line to take, I fancy.'

Part Two

THE LEGAL PROBLEM

'The gladsome light of jurisprudence.'
SIR EDWARD COKE

10

The Will Again

'The will! the will! We will hear Caesar's will!'
Julius Caesar

'Oh, Miss Evelyn, my dear, oh, poor dear!'

The tall girl in black started, and looked round.

'Why, Mrs Gulliver — how very, very kind of you to come and meet me!'

'And glad I am to have the chance, my dear, all owing to these kind gentlemen,' cried the landlady, flinging her arms round the girl and clinging to her to the great annoyance of the other passengers pouring off the gangway. The elder of the two gentlemen referred to gently put his hand on her arm, and drew them out of the stream of traffic.

'Poor lamb!' mourned Mrs Gulliver, 'coming all this way by your lonesome, and poor dear Miss Bertha in her grave and such terrible things said, and her such a good girl always.'

'It's poor Mother I'm thinking about,' said the girl. 'I couldn't rest. I said to my husband, 'I must go,' I said, and he said, 'My honey, if I could come with you I would, but I can't leave the farm, but if you feel you ought to go, you shall,' he said.'

'Dear Mr Cropper — he was always that good

119

and kind,' said Mrs Gulliver, 'but here I am, forgittin' all about the good gentlemen as brought me all this way to see you. This is Lord Peter Wimsey, and this is Mr Murbles, as put in that unfortnit advertisement, as I truly believes was the beginnin' of it all. 'Ow I wish I'd never showed it to your poor sister, not but wot I believe the gentleman acted with the best intentions, 'avin' now seen 'im, which at first I thought 'e was a wrong'un.'

'Pleased to meet you,' said Mrs Cropper, turning with the ready address derived from service in a big restaurant. 'Just before I sailed I got a letter from poor Bertha enclosing your ad. I couldn't make anything of it, but I'd be glad to know anything which can clear up this shocking business. What have they said it is — murder?'

'There was a verdict of natural death at the inquiry,' said Mr Murbles, 'but we feel that the case presents some inconsistencies, and shall be exceedingly grateful for your co-operation in looking into the matter, and also in connection with another matter which may or may not have some bearing upon it.'

'Righto,' said Mrs Cropper. 'I'm sure you're proper gentlemen, if Mrs Gulliver answers for you, for I've never known her mistaken in a person yet, have I, Mrs G.? I'll tell you anything I know, which isn't much, for it's all a horrible mystery to me. Only I don't want you to delay me, for I've got to go straight on down to Mother. She'll be in a dreadful way, so fond as she was of Bertha, and she's all alone except for the young girl that looks after her, and that's not

120

much comfort when you've lost your daughter so sudden.'

'We shall not detain you a moment, Mrs Cropper,' said Mr Murbles. 'We propose, if you will allow us, to accompany you to London, and to ask you a few questions on the way, and then — again with your permission — we should like to see you safely home to Mrs Gotobed's house, wherever that may be.'

'Christchurch, near Bournemouth,' said Lord Peter. 'I'll run you down straight away, if you like. It will save time.'

'I say, you know all about it, don't you?' exclaimed Mrs Cropper with some admiration. 'Well, hadn't we better get a move on, or we'll miss this train?'

'Quite right,' said Mr Murbles. 'Allow me to offer you my arm.'

Mrs Cropper approving of this arrangement, the party made its way to the station, after the usual disembarkation formalities. As they passed the barrier on the platform Mrs Cropper gave a little exclamation and leaned forward as though something had caught her eye.

'What is it, Mrs Cropper?' said Lord Peter's voice in her ear. 'Did you think you recognised somebody?'

'You're a noticing one, aren't you?' said Mrs Cropper. 'Make a good waiter — you would — not meaning any offence, sir, that's a real compliment from one who knows. Yes, I did think I saw someone, but it couldn't be, because the minute she caught my eye she went away.'

'Who did you think it was?'

'Why, I thought it looked like Miss Whittaker, as Bertha and me used to work for.'

'Where was she?'

'Just down by that pillar there, a tall dark lady in a crimson hat and grey fur. But she's gone now.'

'Excuse me.'

Lord Peter unhitched Mrs Gulliver from his arm, hitched her smartly on to the unoccupied arm of Mr Murbles, and plunged into the crowd. Mr Murbles, quite unperturbed by this eccentric behaviour, shepherded the two women into an empty first-class carriage which, Mrs Cropper noted, bore a large label, 'Reserved for Lord Peter Wimsey and party.' Mrs Cropper made some protesting observation about her ticket, but Mr Murbles merely replied that everything was provided for, and that privacy could be more conveniently secured in this way.

'Your friend's going to be left behind,' said Mrs Cropper as the train moved out.

'That would be very unlike him,' replied Mr Murbles, calmly unfolding a couple of rugs and exchanging his old-fashioned top-hat for a curious kind of travelling cap with flaps to it. Mrs Cropper, in the midst of her anxiety, could not help wondering where in the world he had contrived to purchase this Victorian relic. As a matter of fact, Mr Murbles's caps were especially made to his own design by an exceedingly expensive West End hatter, who held Mr Murbles in deep respect as a real gentleman of the old school.

Nothing, however, was seen of Lord Peter for

something like a quarter of an hour, when he suddenly put his head in with an amiable smile and said:

'One red-haired woman in a crimson hat; three dark women in black hats; several nondescript women in those pull-on sort of dust-coloured hats; old women with grey hair, various; sixteen flappers without hats — hats on rack, I mean, but none of 'em crimson; two obvious brides in blue hats; innumerable fair women in hats of all colours; one ash-blonde dressed as a nurse, none of 'em our friend as far as I know. Thought I best just toddle along the train to make sure. There's just one dark sort of female whose hat I can't see because it's tucked down beside her. Wonder if Mrs Cropper would mind doin' a little stagger down the corridor to take a squint at her.'

Mrs Cropper, with some surprise, consented to do so.

'Right you are. 'Splain later. About four carriages along. Now, look here, Mrs Cropper, if it *should* be anybody you know, I'd rather on the whole she didn't spot you watching her. I want you to walk along behind me, just glancin' into the compartments but keepin' your collar turned up. When we come to the party I have in mind, I'll make a screen for you, what?'

These manoeuvres were successfully accomplished, Lord Peter lighting a cigarette opposite the suspected compartment, while Mrs Cropper viewed the hatless lady under cover of his raised elbows. But the result was disappointing. Mrs Cropper had never seen the lady before, and a

123

further promenade from end to end of the train produced no better results.

'We must leave it to Bunter, then,' said his lordship, cheerfully, as they returned to their seats. 'I put him on the trail as soon as you gave me the good word. Now, Mrs Cropper, we really get down to business. First of all, we should be glad of any suggestions you may have to make about your sister's death. We don't want to distress you, but we have got an idea that there might, just possibly, be something behind it.'

'There's just one thing, sir — your lordship, I suppose I should say. Bertha was a real good girl — I can answer for that absolutely. There wouldn't have been any carryings-on with her young man — nothing of that. I know people have been saying all sorts of things, and perhaps, with lots of girls as they are, it isn't to be wondered at. But, believe me, Bertha wouldn't go for to do anything that wasn't right. Perhaps you'd like to see this last letter she wrote to me. I'm sure nothing could be nicer and properer from a girl just looking forward to a happy marriage. Now, a girl as wrote like that wouldn't be going larking about, sir, would she? I couldn't rest, thinking they was saying that about her.'

Lord Peter took the letter, glanced through it, and handed it reverently to Mr Murbles.

'We're not thinking that at all, Mrs Cropper, though of course we're very glad to have your point of view, don't you see. Now, do you think it possible your sister might have been — what shall I say? — got hold of by some woman with a plausible story and all that, and — well

124

— pushed into some position which shocked her very much? Was she cautious and up to the tricks of London people and all that?'

And he outlined Parker's theory of the engaging Mrs Forrest and the supposed dinner in the flat.

'Well, my lord, I wouldn't say Bertha was a very quick girl — not as quick as me, you know. She'd always be ready to believe what she was told and give people credit for the best. Took more after her father, like. I'm Mother's girl, they always said, and I don't trust anybody farther than I can see them. But I'd warned her very careful against taking up with women as talks to a girl in the street, and she did ought to have been on her guard.'

'Of course,' said Peter, 'it may have been somebody she'd got to know quite well — say, at the restaurant, and she thought she was a nice lady and there'd be no harm in going to see her. Or the lady might have suggested taking her into good service. One never knows.'

'I think she'd have mentioned it in her letters if she'd talked to the lady much, my lord. It's wonderful what a lot of things she'd find to tell me about the customers. And I don't think she'd be for going into service again. We got real fed up with service, down in Leahampton.'

'Ah, yes. Now that brings us to quite a different point — the thing we wanted to ask you or your sister about before this sad accident took place. You were in service with this Miss Whittaker whom you mentioned just now. I wonder if you'd mind telling us just exactly why you left. It was a good place, I suppose?'

'Yes, my lord, quite a good place as places go, though of course a girl doesn't get her freedom the way she does in a restaurant. And naturally there was a good deal of waiting on the old lady. Not as we minded that, for she was a very kind, good lady, and generous too.'

'But when she became so ill, I suppose Miss Whittaker managed everything, what?'

'Yes, my lord; but it wasn't a hard place — lots of the girls envied us. Only Miss Whittaker was very particular.'

'Especially about the china, what?'

'Ah, they told you about that, then?'

'I told 'em dearie,' put in Mrs Gulliver, 'I told 'em all about how you come to leave your place and go to London.'

'And it struck us,' put in Mr Murbles, 'that it was, shall we say, somewhat rash of Miss Whittaker to dismiss so competent and, if I may put it so, so well-spoken and personable a pair of maids on so trivial a pretext.'

'You're right there, sir. Bertha — I told you she was the trusting one — she was quite ready to believe as she done wrong, and thought how good it was of Miss Whittaker to forgive her breaking the china, and take so much interest in sending us to London, but I always thought there was something more than met the eye. Didn't I, Mrs Gulliver?'

'That you did, dear; something more than meets the eye, that's what you says to me, and what I agrees with.'

'And did you, in your own mind,' pursued Mr

Murbles, 'connect this sudden dismissal with anything which had taken place?'

'Well, I did then,' replied Mrs Cropper, with some spirit. 'I said to Bertha — but she would hear nothing of it, taking after her father as I tell you — I said, 'Mark my words,' I said, 'Miss Whittaker don't care to have us in the house after the row she had with the old lady.''

'And what row was that?' inquired Mr Murbles.

'Well, I don't know as I ought rightly to tell you about it, seeing it's all over now and we promised to say nothing about it.'

'That, of course,' said Mr Murbles, checking Lord Peter, who was about to burst in impetuously, 'depends upon your own conscience. But, if it will be of any help to you in making up your mind, I think I may say, in the strictest confidence, that this information may be of the utmost importance to use — in a roundabout way which I won't trouble you with — in investigating a very singular set of circumstances which have been brought to our notice. And it is just barely possible — again in a very roundabout way — that it may assist us in throwing some light on the melancholy tragedy of your sister's decease. Further than that I cannot go at the moment.'

'Well, now,' said Mrs Cropper, 'if that's so — though, mind you, I don't see what connection there could be — but if you think that's so, I reckon I'd better come across with it, as my husband would say. After all, I only promised I wouldn't mention about it to the people in Leahampton, as might have made mischief out of it — and a gossipy lot they is, and no mistake.'

'We've nothing to do with the Leahampton crowd,' said his lordship, 'and it won't be passed along unless it turns out to be necessary.'

'Righto. Well, I'll tell you. One morning early in September Miss Whittaker comes along to Bertha and I, and says, 'I want you girls to be just handy on the landing outside Miss Dawson's bedroom,' she says, 'because I may want you to come in and witness her signature to a document. We shall want two witnesses,' she says, 'and you'll have to see her sign; but I don't want to flurry her with a lot of people in the room, so when I give you the tip, I want you to come just inside the door without making a noise, so that you can see her write her name, and then I'll bring it straight across to you and you can write your names where I show you. It's quite easy,' she says, 'nothing to do but just put your names opposite where you see the word Witnesses.'

'Bertha was always a bit the timid sort — afraid of documents and that sort of thing, and she tried to get out of it. 'Couldn't Nurse sign instead of me?' she says. That was Nurse Philliter, you know, the red-haired one as was the doctor's fiancée. She was a very nice woman, and we liked her quite a lot. 'Nurse has gone out for her walk,' says Miss Whittaker, rather sharp, 'I want you and Evelyn to do it,' meaning me, of course. Well, we said we didn't mind, and Miss Whittaker goes upstairs to Miss Dawson with a whole heap of papers, and Bertha and I followed and waited on the landing, like she said.'

'One moment,' said Mr Murbles, 'did Miss Dawson often have documents to sign?'

'Yes, sir, I believe so, quite frequently, but they was usually witnessed by Miss Whittaker or the nurse. There was some leases and things of that sort, or so I heard. Miss Dawson had a little house-property. And then there'd be the cheques for the housekeeping, and some papers as used to come from the Bank and be put away in the safe.'

'Share coupons and so on, I suppose,' said Mr Murbles.

'Very likely, sir, I don't know much about those business matters. I did have to witness a signature once, I remember, a long time back, but that was different. The paper was brought down to me with the signature ready wrote. There wasn't any of this to-do about it.'

'The old lady was capable of dealing with her own affairs, I understand?'

'Up till then, sir. Afterwards, as I understood, she made it all over to Miss Whittaker — that was just before she got feeble-like, and was kept under drugs. Miss Whittaker signed the cheques then.'

'The power of attorney,' said Mr Murbles, with a nod. 'Well, now, did you sign this mysterious paper?'

'No, sir. I'll tell you how that was. When me and Bertha had been waiting a little time, Miss Whittaker comes to the door and makes us a sign to come in quiet. So we comes and stands

129

just inside the door. There was a screen by the head of the bed, so we couldn't see Miss Dawson nor she us, but we could see her reflection quite well in a big looking-glass she had on the left side of the bed.'

Mr Murbles exchanged a significant glance with Lord Peter.

'Now be sure you tell us every detail,' said Wimsey, 'no matter how small and silly it may sound. I believe this is goin' to be very excitin'.'

'Yes, my lord. Well, there wasn't much else, except that just inside the door, on the left-hand side as you went in, there was a little table, where Nurse mostly used to set down trays and things that had to go down, and it was cleared, and a piece of blotting-paper on it and an inkstand and pen, all ready for us to sign with.'

'Could Miss Dawson see that?' asked Mr Marbles.

'No, sir, because of the screen.'

'But it was inside the room?'

'Yes, sir.'

'We want to be quite clear about this. Do you think you could draw — quite roughly — a little plan of the room, showing where the bed was and the screen and the mirror, and so on?'

'I'm not much of a hand at drawing,' said Mrs Cropper dubiously, 'but I'll try.'

Mr Murbles produced a notebook and fountain pen, and after a few false starts, the following rough sketch was produced.

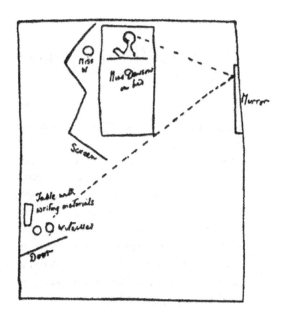

'Thank you, that is very clear indeed. You notice, Lord Peter, the careful arrangements to have the document signed in presence of the witnesses, and witnessed by them in the presence of Miss Dawson and of each other. I needn't tell you for what kind of document that arrangement is indispensable.'

'Was that it, sir? We couldn't understand why it was all arranged like that.'

'It might have happened,' explained Mr Murbles, 'that in case of some dispute about this document, you and your sister would have had to come into court and give evidence about it. And if so, you would have been asked whether you actually saw Miss Dawson write her signature, and whether you and your sister and Miss Dawson were all in the same room together when you signed your names as witnesses. And if that had happened, you could have said yes, couldn't you, and sworn to it?'

131

'Oh, yes.'

'And yet, actually, Miss Dawson would have known nothing about your being there.'

'No, sir.'

'That was it, you see.'

'I see now, sir, but at the time Bertha and me couldn't make nothing of it.'

'But the document, you say, was never signed.'

'No, sir. At any rate, we never witnessed anything. We saw Miss Dawson write her name — at lease, I suppose it was her name — to one or two papers, and then Miss Whittaker puts another lot in front of her and says, 'Here's another little lot, Auntie, some more of those income-tax forms.' So the old lady says, 'What are they exactly, dear, let me see?' So Miss Whittaker says, 'Oh, only the usual things.' And Miss Dawson says, 'Dear dear, what a lot of them. How complicated they do make these things to be sure.' And we could see that Miss Whittaker was giving her several papers, all laid on top of one another, with just the places for the signatures left showing. So Miss Dawson signs the top one, and then lifts up the paper and looks underneath at the next one, and Miss Whittaker says, 'They're all the same,' as if she was in a hurry to get them signed and done with. But Miss Dawson takes them out of her hand and starts looking through them, and suddenly she lets out a screech, and says, 'I won't have it. I won't have it! I'm not dying yet. How dare you, you wicked girl! Can't you wait till I'm dead? — You want to frighten me into my grave before my time. Haven't you got everything you want?'

And Miss Whittaker says, 'Hush, Auntie, you won't let me explain — ' and the old lady says, 'No, I won't, I don't want to hear anything about it. I hate the thought of it. I won't talk about it. You leave me be. I can't get better if you keep frightening me so.' And then she begins to take and carry on dreadful, and Miss Whittaker comes over to us looking awful white and says, 'Run along, you girls,' she says, 'my aunt's taken ill and can't attend to business. I'll call you if I want you,' she says. And I said, 'Can we help with her, miss?' and she says, 'No, it's quite all right. It's just the pain come on again. I'll give her her injection and then she'll be all right.' And she pushes us out of the room, and shuts the door, and we heard the poor old lady crying fit to break anybody's heart. So we went downstairs and met Nurse just coming in, and we told her Miss Dawson was took worse again, and she runs up quick without taking her things off. So we was in the kitchen, just saying it seemed rather funny-like, when Miss Whittaker comes down again and says, 'It's all right now, and Auntie's sleeping quite peaceful, only we'll have to put off business till another day.' And she says, 'Better not say anything about this to anybody, because when the pain comes on Aunt gets frightened and talks a bit wild. She don't mean what she says, but if people was to hear about it they might think it odd.' So I up and says, 'Miss Whittaker,' I says, 'me and Bertha was never ones to talk'; rather stiff, I said it, because I don't hold by gossip and never did. And Miss Whittaker says, 'That's quite all right,' and goes

133

away. And the next day she gives us an afternoon off and a present — ten shillings each, it was, because it was her aunt's birthday, and the old lady wanted us to have a little treat in her honour.'

'A very clear account indeed, Mrs Cropper, and I only wish all witnesses were as sensible and observant as you are. There's just one thing. Did you by any chance get a sight of this paper that upset Miss Dawson so much?'

'No, sir — only from a distance, that is, and in the looking-glass. But I think it was quite short — just a few lines of writing.'

'I see. Was there a typewriter in the house, by the way?'

'Oh, yes, sir. Miss Whittaker used one quite often for business letters and so on. It used to stand in the sitting-room.'

'Quite so. By the way, do you remember Miss Dawson's solicitor calling shortly after this?'

'No, sir. It was only a little time later Bertha broke the teapot and we left. Miss Whittaker gave her her month's warning, but I said no. If she could come down on a girl like that for a little thing, and her such a good worker, Bertha should go at once and me with her. Miss Whittaker said, 'Just as you like,' she said — she never was one to stand any back-chat. So we went that afternoon. But afterwards I think she was sorry, and came over to see us at Christchurch, and suggested why shouldn't we try for a better job in London. Bertha was a bit afraid to go so far — taking after Father, as I mentioned, but Mother, as was always the ambitious one, she says, 'If the lady's kind enough to give you a good start, why not go? There's more chances for a girl in Town.' And I said to Bertha, private-like, afterwards, I says, 'Depend on it, Miss Whittaker wants to see the back of us. She's afraid we'll get talking about the things Miss Dawson said that morning. But,' I says, 'if she's willing to pay us to go, why not go,' I says. 'A girl's got to look out for herself these days, and if we go off to London she'll give us a better character than what she would if we stayed. And anyway,' I said, 'if we don't like it we can always come home again.' So the long and short was, we came to Town, and after a bit we got good jobs with Lyons, what with the good character Miss Whittaker gave us, and I met my husband there and Bertha met her Jim. So we never regretted having taken the chance — not till this dreadful thing happened to Bertha.'

The passionate interest with which her hearers had received this recital must have gratified Mrs Cropper's sense of the dramatic. Mr Murbles was very slowly rotating his hands over one another with a dry, rustling sound — like an old snake, gliding through the long grass in search of prey.

'A little scene after your own heart, Murbles,' said Lord Peter, with a glint under his dropped eyelids. He turned again to Mrs Cropper.

'This is the first time you've told this story?'

'Yes — and I wouldn't have said anything if it hadn't been — '

'I know. Now, if you'll take my advice, Mrs Cropper, you won't tell it again. Stories like that have a nasty way of bein' dangerous. Will you consider it an impertinence if I ask you what your plans are for the next week or two?'

'I'm going to see Mother and get her to come back to Canada with me. I wanted her to come when I got married, but she didn't like going so far away from Bertha. She was always Mother's favourite — taking so much after Father, you see. Mother and me was always too much alike to get on. But now she's got nobody else, and it isn't right for her to be all alone, so I think she'll come with me. It's a long journey for an ailing old woman, but I reckon blood's thicker than water. My husband said, 'Bring her back fast-class, my girl, and I'll find the money.' He's a good sort, is my husband.'

'You couldn't do better,' said Wimsey, 'and if you'll allow me, I'll send a friend to look after you both on the train journey and see you safe on to the boat. And don't stop long in England. Excuse me buttin' in on your affairs like this, but honestly I think you'd be safer elsewhere.'

'You don't think that Bertha — ?'

Her eyes widened with alarm.

'I don't like to say quite what I think, because I don't know. But I'll see you and your mother are safe, whatever happens.'

'And Bertha? Can I do anything about that?'

'Well, you'll have to come and see my friends at Scotland Yard, I think, and tell them what you've told me. They'll be interested.'

'And will something be done about it?'

'I'm sure, if we can prove there's been any foul play, the police won't rest till it's been tracked

136

down to the right person. But the difficulty is, you see, to prove that the death wasn't natural.'

'I observe in today's paper,' said Mr Murbles, 'that the local superintendent is now satisfied that Miss Gotobed came down alone for a quiet picnic and died of a heart attack.'

'That man would say anything,' said Wimsey. 'We know from the post-mortem that she had recently had a heavy meal — forgive these distressin' details, Mrs Cropper — so why the picnic?'

'I suppose they had the sandwiches and the beer-bottle in mind,' said Mr Murbles, mildly.

'I see. I suppose she went down to Epping alone with a bottle of Bass and took out the cork with her fingers. Ever tried doing it, Murbles? No? Well, when they find the corkscrew I'll believe she went there alone. In the meantime, I hope the papers will publish a few more theories like that. Nothin' like inspiring criminals with confidence, Murbles — it goes to their heads, you know.'

11

Cross-Roads

'Patience — and shuffle the cards.'
Don Quixote

Lord Peter took Mrs Cropper down to Christchurch and returned to town to have a conference with Mr Parker. The latter had just listened to his recital of Mrs Cropper's story, when the discreet opening and closing of the flat door announced the return of Bunter.

'Any luck?' inquired Wimsey.

'I regret exceedingly to have to inform your lordship that I lost track of the lady. In fact, if your lordship will kindly excuse the expression, I was completely done in the eye.'

'Thank God, Bunter, you're human after all. I didn't know anybody could do you. Have a drink.'

'I am much obliged to your lordship. According to instructions, I searched the platform for a lady in a crimson hat and a grey fur, and at length was fortunate enough to observe her making her way out by the station entrance towards the big bookstall. She was some way ahead of me, but the hat was very conspicuous, and, in the words of the poet, if I may so express myself, I followed the gleam.'

'Stout fellow.'

'Thank you, my lord. The lady walked into the Station Hotel, which, as you know, has two entrances, one upon the platform, and the other upon the street. I hurried after her for fear she should give me the slip, and made my way through the revolving doors just in time to see her back disappearing into the Ladies' Retiring Room.'

'Whither, as a modest man, you could not follow her. I quite understand.'

'Quite so, my lord. I took a seat in the entrance hall, in a position from which I could watch the door without appearing to do so.'

'And discovered too late that the place had two exits, I suppose. Unusual and distressin'.'

'No, my lord. That was not the trouble. I sat watching for three quarters of an hour, but the crimson hat did not reappear. Your lordship will bear in mind that I had never seen the lady's face.'

Lord Peter groaned.

'I foresee the end of this story, Bunter. Not your fault. Proceed.'

'At the end of this time, my lord, I felt bound to conclude either that the lady had been taken ill or that something untoward had occurred. I summoned a female attendant who happened to cross the hall and informed her that I had been entrusted with a message for a lady whose dress I described. I begged her to ascertain from the attendant in the Ladies' Room whether the lady in question was still there. The girl went away and presently returned to say that the lady had changed her costume in the cloakroom and had gone out half an hour previously.'

'Oh, Bunter, Bunter. Didn't you spot the suitcase or whatever it was when she came out again?'

'Excuse me, my lord. The lady had come in earlier in the day and had left an attaché-case in charge of the attendant. On returning, she had transferred her hat and fur to the attaché-case and put on a small black felt hat and a lightweight raincoat which she had packed there in readiness. So that her dress was concealed when she emerged and she was carrying the attaché-case, whereas, when I first saw her, she had been empty-handed.'

'Everything foreseen. What a woman!'

'I made immediate inquiries, my lord, in the region of the hotel and the station, but without result. The black hat and raincoat were entirely inconspicuous, and no one remembered having seen her. I went to the Central Station to discover if she had travelled by any train. Several women answering to the description had taken tickets for various destinations, but I could get no definite information. I also visited all the garages in Liverpool, with the same lack of success. I am greatly distressed to have failed your lordship.'

'Can't be helped. You did everything you could do. Cheer up. Never say die. And you must be tired to death. Take the day off and go to bed.'

'I thank your lordship, but I slept excellently in the train on the way up.'

'Just as you like, Bunter. But I did hope you sometimes got tired like other people.'

Bunter smiled discreetly and withdrew.

140

'Well, we've gained this much, anyhow,' said Parker. 'We know that this Miss Whittaker has something to conceal, since she takes such precautions to avoid being followed.'

'We know more than that. We know that she was desperately anxious to get hold of the Cropper woman before anybody else could see her, no doubt to stop her mouth by bribery or by worse means. By the way, how did she know she was coming by that boat?'

'Mrs Cropper sent a cable, which was read at the inquest.'

'Damn these inquiries. They give away all the information one wants kept quiet, and produce no evidence worth having.'

'Hear, hear,' said Parker, with emphasis, 'not to mention that we had to sit through a lot of moral punk by the Coroner, about the prevalence of jazz and the immoral behaviour of modern girls in going off alone with young men to Epping Forest.'

'It's a pity these busy-bodies can't be had up for libel. Never mind. We'll get the Whittaker woman yet.'

'Always provided it was the Whittaker woman. After all, Mrs Cropper may have been mistaken. Lots of people do change their hats in cloakrooms without any criminal intention.'

'Oh, of course. Miss Whittaker's supposed to be in the country with Miss Findlater, isn't she? We'll get the invaluable Miss Climpson to pump the girl when they turn up again. Meanwhile, what do you think of Mrs Cropper's story?'

'There's no doubt about what happened there.

Miss Whittaker was trying to get the old lady to sign a will without knowing it. She gave it to her all mixed up with the income-tax papers, hoping she'd put her name to it without reading it. It must have been a will, I think, because that's the only document I know of which is invalid unless it's witnessed by two persons in the presence of the testatrix and of each other.'

'Exactly. And since Miss Whittaker couldn't be one of the witnesses herself, but had to get the two maids to sign, the will must have been in Miss Whittaker's favour.'

'Obviously. She wouldn't go to all that trouble to disinherit herself.'

'But that brings us to another difficulty. Miss Whittaker, as next of kin, would have taken all the old lady had to leave in any case. As a matter of fact, she did. Why bother about a will?'

'Perhaps, as we said before, she was afraid Miss Dawson would change her mind, and wanted to get a will made out before — no, that won't work.'

'No — because, anyhow, any will made later would invalidate the first will. Besides, the old lady sent for her solicitor some time later, and Miss Whittaker put no obstacle of any kind in her way.'

'According to Nurse Forbes, she was particularly anxious that every facility should be given.'

'Seeing how Miss Dawson distrusted her niece, it's a bit surprising, really, that she didn't will the money away. Then it would have been to Miss Whittaker's advantage to keep her alive as long as possible.'

'I don't suppose she really distrusted her — not to the extent of expecting to be made away with. She was excited and said more than she meant — we often do.'

'Yes, but she evidently thought there'd be other attempts to get a will signed.'

'How do you make that out?'

'Don't you remember the power of attorney? The old girl evidently thought that out and decided to give Miss Whittaker authority to sign everything for her so that there couldn't possibly be any jiggery-pokery about papers in future.'

'Of course. Cute old lady. How very irritating for Miss Whittaker. And after that very hopeful visit of the solicitor, too. So disappointing. Instead of the expected will, a very carefully planted spoke in her wheel.'

'Yes. But we're still brought up against the problem, why a will at all?'

'So we are.'

The two men pulled at their pipes for some time in silence.

'The aunt evidently intended the money to go to Mary Whittaker all right,' remarked Parker at last. 'She promised it so often — besides, I daresay she was a just-minded old thing, and remembered that it was really Whittaker money which had come to her over the head of the Rev Charles, or whatever his name was.'

'That's so. Well, there's only one thing that could prevent that happening, and that's — oh, lord! old son. Do you know what it works out at? — The old, old story, beloved of novelists — the missing heir!'

143

'Good lord, yes, you're right. Damn it all, what fools we were not to think of it before. Mary Whittaker possibly found out that there was some nearer relative left, who would scoop the lot. Maybe she was afraid that if Miss Dawson got to know about it, she'd divide the money or disinherit Mary altogether. Or perhaps she just despaired of hammering the story into the old lady's head, and so hit on the idea of getting her to make the will unbeknownst to herself in Mary's favour.'

'What a brain you've got, Charles. Or, see here, Miss Dawson may have known all about it, sly old thing, and determined to pay Miss Whittaker out for her indecent urgency in the matter of will-makin' by just dyin' intestate in the other chappie's favour.'

'If she did, she deserved anything she got,' said Parker, rather viciously. 'After taking the poor girl away from her job under promise of leaving her the dibs.'

'Teach the young woman not to be so mercenary,' retorted Wimsey, with the cheerful brutality of the man who has never in his life been short of money.

'If this bright idea is correct,' said Parker, 'it rather messes up your murder theory, doesn't it? Because Mary would obviously take the line of keeping her aunt alive as long as possible, in hopes she might make a will after all.'

'That's true. Curse you, Charles. I see that bet of mine going west. What a blow for friend Carr, too. I did hope I was going to vindicate him and have him played home by the village band under

144

a triumphal arch with 'Welcome, Champion of Truth!' picked out in red-white-and-blue electric bulbs. Never mind. It's better to lose a wager and see the light than walk in ignorance bloated with gold. — O stop! — why shouldn't Carr be right after all? Perhaps it's just my choice of a murderer that's wrong. Aha! I see a new and even more sinister villain step upon the scene. The new claimant, warned by his minions — '

'What minions?'

'Oh, don't be so pernickety, Charles. Nurse Forbes, probably. I shouldn't wonder if she's in his pay. Where was I? I wish you wouldn't interrupt.'

'Warned by his minions — ' prompted Parker.

'Oh, yes — warned by his minions that Miss Dawson is hobnobbing with solicitors and being tempted into making wills and things, get the minions to polish her off before she can do any mischief.'

'Yes, but how?'

'Oh, by one of those native poisons which slay in a split second and defy the skill of the analyst. They are familiar to the meanest writer of mystery stories. I'm not going to let a trifle like that stand in my way.'

'And why hasn't this hypothetical gentleman brought forward any claim to the property so far?'

'He's biding his time. The fuss about the death scared him, and he's lying low till it's all blown over.'

'He'll find it much more awkward to dispossess Miss Whittaker now she's taken possession. Possession is nine points of the law, you know.'

'I know, but he's going to pretend he wasn't anywhere near at the time of Miss Dawson's death. He only read about it a few weeks ago in a sheet of newspaper wrapped round a salmon-tin, and now he's rushing home from his distant farm in thing-ma-jig to proclaim himself as the long-lost Cousin Tom . . . Great Scott! that reminds me.'

He plunged his hand into his pocket and pulled out a letter.

'This came this morning just as I was going out, and I met Freddy Arbuthnot on the doorstep and shoved it into my pocket before I'd read it properly. But I do believe there was something in it about a Cousin Somebody from some god-forsaken spot. Let's see.'

He unfolded the letter, which was written in Miss Climpson's old-fashioned flowing hand, and ornamented with such a variety of underlinings and exclamation marks as to look like an exercise in musical notation.

'Oh, lord!' said Parker.

'Yes, it's worse than usual, isn't it? — it must be of desperate importance. Luckily it's comparatively short.'

MY DEAR LORD PETER,

'I heard something this morning which MAY be of *use*, so I HASTEN to communicate it!! You remember I *mentioned before* that Mrs Budge's maid is the SISTER of the present maid at Miss *Whittaker's?* WELL!!! The AUNT of these two girls came to *pay a visit* to Mrs Budge's girl this afternoon, and was *introduced* to *me* — of

146

course, as *boarder* at Mrs Budge's I am naturally an *object of local interest* — and bearing *your instructions* in mind, I *encouraged* this to an extent I should not otherwise do!!

'It appears that this *aunt* was well acquainted with a *former housekeeper* of Miss Dawson's — *before* the time of the Gotobed girls, I mean. The *aunt* is a highly *respectable* person of FORBIDDING ASPECT! — with a *bonnet(!)*, and to my mind, a most *disagreeable* CENSORIOUS woman. However! — We got to speaking of Miss Dawson's death, and this aunt — her name is Timmins — *primmed* up her mouth and said: 'No unpleasant scandal would surprise me about *that* family, Miss Climpson. They were most UNDESIRABLY connected! You recollect, Mrs Budge that I felt *obliged to leave* after the appearance of that *most* EXTRAORDINARY person who announced himself as Miss Dawson's cousin.' Naturally, I asked *who* this *might be*, not having heard of any *other relations*! She said that this person, whom she described as a *nasty*, DIRTY *NIGGER* (!!!) arrived one morning, dressed up as a CLERGYMAN!!! and sent her — Miss Timmins — to announce him to Miss Dawson as her COUSIN HALLELUJAH!!! Miss Timmins showed him up, *much against her will*, she said, into the *nice*, CLEAN drawing-room! Miss Dawson, she said, actually *came down* to see this 'creature' instead of sending him about his 'black business' *(!)*, and as a *crowning scandal*, asked him to *stay* to lunch! — 'with her niece there, too,' Miss Timmins said, 'and this horrible *blackamoor* ROLLING his

147

dreadful eyes at her.' Miss Timmins said that it 'regularly turned her stomach' — that was her phrase, and I trust you will excuse it — I understand that these *parts of the body* are frequently referred to in polite *(!)* society nowadays. In fact, it appears she *refused to cook the lunch* for the poor black man — (after all, even *blacks are God's creatures* and we might *all* be *black* OURSELVES if He had not in His infinite kindness seen fit to *favour us* with *white* skins!!) — and walked straight out of the house!!! So that unfortunately she cannot tell us anything *further* about this *remarkable* incident! She is *certain*, however, that the 'nigger' had a *visiting-card*, with the name 'Rev H. Dawson' upon it, but an address in foreign parts. It does seem *strange*, does it not, but I believe many of these *native preachers* are called to do *splendid work* among their own people, and no doubt a MINISTER is entitled to have a *visiting-card*, even when black!!!

'In great haste,
'Sincerely yours,
'A. K. CLIMPSON.'

'God bless my soul,' said Lord Peter, when he had disentangled this screed — 'here's our claimant ready made.'

'With a hide as black as his heart, apparently,' replied Parker. 'I wonder where the Rev Hallelujah has got to — and where he came from. He — er — he wouldn't be in 'Crockford', I suppose.'

'He would be, probably, if he's Church of

England,' said Lord Peter, dubiously, going in search of that valuable work of reference. 'Dawson — Rev George, Rev Gordon, Rev Gurney, Rev Habbakuk, Rev Hadrian, Rev Hammond — no, there's no Rev Hallelujah. I was afraid the name hadn't altogether an established sound. It would be easier if we had an idea what part of the world the gentleman came from. 'Nigger', to a Miss Timmins, may mean anything from a high-caste Brahmin to Sambo and Rastus at the Coliseum — it may even, at a pinch, be an Argentine or an Esquimaux.'

'I suppose other religious bodies have their Crockfords,' suggested Parker, a little hopelessly.

'Yes, no doubt — except perhaps the more exclusive sects — like the Agapemonites and those people who gather together to say OM. Was it Voltaire who said that the English had three hundred and sixty-five religions and only one sauce?'

'Judging from the War Tribunals,' said Parker, 'I should say that was an understatement. And then there's America — a country, I understand, remarkably well supplied with religions.'

'Too true. Hunting for a single dog-collar in the States must be like the proverbial needle. Still, we could make a few discreet inquiries, and meanwhile I'm going to totter up to Crofton with the jolly old bus.'

'Crofton?'

'Where Miss Clara Whittaker and Miss Dawson used to live. I'm going to look for the man with the little black bag — the strange, suspicious solicitor, you remember, who came to see Miss Dawson two years ago, and was so anxious that she should make a will. I fancy he knows all there is to know about the Rev Hallelujah and his claim. Will you come too?'

'Can't — not without special permission. I'm not officially on this case, you know.'

'You're in the Gotobed business. Tell the Chief you think they're connected. I shall need your restraining presence. No less ignoble pressure than that of the regular police force will induce a smoke-dried family lawyer to spill the beans.'

'Well, I'll try — if you'll promise to drive with reasonable precaution.'

'Be thou as chaste as ice and have a licence as pure as snow, thou shalt not escape calumny. I am *not* a dangerous driver. Buck up and get your leave. The snow-white horsepower foams and frets and the blue bonnet — black in this case — is already, in a manner of speaking, over the border.'

'You'll drive me over the border one of these days,' grumbled Parker, and went to the phone to call up Sir Andrew Mackenzie at Scotland Yard.

★ ★ ★

Crofton is a delightful little old-world village, tucked away amid the maze of criss-cross country roads which fills the triangle of which Coventry, Warwick, and Birmingham mark the angles. Through the falling night, 'Mrs Merdle' purred her way delicately round hedge-blinded corners and down devious lanes, her quest made no easier by the fact that the Warwick County Council had pitched upon that particular week for a grand repairing of signposts and had reached the preliminary stage of laying a couple of thick coats of gleaming white paint over all the lettering. At intervals the patient Bunter unpacked himself from the back seat and climbed one of these uncommunicative guides to peer at its blank surface with a torch — a process which reminded Parker of Alan Quartermaine trying to trace the features of the departed Kings of the Kukuanas under their calcareous shrouds of stalactite. One of the posts turned out to be in the wet-paint stage, which added to the depression of the party. Finally, after several misdirections, blind alleys and reversings back to the main road, they came to a fourways. The signpost here must have been in extra need of repairs, for its arms had been removed bodily; it stood stark and ghastly — a long, livid finger erected in wild protest to the unsympathetic heavens.

'It's starting to rain,' observed Parker, conversationally.

'Look here, Charles, if you're going to bear up cheerfully and be the life and soul of the expedition, say so and have done with it. I've got a good, heavy spanner handy under the seat, and Bunter can help to bury the body.'

'I think this must be Brushwood Cross,' resumed Parker, who had the map on his knee. 'If so, and if it's not Covert Corner, which I thought we passed half an hour ago, one of these

151

roads leads directly to Crofton.'

'That would be highly encouraging if we knew which road we were on.'

'We can always try them in turn, and come back if we find we're going wrong.'

'They bury *suicides* at crossroads,' replied Wimsey, dangerously.

'There's a man sitting under that tree,' pursued Parker. 'We can ask him.'

'He's lost his way too, or he wouldn't be sitting there,' retorted the other. 'People don't sit about in the rain for fun.'

At this moment the man observed their approach and, rising, advanced to meet them with raised, arresting hand.

Wimsey brought the car to a standstill.

'Excuse me,' said the stranger, who turned out to be a youth in motor-cycling kit, 'but could you give me a hand with my bus?'

'What's the matter with her?'

'Well, she won't go.'

'I guessed as much,' said Wimsey. 'Though why she should wish to linger in a place like this beats me.' He got out of the car, and the youth, diving into the hedge, produced the patient for inspection.

'Did you tumble there or put her there?' inquired Wimsey, eyeing the machine distastefully.

'I put her there. I've been kicking the starter for hours but nothing happened, so I thought I'd wait till somebody came along.'

'I see. What is the matter, exactly?'

'I don't know. She was going beautifully and

then she conked out suddenly.'

'Have you run out of petrol?'

'Oh, no. I'm sure there's plenty in.'

'Plug all right?'

'I don't know.' The youth looked unhappy. 'It's only my second time out, you see.'

'Oh! well — there can't be much wrong. We'll just make sure about the petrol first,' said Wimsey, more cheerfully. He unscrewed the filler-cap and turned his torch upon the interior of the tank. 'Seems all right.' He bent over again, whistling, and replaced the cap. 'Let's give her another kick for luck and then we'll look at the plug.'

The young man, thus urged, grasped the handle-bars, and with the energy of despair delivered a kick which would have done credit to an army mule. The engine roared into life in a fury of vibration, racing heart-rendingly.

'Good God!' said the youth, 'it's a miracle.'

Lord Peter laid a gentle hand on the throttle-lever and the shattering bellow calmed into a grateful purr.

'What did you do to it?' demanded the cyclist.

'Blew through the filler-cap,' said his lordship with a grin. 'Air-lock in the feed, old son, that's all.'

'I'm frightfully grateful.'

'That's all right. Look here, can you tell us the way to Crofton?'

'Sure. Straight down here. I'm going there, as a matter of fact.'

'Thank Heaven. Lead and I follow, as Sir Galahad says. How far?'

'Five miles.'

'Decent inn?'

'My governor keeps the 'Fox-and-Hounds'. Would that do? We'd give you awfully decent grub.'

'Sorrow vanquished, labour ended, Jordan passed. Buzz off, my lad. No, Charles, I will *not* wait while you put on a Burberry. Back and side go bare, go bare, hand and foot go cold, so belly-god send us good ale enough, whether it be new or old.'

The starter hummed — the youth mounted his machine and led off down the lane after one alarming wobble — Wimsey slipped in the clutch and followed in his wake.

The 'Fox-and-Hounds' turned out to be one of the pleasant, old-fashioned inns where everything is upholstered in horsehair and it is never too late to obtain a good meal of cold roast sirloin and home-grown salad. The landlady, Mrs Piggin, served the travellers herself. She wore a decent black satin dress and a front of curls of the fashion favoured by the Royal Family. Her round, cheerful face glowed in the firelight, seeming to reflect the radiance of the scarlet-coated huntsmen who galloped and leapt and fell on every wall through a series of sporting prints. Lord Peter's mood softened under the influence of the atmosphere and the house's excellent ale, and by a series of inquiries directed to the hunting-season, just concluded, the neighbouring families and the price of horseflesh, he dexterously led the conversation round to the subject of the late Miss Clara Whittaker.

'Oh, dear, yes,' said Mrs Piggin, 'to be sure, we knew Miss Whittaker. Everybody knew her in these parts. A wonderful old lady she was. There's many of her horses still in the country. Mr Cleveland, he bought the best part of the stock, and is doin' well with them. Fine honest stock she bred, and they all used to say she was a woman of wonderful judgement with a horse — or a man either. Nobody ever got the better of her twice, and very few, once.

'Ah!' said Lord Peter, sagaciously.

'I remember her well, riding to hounds when she was well over sixty,' went on Mrs Piggin, 'and she wasn't one to wait for a gap, neither. Now Miss Dawson — that was her friend as lived with her — over at the Manor beyond the stone bridge — she was more timid-like. She'd go by the gates, and we often used to say she'd never be riding at all, but for bein' that fond of Miss Whittaker and not wanting to let her out of her sight. But there, we can't all be alike, can we, sir? — and Miss Whittaker was altogether out of the way. They don't make them like that nowadays. Not but what these modern girls are good goers, many of them, and does a lot of things as would have been thought very fast in the old days, but Miss Whittaker had the knowledge as well. Bought her own horses and physicked 'em and bred 'em, and needed no advice from anybody.'

'She sounds a wonderful old girl,' said Wimsey, heartily. 'I'd have liked to know her. I've got some friends who knew Miss Dawson quite well — when she was living in Hampshire, you know.'

'Indeed, sir? Well, that's strange, isn't it? She was a very kind, nice lady. We heard she'd died, too. Of this cancer, was it? That's a terrible thing, poor soul. And fancy you being connected with her, so to speak. I expect you'd be interested in some of our photographs of the Crofton Hunt. Jim?'

'Hullo!'

'Show these gentlemen the photographs of Miss Whittaker and Miss Dawson. They're acquainted with some friends of Miss Dawson down in Hampshire. Step this way — if you're sure you won't take anything more, sir.'

Mrs Piggin led the way into a cosy little private bar, where a number of hunting-looking gentlemen were enjoying a final glass before closing-time. Mr Piggin, stout and genial as his wife, moved forward to do the honours.

'What'll you have, gentlemen? — Joe, two pints of the winter ale. And fancy you knowing our Miss Dawson. Dear me, the world's a very small place, as I often says to my wife. Here's the last group as was ever took of them, when the meet was held at the Manor in 1918. Of course, you'll understand, it wasn't a regular meet, like, owing to the War and the gentlemen being away and the horses too — we couldn't keep things up regular like in the old days. But what with the foxes gettin' so terrible many, and the packs all going to the dogs — ha! ha! — that's what I often used to say in this bar — the 'ounds is going to the dogs, I says. Very good, they used to think it. There's many a gentleman has laughed at me sayin' that — the 'ounds, I says, is goin' to

156

the dogs — well, as I was sayin', Colonel Fletcher and some of the older gentlemen, they says, we must carry on somehow, they says, and so they 'ad one or two scratch meets as you might say, just to keep the pack from fallin' to pieces, as you might say. And Miss Whittaker, she says, "Ave the meet at the Manor, Colonel,' she says, 'it's the last meet I'll ever see, perhaps,' she says. And so it was, poor lady, for she 'ad a stroke in the New Year. She died in 1922. That's 'er, sitting in the pony-carriage and Miss Dawson beside 'er. Of course, Miss Whittaker 'ad 'ad to give up riding to 'ounds some years before. She was gettin' on, but she always followed in the trap, up to the very last. 'Andsome old lady, ain't she, sir?'

Lord Peter and Parker looked with considerable interest at the rather grim old woman sitting so uncompromisingly upright with the reins in her hand. A dour, weather-beaten old face, but certainly handsome still, with its large nose and straight, heavy eyebrows. And beside her, smaller, plumper and more feminine, was the Agatha Dawson whose curious death had led them to this quiet country place. She had a sweet, smiling face — less dominating than that of her redoubtable friend, but full of spirit and character. Without doubt they had been a remarkable pair of old ladies.

Lord Peter asked a question or two about the family.

'Well, sir, I can't say as I knows about that. We always understood as Miss Whittaker had quarrelled with her people on account of comin' here and settin' up for herself. It wasn't usual in them days for girls to leave home the way it is now. But if you're particularly interested, sir, there's an old gentleman here as can tell you all about the Whittakers and the Dawsons too, and that's Ben Cobling. He was Miss Whittaker's groom for forty years, and he married Miss Dawson's maid as come with her from Norfolk. Eighty-six 'e was, last birthday, but a grand old fellow still. We thinks a lot of Ben Cobling in these parts. 'Im and his wife lives in the little cottage what Miss Whittaker left them when she died. If you'd like to go round and see them tomorrow, sir, you'll find Ben's memory as good as ever it was. Excuse me, sir, but it's time. I must get 'em out of the bar. Time, gentlemen, please! Three and eightpence, sir, thank you, sir. Hurry up, gentlemen, please. Now then, Joe, look sharp.'

'Great place, Crofton,' said Lord Peter, when he and Parker were left alone in a great, low-ceilinged bedroom, where the sheets smelt of lavender. 'Ben Cobling's sure to know all about Cousin Hallelujah. I'm looking forward to Ben Cobling.'

12

A Tale of Two Spinsters

'The power of perpetuating our property in our families is one of the most valuable and interesting circumstances belonging to it.'

BURKE: *Reflections on the Revolution*

The rainy night was followed by a sun-streaked morning. Lord Peter, having wrapped himself affectionately round an abnormal quantity of bacon and eggs, strolled out to bask at the door of the 'Fox-and-Hounds'. He filled a pipe slowly, and meditated. Within, a cheerful bustle in the bar announced the near arrival of opening time. Eight ducks crossed the road in Indian file. A cat sprang up upon the bench, stretched herself, tucked her hind legs under her and coiled her tail tightly round them as though to prevent them from accidentally working loose. A groom passed, riding a tall bay horse and leading a chestnut with a hogged mane; a spaniel followed them, running ridiculously, with one ear flopped inside-out over his foolish head.

Lord Peter said, 'Hah!'

The inn door was set hospitably open by the barman, who said, 'Good morning, sir; fine morning, sir,' and vanished within again.

Lord Peter said, 'Umph.' He uncrossed his

right foot from over his left and straddled happily across the threshold.

Round the corner by the churchyard wall a little bent figure hove into sight — an aged man with a wrinkled face and legs incredibly bowed, his spare shanks enclosed in leather gaiters. He advanced at a kind of brisk totter and civilly bared his ancient head before lowering himself with an audible creak on to the bench beside the cat.

'Good morning, sir,' said he.

'Good morning,' said Lord Peter. 'A beautiful day.'

'That it be, sir, that it be,' said the old man, heartily. 'When I sees a beautiful May day like this, I pray the Lord He'll spare me to live in this wonderful world of His a few years longer. I do indeed.'

'You look uncommonly fit,' said his lordship; 'I should think there was every chance of it.'

'I'm still very hearty, sir, thank you, though I'm eighty-seven next Michaelmas.'

Lord Peter expressed a proper astonishment.

'Yes, sir, eighty-seven, and if it wasn't for the rheumatics I'd have nothin' to complain on. I'm stronger maybe than what I look. I knows I'm a bit bent, sir, but that's the 'osses, sir, more than age. Regular brought up with 'osses I've been all my life. Worked with 'em, slept with 'em — lived in a stable, you might say, sir.'

'You couldn't have better company,' said Lord Peter.

'That's right, sir, you couldn't. My wife always used to say she was jealous of the 'osses. Said I preferred their conversation to hers. Well, maybe she was right, sir. A 'oss never talks no foolishness, I says to her, and that's more than you can always say of women, ain't it, sir?'

'It is indeed,' said Wimsey. 'What are you going to have?'

'Thank you, sir, I'll have my usual pint of bitter. Jim knows. Jim! Always start the day with a pint of bitter, sir. It's 'olesomer than tea to my mind and don't fret the coats of the stomach.'

'I dare say you're right,' said Wimsey. 'Now you mention it, there is something fretful about tea. Mr Piggin, two pints of bitter, please, and will you join us?'

'Thank you, my lord,' said the landlord. 'Joe! Two large bitters and a Guinness. Beautiful morning, my lord — 'morning, Mr Cobling — I see you've made each other's acquaintance already.'

'By Jove! so this is Mr Cobling. I'm delighted to see you. I wanted particularly to have a chat with you.'

'Indeed, sir?'

'I was telling this gentleman — Lord Peter Wimsey his name is — as you could tell him about Miss Whittaker and Miss Dawson. He knows friends of Miss Dawson's.'

'Indeed? Ah! There ain't much I *couldn't* tell you about them ladies. And proud I'd be to do it. Fifty years I was with Miss Whittaker. I come to her as under-groom in old Johnny Black-thorn's time, and stayed on as head-groom after he died. A rare young lady she was in them days. Deary me. Straight as a switch, with a fine, high colour in her cheeks and shiny black hair — just like a beautiful two-year-old filly she was. And very sperrited. Wonnerful sperrited. There was many a gentleman as would have been glad to hitch up with her, but she was never broke to harness. Like dirt, she treated 'em. Wouldn't look at 'em, except it might be the grooms and stable-hands in a matter of 'osses. And in the way of business, of course. Well, there is some creatures like that. I 'ad a terrier-bitch that way. Great ratter she was. But a business woman — nothin' else. I tried 'er with all the dogs I could lay 'and to, but it weren't no good. Bloodshed there was an' sich a row — you never 'eard. The Lord makes a few of 'em that way to suit 'Is own purposes, I suppose. There ain't no arguin' with females.'

Lord Peter said, 'Ah!'

The ale went down in silence.

Mr Piggin roused himself presently from contemplation to tell a story of Miss Whittaker in the hunting-field. Mr Cobling capped this by another. Lord Peter said, 'Ah!' Parker then emerged and was introduced, and Mr Cobling begged the privilege of standing a round of drinks. This ritual accomplished, Mr Piggin begged the company would be his guests for a third round, and then excused himself on the plea of customers to attend to.

He went in, and Lord Peter, by skilful and maddeningly slow degrees, began to work his way back to the history of the Dawson family. Parker — educated at Barrow-in-Furness grammar school and with his wits further sharpened

162

in the London police service — endeavoured now and again to get matters along faster by a brisk question. The result, every time, was to make Mr Cobling lose the thread of his remarks and start him off into a series of interminable sidetracks. Wimsey kicked his friend viciously on the ankle-bone to keep him quiet, and with endless patience worked the conversation back to the main road again.

At the end of an hour or so, Mr Cobling explained that his wife could tell them a great deal more about Miss Dawson than what he could, and invited them to visit his cottage. This invitation being accepted with alacrity, the party started off, Mr Cobling explaining to Parker that he was eighty-seven come next Michaelmas, and hearty still, indeed, stronger than he appeared, bar the rheumatics that troubled him. 'I'm not saying as I'm not bent,' said Mr Cobling, 'but that's more the work of the 'osses. Regular lived with 'osses all my life — '

'Don't look so fretful, Charles,' murmured Wimsey in his ear; 'it must be the tea at breakfast — it frets the coats of the stomach.'

Mrs Cobling turned out to be a delightful old lady, exactly like a dried-up pippin and only two years younger than her husband. She was entranced at getting an opportunity to talk about her darling Miss Agatha. Parker, thinking it necessary to put forward some reason for the inquiry, started on an involved explanation, and was kicked again. To Mrs Cobling, nothing could be more natural than that all the world should be interested in the Dawsons, and she prattled gaily on without prompting.

She had been in the Dawson family service as a girl — almost born in it as you might say. Hadn't her mother been housekeeper to Mr Henry Dawson, Miss Agatha's papa, and to his father before him? She herself had gone to the big house as stillroom maid when she wasn't but fifteen. That was when Miss Harriet was only three years old — her as afterwards married Mr James Whittaker. Yes, and she'd been there when the rest of the family was born. Mr Stephen — him as should have been the heir — ah dear! only the trouble came and that killed his poor father and there was nothing left. Yes, a sad business that was. Poor Mr Henry speculated with something — Mrs Cobling wasn't clear what, but it was all very wicked and happened in London where there were so many wicked people — and the long and the short was, he lost it all, poor gentleman, and never held up his head again. Only fifty-four he was when he died; such a fine upright gentleman with a pleasant word for everybody. And his wife didn't live long after him, poor lamb. She was a Frenchwoman and a sweet lady, but she was very lonely in England, having no family and her two sisters walled up alive in one of them dreadful Romish Convents.

'And what did Mr Stephen do when the money went?' asked Wimsey.

'Him? Oh, he went into business — a strange thing that did seem, though I have heard tell as old Barnabas Dawson, Mr Henry's grandfather that was, was nought but a grocer or something

164

of that — and they do say, don't they, that from shirtsleeves to shirtsleeves is three generations? Still, it was very hard on Mr Stephen, as had always been brought up to have everything of the best. And engaged to be married to a beautiful lady, too, and a very rich heiress. But it was all for the best, for when she heard Mr Stephen was a poor man after all, she threw him over, and that showed she had no heart in her at all. Mr Stephen never married till he was over forty, and then it was a lady with no family at all — not lawful, that is, though she was a dear, sweet girl and made Mr Stephen a most splendid wife — she did indeed. And Mr John, he was their only son. They thought the world of him. It was a terrible day when the news came that he was killed in the War. A cruel business that was, sir, wasn't it? — and nobody the better for it as I can see, but all these shocking hard taxes, and the price of everything gone up so, and so many out of work.'

'So he was killed? That must have been a terrible grief to his parents.'

'Yes, sir, terrible. Oh, it was an awful thing altogether, sir, for poor Mr Stephen, as had had so much trouble all his life, he went out of his poor mind and shot hisself. Out of his mind he must have been, sir, to do it — and what was more dreadful still, he shot his dear lady as well. You may remember it, sir. There was pieces in the paper about it.'

'I seem to have some vague recollection of it,' said Peter, quite untruthfully, but anxious not to seem to belittle the local tragedy. 'And young

John — he wasn't married, I suppose.'

'No, sir. That was very sad, too. He was engaged to a young lady — a nurse in one of the English hospitals, as we understood, and he was hoping to get back and be married to her on his next leave. Everything did seem to go all wrong together them terrible years.'

The old lady sighed, and wiped her eyes.

'Mr Stephen was the only son, then?'

'Well, not exactly, sir. There was the darling twins. Such pretty children, but they only lived two days. They come four years after Miss Harriet — her as married Mr James Whittaker.'

'Yes, of course. That was how the families became connected.'

'Yes, sir. Miss Agatha and Miss Harriet and Miss Clara Whittaker was all at the same school together, and Mrs Whittaker asked the two young ladies to go and spend their holidays with Miss Clara, and that was when Mr James fell in love with Miss Harriet. She wasn't as pretty as Miss Agatha, to my thinking, but she was livelier and quicker — and then, of course, Miss Agatha was never one for flirting and foolishness. Often she used to say to me, 'Betty,' she said, 'I mean to be an old maid and so does Miss Clara, and we're going to live together and be ever so happy, without any stupid, tiresome gentlemen.' And so it turned out, sir, as you know, for Miss Agatha, for all she was so quiet, was very determined. Once she'd said a thing, you couldn't turn her from it — not with reasons, nor with threats, nor with coaxings — nothing! Many's the time I've tried when she was a child

166

— for I used to give a little help in the nursery sometimes, sir. You might drive her into a temper or into the sulks, but you couldn't make her change her little mind, even then.'

There came to Wimsey's mind the picture of the stricken, helpless old woman, holding to her own way in spite of her lawyer's reasoning and her niece's subterfuge. A remarkable old lady, certainly, in her way.

'I suppose the Dawson family has practically died out, then,' he said.

'Oh, yes, sir. There's only Miss Mary now — and she's a Whittaker, of course. She is Miss Harriet's granddaughter, Mr Charles Whittaker's only child. She was left all alone, too, when she went to live with Miss Dawson. Mr Charles and his wife was killed in one of those dreadful motors — dear, dear — it seemed we was fated to have nothing but one tragedy after another. Just to think of Ben and me outliving them all.'

'Cheer up, Mother,' said Ben, laying his hand on hers. 'The Lord have been wonderful good to us.'

'That He have. Three sons we have, sir, and two daughters, and fourteen grandchildren and three great-grandchildren. Maybe you'd like to see their pictures, sir.'

Lord Peter said he should like to very much, and Parker made confirmatory noises. The life-histories of all the children and descendants were detailed at suitable length. Whenever a pause seemed discernible, Parker would mutter hopefully in Wimsey's ear, 'How about Cousin Hallelujah?' but before a question could be put,

167

the interminable family chronicle was resumed.

'And for God's sake, Charles,' whispered Peter, savagely, when Mrs Cobling had risen to hunt for the shawl which Grandson William had sent home from the Dardanelles, 'don't keep saying Hallelujah at me! I'm not a revival meeting.'

The shawl being duly admired, the conversation turned upon foreign parts, natives and black people generally, following on which, Lord Peter added carelessly:

'By the way, hasn't the Dawson family got some sort of connections in those foreign countries somewhere?'

'Well, yes,' said Mrs Cobling, in rather a shocked tone. There had been Mr Paul, Mr Henry's brother. But he was not mentioned much. He had been a terrible shock to his family. In fact — a gasp here, and a lowering of the voice — he had *turned Papist* and become — a monk! (Had he become a murderer, apparently, he could hardly have done worse.) Mr Henry had always blamed himself very much in the matter.

'How was it his fault?'

'Well, of course, Mr Henry's wife — my dear mistress, you see, sir — she was French, as I told you, and of course, *she* was a Papist. Being brought up that way, she wouldn't know any better, naturally, and she was very young when she was married. But Mr Henry soon taught her to be a Christian, and she put away her idolatrous ideas and went to the parish church. But Mr Paul, *he* fell in love with one of her

168

sisters, and the sister had been vowed to religion, as they call it, and had shut herself up in a nunnery.' And then Mr Paul had broken his heart and 'gone over' to the Scarlet Woman and — again the pause and the hush — become a monk. A terrible to-do it made. And he'd lived to be a very old man, and for all Mrs Cobling knew was living yet, still in the error of his ways.

'If he's alive,' murmured Parker, 'he's probably the real heir. He'd be Agatha Dawson's uncle and her nearest relation.'

Wimsey frowned and returned to the charge.

'Well, it couldn't have been Mr Paul I had in mind,' he said, 'because this sort of relation of Miss Agatha Dawson's that I heard about was a real foreigner — in fact, a very dark-complexioned man — almost a black man, or so I was told.'

'Black?' cried the old lady — 'oh, no, sir — that couldn't be. Unless — dear Lord a' mercy, it couldn't be that, surely! Ben, do you think it could be that? — Old Simon, you know?'

Ben shook his head. 'I never heard tell much about him.'

'Nor nobody did,' replied Mrs Cobling, energetically. 'He was a long way back, but they had tales of him in the family. 'Wicked Simon', they called him. He sailed away to the Indies, many years ago, and nobody knew what became of him. Wouldn't it be a queer thing, like, if he was to have married a black wife out in them parts, and this was his — oh, dear — his grandson it 'ud have to be, if not his great-grandson, for he was Mr Henry's uncle,

169

and that's a long time ago.'

This was disappointing. A grandson of 'old Simon's' would surely be too distant a relative to dispute Mary Whittaker's title. However:

'That's very interesting,' said Wimsey. 'Was it the East Indies or the West Indies he went to, I wonder?'

Mrs Cobling didn't know, but she believed it was something to do with America.

'It's a pity as Mr Probyn ain't in England any longer. He could have told you more about the family than what I can. But he retired last year and went away to Italy or some such place.'

'Who was he?'

'He was Miss Whittaker's solicitor,' said Ben, 'and he managed all Miss Dawson's business, too. A nice gentleman he was, but uncommon sharp — ha, ha! Never gave nothing away. But that's lawyers all the world over,' added he, shrewdly, 'take all and give nothing.'

'Did he live in Crofton?'

'No, sir, in Crofton Magna, twelve miles from here. Pointer & Winkin have his business now, but they're young men, and I don't know much about them.'

Having by this time heard all the Coblings had to tell, Wimsey and Parker gradually disentangled themselves and took their leave.

'Well, Cousin Hallelujah's a wash-out,' said Parker.

'Possibly — possibly not. There may be some connection. Still, I certainly think the disgraceful and papistical Mr Paul is more promising. Obviously Mr Probyn is the bird to get hold of.

You realise who he is?'

'He's the mysterious solicitor, I suppose.'

'Of course he is. He knows why Miss Dawson ought to have made her will. And we're going straight off to Crofton Magna to look up Messrs Pointer & Winkin, and see what they have to say about it.'

Unhappily, Messrs Pointer & Winkin had nothing to say whatever. Miss Dawson had withdrawn her affairs from Mr Probyn's hands and had lodged all the papers with her new solicitor. Messrs Pointer & Winkin had never had any connection with the Dawson family. They had no objection, however, to furnishing Mr Probyn's address — Villa Bianca, Fiesole. They regretted that they could be of no further assistance to Lord Peter Wimsey and Mr Parker. Good morning.

'Short and sour,' was his lordship's comment. 'Well, well — we'll have a spot of lunch and write a letter to Mr Probyn and another to my good friend Bishop Lambert of the Orinoco Mission to get a line on Cousin Hallelujah. Smile, smile, smile. As Ingoldsby says: 'The breezes are blowing a race, a race! The breezes are blowing — we near the chase!' Do ye ken John Peel? Likewise, know'st thou the land where blooms the citron-flower? Well, never mind if you don't — you can always look forward to going there for your honeymoon.'

13

Hallelujah

'Our ancestors are very good kind of folks,
but they are the last people I should choose
to have a visiting acquaintance with.'
SHERIDAN: *The Rivals*

That excellent prelate, Bishop Lambert of the
Orinoco Mission, proved to be a practical and
kind man. He did not personally know the Rev
Hallelujah Dawson, but thought he might belong
to the Tabernacle Mission — a Nonconformist
body which was doing very valuable work in
those parts. He would himself communicate with
the London Headquarters of this community
and let Lord Peter know the result. Two hours
later, Bishop Lambert's secretary had duly rung
up the Tabernacle Mission and received the very
satisfactory information that the Rev Hallelujah
Dawson was in England, and, indeed, available at
their Mission House in Stepney. He was an elderly minister, living in very reduced circumstances
— in fact, the Bishop rather gathered that the
story was a sad one — Oh, not at all, pray, no
thanks. The Bishop's poor miserable slave of a
secretary did all the work. Very glad to hear from
Lord Peter, and was he being good? Ha, ha! and
when was he coming to dine with the Bishop?
Lord Peter promptly gathered up Parker and

swooped down with him upon the Tabernacle Mission, before whose dim and grim frontage Mrs Merdle's long black bonnet and sweeping copper exhaust made an immense impression. The small fry of the neighbourhood had clustered about her and were practising horn solos almost before Wimsey had rung the bell. On Parker's threatening them with punishment and casually informing them that he was a police officer, they burst into ecstasies of delight, and joining hands, formed a ring-o'-roses round him, under the guidance of a sprightly young woman of twelve years old or thereabouts. Parker made a few harassed darts at them, but the ring only broke up, shrieking with laughter, and reformed, singing. The Mission door opened at the moment, displaying this undignified exhibition to the eyes of a lank young man in spectacles, who shook a long finger disapprovingly and said, 'Now, you children,' without the slightest effect and apparently without the faintest expectation of producing any.

Lord Peter explained his errand.

'Oh, come in, please,' said the young man, who had one finger in a book of theology. 'I'm afraid your friend — er — this is rather a noisy district.'

Parker shook himself free from his tormentors, and advanced, breathing threatenings and slaughter, to which the enemy responded by a derisive blast of the horn.

'They'll run those batteries down,' said Wimsey.

'You can't do anything with the little devils,' growled Parker.

'Why don't you treat them as human beings?' retorted Wimsey. 'Children are creatures of like passions with politicians and financiers. Here, Esmeralda!' he added, beckoning to the ring-leader.

The young woman put her tongue out and made a rude gesture, but observing the glint of coin in the outstretched hand, suddenly approached and stood challengingly before them.

'Look here,' said Wimsey, 'here's half a crown — thirty pennies, you know. Any use to you?'

The child promptly proved her kinship with humanity. She became abashed in the presence of wealth, and was silent, rubbing one dusty shoe upon the calf of her stocking.

'You appear,' pursued Lord Peter, 'to be able to keep your young friends in order if you choose. I take you, in fact, for a woman of character. Very well, if you keep them from touching my car while I'm in the house, you get this half-crown, see? But if you let 'em blow the horn, I shall hear it. Every time the horn goes, you lose a penny, got that? If the horn blows six times, you only get two bob. If I hear it thirty times, you don't get anything. And I shall look out from time to time, and if I see anybody mauling the car about, or sitting in it *then* you don't get anything. Do I make myself clear?'

'I takes care o' yer car fer 'arf a crahn. An' ef the 'orn goes, you docks a copper 'orf of it.'

'That's right.'

'Right you are, mister. I'll see none of 'em touches it.'

'Good girl. Now, sir.'

174

The spectacled young man led them into a gloomy little waiting-room, suggestive of a railway station and hung with Old Testament prints.

'I'll tell Mr Dawson you're here,' said he, and vanished, with the volume of theology still clutched in his hand.

Presently a shuffling step was heard on the coconut matting, and Wimsey and Parker braced themselves to confront the villainous claimant.

The door, however, opened to admit an elderly West Indian, of so humble and inoffensive an appearance that the hearts of the two detectives sank into their boots. Anything less murderous could scarcely be imagined, as he stood blinking nervously at them from behind a pair of steel-rimmed spectacles, the frames of which had at one time been broken and bound with wire.

The Rev Hallelujah Dawson was undoubtedly a man of colour. He had the pleasant, slightly aquiline features and brown-olive skin of the Polynesian. His hair was scanty and greyish — not woolly, but closely curled. His stooping shoulders were clad in a threadbare clerical coat. His black eyes, yellow about the whites and slightly protruding, rolled amiably at them, and his smile was open and frank.

'You asked to see me?' he began, in perfect English, but with the soft native intonation. 'I think I have not the pleasure — ?'

'How do you do, Mr Dawson? Yes. We are — er — makin' certain inquiries — er — in connection with the family of the Dawsons of

Crofton in Warwickshire, and it has been suggested that you might be able to enlighten us, what? as to their West Indian connections — if you would be so good.'

'Ah, yes!' The old man drew himself up slightly. 'I am myself — in a way — a descendant of the family. Won't you sit down?'

'Thank you. We thought you might be.'

'You do not come from Miss Whittaker?'

There was something eager, yet defensive in the tone. Wimsey, not quite knowing what was behind it, chose the discreeter part.

'Oh, no. We are — preparin' a work on Country Families, don't you know. Tombstones and genealogies and that sort of thing.'

'Oh! — yes — I hoped perhaps — ' The mild tones died away in a sigh. 'But I shall be very happy to help you in any way.'

'Well, the question now is, what became of Simon Dawson? We know that he left his family and sailed for the West Indies in — ah! — in seventeen — '

'Eighteen hundred and ten,' said the old man, with surprising quickness. 'Yes. He got into trouble when he was a lad of sixteen. He took up with bad men older than himself, and became involved in a very terrible affair. It had to do with gaming, and a man was killed. Not in a duel — in those days that would not have been considered disgraceful — though violence is always displeasing to the Lord — but the man was foully murdered and Simon Dawson and his friends fled from justice. Simon fell in with the press-gang and was carried off to sea. He served

176

fifteen years and was then taken by a French privateer. Later on he escaped and — to cut a long story short — got away to Trinidad under another name. Some English people there were kind to him and gave him work on their sugar plantation. He did well there and eventually became owner of a small plantation of his own.'

'What was the name he went by?'

'Harkaway. I suppose he was afraid that they would get hold of him as a deserter from the Navy if he went by his own name. No doubt he should have reported his escape. Anyway, he liked plantation life and was quite satisfied to stay where he was. I don't suppose he would have cared to go home, even to claim his inheritance. And then, there was always the matter of the murder, you know — though I daresay they would not have brought that trouble up against him, seeing he was so young when it happened and it was not his hand that did the awful deed.'

'His inheritance? Was he the eldest son, then?'

'No. Barnabas was the eldest, but he was killed at Waterloo and left no family. Then there was a second son, Roger, but he died of smallpox as a child. Simon was the third son.'

'Then it was the fourth son who took the estate?'

'Yes, Frederick. He was Henry Dawson's father. They tried, of course, to find out what became of Simon, but in those days it was very difficult, you understand, to get information from foreign places, and Simon had quite disappeared. So they had to pass him over.'

'And what happened to Simon's children?' asked Parker. 'Did he have any?'

The clergyman nodded, and a deep, dusky flush showed under his dark skin.

'I am his grandson,' he said, simply. 'That is why I came over to England. When the Lord called me to feed His lambs among my own people, I was in quite good circumstances. I had the little sugar plantation which had come down to me through my father, and I married and was very happy. But we fell on bad times — the sugar crop failed, and our little flock became smaller and poorer and could not give so much support to their minister. Besides, I was getting too old and frail to do my work — and I have a sick wife, too, and God has blessed us with many daughters, who needed our care. I was in great straits. And then I came upon some old family papers belonging to my grandfather, Simon, and learned that his name was not Harkaway but Dawson, and I thought, maybe, I had a family in England and that God would yet raise up a table in the wilderness. Accordingly, when the time came to send a representative home to our London Headquarters, I asked permission to resign my ministry out there and come over to England.'

'Did you get in touch with anybody?'

'Yes. I went to Crofton — which was mentioned in my grandfather's letters — and saw a lawyer in the town there — a Mr Probyn of Croftover. You know him?'

'I've heard of him.'

'Yes. He was very kind, and very much

178

interested to see me. He showed me the genealogy of the family, and how my grandfather should have been the heir to the property.'

'But the property had been lost by that time, had it not?'

'Yes. And, unfortunately — when I showed him my grandmother's marriage certificate, he — he told me that it was no certificate at all. I fear that Simon Dawson was a sad sinner. He took my grandmother to live with him, as many of the planters did take women of colour, and he gave her a document which was supposed to be a certificate of marriage signed by the Governor of the country. But when Mr Probyn inquired into it, he found that it was all a sham, and no such governor had ever existed. It was distressing to my feelings as a Christian, of course — but since there was no property, it didn't make any actual difference to us.'

'That was bad luck,' said Peter, sympathetically.

'I called resignation to my aid,' said the old Indian, with a dignified little bow. 'Mr Probyn was also good enough to send me with a letter of introduction to Miss Agatha Dawson, the only surviving member of our family.'

'Yes, she lived at Leahampton.'

'She received me in the most charming way, and when I told her who I was — acknowledging, of course, that I had not the slightest claim upon her — she was good enough to make an allowance of £100 a year, which she continued till her death.'

'Was that the only time you saw her?'

'Oh, yes. I would not intrude upon her. It could not be agreeable to her to have a relative of my complexion continually at her house,' said the Rev Hallelujah, with a kind of proud humility. 'But she gave me lunch, and spoke very kindly.'

'And — forgive my askin' — hope it isn't impertinent — but does Miss Whittaker keep up the allowance?'

'Well, no — I — perhaps I should not expect it, but it would have made a great difference to our circumstances. And Miss Dawson rather led me to hope that it might be continued. She told me that she did not like the idea of making a will, but, she said, 'It is not necessary at all, Cousin Hallelujah; Mary will have my money when I am gone, and she can continue the allowance on my behalf.' But perhaps Miss Whittaker did not get the money after all?'

'Oh, yes, she did. It is very odd. She may have forgotten about it.'

'I took the liberty of writing her a few words of spiritual comfort when her aunt died. Perhaps that did not please her. Of course, I did not write again. Yet I am loath to believe that she has hardened her heart against the unfortunate. No doubt there is some explanation.'

'No doubt,' said Lord Peter. 'Well, I'm very grateful to you for your kindness. That has quite cleared up the little matter of Simon and his descendants. I'll just make a note of the names and dates, if I may.'

'Certainly. I will bring you the paper which Mr Probyn kindly made out for me, showing the

180

whole of the family. Excuse me.'

He was not gone long, and soon reappeared with a genealogy, neatly typed out on a legal-looking sheet of blue paper.

Wimsey began to note down the particulars concerning Simon Dawson and his son, Bosun, and his grandson, Hallelujah. Suddenly he put his finger on an entry farther along.

'Look here, Charles,' he said. 'Here is our Father Paul — the bad boy who turned RC and became a monk.'

'So he is. But — he's dead, Peter — died in 1922, three years before Agatha Dawson.'

'Yes. We must wash him out. Well, these little setbacks will occur.'

They finished their notes, bade farewell to the Rev Hallelujah, and emerged to find Esmeralda valiantly defending Mrs Merdle against all-comers. Lord Peter handed over the half-crown and took delivery of the car.

'The more I hear of Mary Whittaker,' he said, 'the less I like her. She might at least have given poor old Cousin Hallelujah his hundred quid.'

'She's a rapacious female,' agreed Parker. 'Well, anyway, Father Paul's safely dead, and Cousin Hallelujah is illegitimately descended. So there's an end of the long-lost claimant from overseas.'

'Damn it all!' cried Wimsey, taking both hands from the steering wheel and scratching his head, to Parker's extreme alarm, 'that strikes a familiar chord. Now where in thunder have I heard those words before?'

181

14

Sharp Quillets of the Law

'Things done without example — in their issue
Are to be feared.'

Henry VIII, 1, 2

'Murbles is coming round to dinner tonight,
Charles,' said Wimsey. 'I wish you'd stop and
have grub with us too. I want to put all this
family history business before him.'

'Where are you dining?'

'Oh, at the flat. I'm sick of restaurant meals.
Bunter does a wonderful bloody steak and there
are new peas and potatoes and genuine English
grass. Gerald sent it up from Denver specially.
You can't buy it. Come along. Ye olde English
fare, don't you know, and a bottle of what Pepys
calls Ho Bryon. Do you good.'

Parker accepted. But he noticed that, even
when speaking on his beloved subject of food,
Wimsey was vague and abstracted. Something
seemed to be worrying at the back of his mind,
and even when Mr Murbles appeared, full of
mild legal humour, Wimsey listened to him with
extreme courtesy indeed, but with only half his
attention.

They were partly through dinner when,
apropos of nothing, Wimsey suddenly brought
his fist down on the mahogany with a crash that

182

startled even Bunter, causing him to jerk a great crimson splash of the Haut Brion over the edge of the glass upon the tablecloth.

'Got it!' said Lord Peter.

Bunter, in a low shocked voice, begged his lordship's pardon.

'Murbles,' said Wimsey, without heeding him, 'isn't there a new Property Act?'

'Why, yes,' said Mr Murbles, in some surprise. He had been in the middle of a story about a young barrister and a Jewish pawnbroker when the interruption occurred, and was a little put out.

'I knew I'd read that sentence somewhere — you know, Charles — about doing away with the long-lost claimant from overseas. It was in some paper or other about a couple of years ago, and it had to do with the new Act. Of course, it said what a blow it would be to romantic novelists. Doesn't the Act wash out the claims of distant relatives, Murbles?'

'In a sense, it does,' replied the solicitor. 'Not, of course, in the case of entailed property, which has its own rules. But I understand you to refer to ordinary personal property or real estate not entailed.'

'Yes — what happens to that, now, if the owner of the property dies without making a will?'

'It is rather a complicated matter,' began Mr Murbles.

'Well, look here, first of all — before the jolly old Act was passed, the next-of-kin got it all, didn't he — no matter if he was only a seventh

183

cousin fifteen times removed?'

'In a general way, that is correct. If there was a husband or wife — '

'Wash out the husband and wife. Suppose the person is unmarried and has no near relations living. It would have gone — '

'To the next-of-kin, whoever that was, if he or she could be traced.'

'Even if you had to burrow back to William the Conqueror to get at the relationship?'

'Always supposing you could get a clear record back to so very early a date,' replied Mr Murbles. 'It is, of course, in the highest degree improbable — '

'Yes, yes, I know, sir. But what happens now in such a case?'

'The new Act makes inheritance on intestacy very much simpler,' said Mr Murbles, setting his knife and fork together, placing both elbows on the table and laying the index-finger of his right hand against his left thumb in a gesture of tabulation.

'I bet it does,' interpolated Wimsey. 'I know what an Act to make things simpler means. It means that the people who drew it up don't understand it themselves and that every one of its clauses needs a law-suit to disentangle it. But do go on.'

'Under the new Act,' pursued Mr Murbles, 'one half of the property goes to the husband and wife, if living, and subject to his or her life-time interest, then all to the children equally. But if there be no spouse and no children, then it goes to the father or mother of the deceased. If

184

the father and mother are both dead, then everything goes to the brothers and sisters of the whole blood who are living at the time, but if any brother or sister dies before the intestate, then to his or her issue. In case there are no brothers or sisters of the — '

'Stop, stop! you needn't go any further. You're absolutely sure of that? It goes to the brothers' or sisters' issue?'

'Yes. That is to say, if it were you that died intestate and your brother Gerald and your sister Mary were already dead, your money would be equally divided among your nieces and nephews.'

'Yes, but suppose they were already dead too — suppose I'd gone tediously living on till I'd nothing left but great-nephews and great-nieces — would they inherit?'

'Why — why, yes, I suppose they would,' said Mr Murbles, with less certainty, however. 'Oh, yes, I think they would.'

'Clearly they would,' said Parker, a little impatiently, 'if it says to the issue of the deceased's brothers and sisters.'

'Ah! but we must not be precipitate,' said Mr Murbles, rounding upon him. 'To the lay mind, doubtless the word 'issue' appears a simple one. But in law' — (Mr Murbles, who up to this point had held the index-finger of the right hand poised against the ring-finger of the left, in recognition of the claims of the brothers and sisters of the half-blood, now placed his left palm upon the table and wagged his right index-finger admonishingly in Parker's direction) — 'in *law*

185

the word may bear one of two, or indeed several interpretations, according to the nature of the document in which it occurs and the date of that document.'

'But in the new Act — ' urged Lord Peter.

'I am not, particularly,' said Mr Murbles, 'a specialist in the law concerning property, and I should not like to give a decided opinion as to its interpretation, all the more as, up to the present, no case has come before the Courts bearing on the present issue — no pun intended, ha, ha, ha! But my immediate and entirely tentative opinion — which, however, I should advise you not to accept without the support of some weightier authority — would be, I *think*, that issue in this case means issue *ad infinitum*, and that therefore the great-nephews and great-nieces would be entitled to inherit.'

'But there might be another opinion?'

'Yes — the question is a complicated one — '

'What did I tell you?' groaned Peter. 'I *knew* this simplifying Act would cause a shockin' lot of muddle.'

'May I ask,' said Mr Murbles, 'exactly why you want to know all this?'

'Why, sir,' said Wimsey, taking from his pocket-book the genealogy of the Dawson family which he had received from the Rev Hallelujah Dawson, 'here is the point. We have always talked about Mary Whittaker as Agatha Dawson's niece; she was always called so and speaks of the dear old lady as her aunt. But if you look at this, you will see that actually she was no nearer to her than great-niece; she was the granddaughter of Agatha's sister Harriet.'

'Quite true,' said Mr Murbles, 'but still, she was apparently the nearest surviving relative, and since Agatha Dawson died in 1925, the money passed without any question to Mary Whittaker under the old Property Act. There's no ambiguity there.'

'No,' said Wimsey, 'none whatever, that's the point. But — '

'Good God!' broke in Parker, 'I see what you're driving at. When did the new Act come into force, sir?'

'In January, 1926,' replied Mr Murbles.

'And Miss Dawson died, rather unexpectedly, as we know, in November, 1925,' went on Peter. 'But supposing she had lived, as the doctor fully expected her to do, till February or March, 1926 — are you absolutely positive, sir, that Mary Whittaker would have inherited then?'

Mr Murbles opened his mouth to speak — and shut it again. He removed his eyeglasses and resettled them more firmly on his nose. Then:

'You are quite right, Lord Peter,' he said in a grave tone, 'this is a very serious and important point. Much too serious for me to give an opinion on. If I understand you rightly, you are suggesting that any ambiguity in the interpretation of the new Act might provide an interested party with a very good and sufficient motive for hastening the death of Agatha Dawson.'

'I do mean exactly that. Of course, if the great-niece inherits anyhow, the old lady might as well die under the new Act as under the old.

But if there was any doubt about it — tempting, don't you see, to give her a little push over the edge, so as to make her die in 1925. Especially as she couldn't live long anyhow, and there were no other relatives to be defrauded.'

'That reminds me,' put in Parker, 'suppose the great-niece is excluded from the inheritance, where does the money go?'

'It goes to the Duchy of Lancaster — or, in other words, to the Crown.'

'In fact,' said Wimsey, 'to no one in particular. Upon my soul, I really can't see that it's very much of a crime to bump a poor old thing off a bit previously when she's sufferin' horribly, just to get the money she intends you to have. Why the devil should the Duchy of Lancaster have it? Who cares about the Duchy of Lancaster? It's like defrauding the Income Tax.'

'Ethically,' observed Mr Murbles, 'there may be much to be said for your point of view. Legally, I am afraid, murder is murder, however frail the victim or convenient the result.'

'And Agatha Dawson didn't want to die,' added Parker, 'she said so.'

'No,' said Wimsey, thoughtfully, 'and I suppose she had a right to an opinion.'

'I think,' said Mr Murbles, 'that before we go any further, we ought to consult a specialist in this branch of the law. I wonder whether Towkington is at home. He is quite the ablest authority I could name. Greatly as I dislike that modern invention, the telephone, I think it might be advisable to ring him up.'

Mr Towkington proved to be at home and at

liberty. The case of the great-niece was put to him over the phone. Mr Towkington, taken at a disadvantage without his authorities, and hazarding an opinion on the spur of the moment, thought that in all probability the great-niece would be excluded from the succession under the new Act. But it was an interesting point, and he would be glad of an opportunity to verify his references. Would not Mr Murbles come round and talk it over with him? Mr Murbles explained that he was at that moment dining with two friends who were interested in the question. In that case, would not the two friends also come and see Mr Towkington?

'Towkington has some very excellent port,' said Mr Murbles, in a cautious aside, and clapping his hand over the mouthpiece of the telephone.

'Then why not go and try it?' said Wimsey, cheerfully.

'It's only as far as Gray's Inn,' continued Mr Murbles.

'All the better,' said Lord Peter.

Mr Murbles released the telephone and thanked Mr Towkington. The party would start at once for Gray's Inn. Mr Towkington was heard to say, 'Good, good,' in a hearty manner before ringing off.

On their arrival at Mr Towkington's chambers the oak was found to be hospitably unsported, and almost before they could knock, Mr Towkington himself flung open the door and greeted them in a loud and cheerful tone. He was a large, square man with a florid face and a harsh voice. In court, he was famous for a way of saying, 'Come now,' as a preface to tying recalcitrant witnesses into tight knots, which he would then proceed to slash open with a brilliant confutation. He knew Wimsey by sight, expressed himself delighted to meet Inspector Parker, and bustled his guests into the room with jovial shouts.

'I've been going into this little matter while you were coming along,' he said. 'Awkward, eh? ha! Astonishing thing that people can't say what they mean when they draw Acts, eh? ha! Why do you suppose it is, Lord Peter, eh? ha! Come now!'

'I suspect it's because Acts are drawn up by lawyers,' said Wimsey with a grin.

'To make work for themselves, eh? I daresay you're right. Even lawyers must live, eh? ha! Very good. Well now, Murbles, let's just have this case again, in greater detail, d'you mind?'

Mr Murbles explained the matter again, displaying the genealogical table and putting forward the point as regards a possible motive for murder.

'Eh, ha!' exclaimed Mr Towkington, much delighted, 'that's good — very good — your idea, Lord Peter? Very ingenious. Too ingenious. The dock at the Old Bailey is peopled by gentlemen who are too ingenious. Ha! Come to a bad end one of these days, young man. Eh? Yes — well, now, Murbles, the question here turns on the interpretation of the word 'issue' — you grasp that, eh, ha! Yes. Well, you seem to think it means issue ad infinitum. How do you make that out, come now?'

'I didn't say I thought it did; I said I thought it

190

might,' remonstrated Mr Murbles, mildly. 'The general intention of the Act appears to be to exclude any remote kin where the common ancestor is farther back than the grandparents — not to cut off the descendants of the brothers and sisters.'

'Intention?' snapped Mr Towkington. 'I'm astonished at you, Murbles! The law has nothing to do with good intentions. What does the Act say? It says, 'To the brothers and sisters of the whole blood and their issue.' Now in the absence of any new definition, I should say that the word is here to be construed as before the Act it was construed on intestacy — in so far, at any rate, as it refers to personal property, which I under-stand the property in question to be, eh?'

'Yes,' said Mr Murbles.

'Then I don't see that you and your great-niece have a leg to stand on — come now!'

'Excuse me,' said Wimsey, 'but d'you mind — I know lay people are awful ignorant nuisances — but if you *would* be so good as to explain what the beastly word did or does mean, it would be frightfully helpful, don't you know.'

'Ha! Well, it's like this,' said Mr Towkington, graciously. 'Before 1837 — '

'Queen Victoria, I know,' said Peter, intelli-gently.

'Quite so. At the time when Queen Victoria came to the throne, the word 'issue' had no legal meaning — no legal meaning at all.'

'You surprise me!'

'You are too easily surprised,' said Mr Towkington. 'Many words have no legal

191

meaning. Others have a legal meaning very unlike their ordinary meaning. For example, the word 'daffy-down-dilly'. It is a criminal libel to call a lawyer a daffy-down-dilly. Ha! Yes, I advise you never to do such a thing. No, I certainly advise you *never* to do it. Then again, words which are quite meaningless in your ordinary conversation may have a meaning in law. For instance, I might say to a young man like yourself, 'You wish to leave such-and-such property to so-and-so.' And you would very likely reply, 'Oh, yes, absolutely' — meaning nothing in particular by that. But if you were to write in your will, 'I leave such-and-such property to so-and-so *absolutely*,' then that word would bear a definite legal meaning, and would condition your bequest in a certain manner, and might even prove an embarrassment and produce results very far from your actual intentions. Eh, ha! You see?'

'Quite.'

'Very well. Prior to 1837, the word 'issue' meant nothing. A grant 'to A. and his issue' merely gave A. a life estate. Ha! But this was altered by the Wills Act of 1837.'

'As far as a will was concerned,' put in Mr Murbles.

'Precisely. After 1837, in a will, 'issue' means 'heirs of the body' — that is to say, 'issue *ad infinitum*'. In a deed, on the other hand, 'issue' retained its old meaning — or lack of meaning, eh, ha! You follow?'

'Yes,' said Mr Murbles, 'and on intestacy of personal property — '

'I am coming to that,' said Mr Towkington.

' — the word 'issue' continued to mean 'heirs of the body', and that held good till 1926.'

'Stop!' said Mr Towkington, 'issue of the child or children of the deceased certainly meant 'issue *ad infinitum*' — *but* — issue of any person *not* a child of the deceased only meant the child of that person and did not include other descendants. And that undoubtedly held good till 1926. And since the new Act contains no statement to the contrary, I think we must presume that it continues to hold good. Ha! Come now! In the case before us, you observe that the claimant is *not* the child of the deceased nor issue of the child of the deceased; nor is she the child of the deceased's sister. She is merely the grandchild of the deceased sister of the deceased. Accordingly, I think she is debarred from inheriting under the new Act, eh? ha!'

'I see your point,' said Mr Murbles.

'And moreover,' went on Mr Towkington, 'after 1925, 'issue' in a will or deed does *not* mean 'issue *ad infinitum*'. That at least is clearly stated, and the Wills Act of 1837 is revoked on that point. Not that that has any direct bearing on the question. But it may be an indication of the tendency of modern interpretation, and might possibly affect the mind of the court in deciding how the word 'issue' was to be construed for the purpose of the new Act!'

'Well,' said Mr Murbles, 'I bow to your superior knowledge.'

'In any case,' broke in Parker, 'any uncertainty in the matter would provide as good a motive for murder as the certainty of exclusion from inheritance. If Mary Whittaker only *thought* she might lose the money in the event of her great-aunt's surviving into 1926, she might quite well be tempted to polish her off a little earlier, and make sure.'

'That's true enough,' said Mr Murbles.

'Shrewd, very shrewd, ha!' added Mr Towkington. 'But you realise that all this theory of yours depends on Mary Whittaker's having known about the new Act and its probable consequences as early as October, 1925, eh, ha!'

'There's no reason why she shouldn't,' said Wimsey. 'I remember reading an article in the *Evening Banner*, I think it was, some months earlier — about the time when the Act was having its second reading. That's what put the thing into my head — I was trying to remember all evening where I'd seen that thing about washing out the long-lost heir, you know. Mary Whittaker may easily have seen it too.'

'Well, she'd probably have taken advice about it if she did,' said Mr Murbles. 'Who is her usual man of affairs?'

Wimsey shook his head.

'I don't think she'd have asked him,' he objected. 'Not if she was wise, that is. You see, if she did, and he said she probably wouldn't get anything unless Miss Dawson either made a will or died before January, 1926, and if after that the old lady did unexpectedly pop off in October, 1925, wouldn't the solicitor-johnnie feel inclined to ask questions? It wouldn't be safe, don't y'know. I 'xpect she went to some stranger, and

194

asked a few innocent little questions under another name, what?'

'Probably,' said Mr Towkington. 'You show a remarkable disposition for crime, don't you, eh?'

'Well, if I did go in for it, I'd take reasonable precautions,' retorted Wimsey. ''S wonderful, of course, the tomfool things murderers *do* do. But I have the highest opinion of Miss Whittaker's brains. I bet she covered her tracks pretty well.'

'You don't think Mr Probyn mentioned the matter,' suggested Parker, 'the time he went down and tried to get Miss Dawson to make her will.'

'I *don't*,' said Wimsey, with energy, 'but I'm pretty certain he tried to explain matters to the old lady, only she was so terrified of the very idea of a will she wouldn't let him get a word in. But I fancy old Probyn was too downy a bird to tell the heir that her only chance of gettin' the dollars was to see that her great-aunt died off before the Act went through. Would *you* tell anybody that, Mr Towkington?'

'Not if I knew it,' said that gentleman, grinning.

'It would be highly undesirable,' agreed Mr Murbles.

'Anyway,' said Wimsey, 'we can easily find out. Probyn's in Italy — I was going to write to him, but perhaps you'd better do it, Murbles. And, in the meanwhile, Charles and I will think up a way to find whoever it was that did give Miss Whittaker an opinion on the matter.'

'You're not forgetting, I suppose,' said Parker, rather drily, 'that before pinning down a murder

195

to any particular motive, it is usual to ascertain that a murder has been committed? So far, all we know is that, after a careful post-mortem analysis, two qualified doctors have agreed that Miss Dawson died a natural death.'

'I wish you wouldn't keep on saying the same thing, Charles. It bores me so. It's like the Raven never flitting which, as the poet observes, still is sitting, still is sitting, inviting one to heave the pallid bust of Pallas at him and have done with it. You wait till I publish my epoch-making work: *The Murderer's Vade-Mecum, or 101 Ways of Causing Sudden Death*. That'll show you I'm not a man to be trifled with.'

'Oh, well!' said Parker.

But he saw the Chief Commissioner next morning and reported that he was at last disposed to take the Dawson case seriously.

15

Temptation of St Peter

PIERROT: 'Scaramel, I am tempted.'
SCARAMEL: 'Always yield to temptation.'
L. HOUSMAN: *Prunella*

As Parker came out from the Chief Commissioner's room, he was caught by an officer.

'There's been a lady on the phone to you,' he said. 'I told her to ring up at 10.30. It's about that now.'

'What name?'

'A Mrs Forrest. She wouldn't say what she wanted.'

'Odd,' thought Parker. His researches in the matter had been so unfruitful that he had practically eliminated Mrs Forrest from the Gotobed mystery — merely keeping her filed, as it were, in the back of his mind for future reference. It occurred to him, whimsically, that she had at length discovered the absence of one of her wine-glasses and was ringing him up in a professional capacity. His conjectures were interrupted by his being called to the telephone to answer Mrs Forrest's call.

'Is that Detective-Inspector Parker? — I'm so sorry to trouble you, but could you possibly give me Mr Templeton's address?'

'Templeton?' said Parker, momentarily puzzled.

'Wasn't it Templeton — the gentleman who

came with you to see me?'

'Oh, yes, of course — I beg your pardon — I — the matter had slipped my memory. Er — you want his address?'

'I have some information which I think he will be glad to hear.'

'Oh, yes. You can speak quite freely to me, you know, Mrs Forrest.'

'Not *quite* freely,' purred the voice at the other end of the wire, 'you are rather official, you know. I should prefer just to write to Mr Templeton privately, and leave it to him to take up with you.'

'I see.' Parker's brain worked briskly. It might be inconvenient to have Mrs Forrest writing to Mr Templeton at 110A, Piccadilly. The letter might not be delivered. Or, if the lady were to take it into her head to call and discovered that Mr Templeton was not known to the porter, she might take alarm and bottle up her valuable information.

'I think,' said Parker, 'I ought not, perhaps, to give you Mr Templeton's address without consulting him. But you could phone him — '

'Oh, yes, that would do. Is he in the book?'

'No — but I can give you his private number.'

'Thank you very much. You'll forgive my bothering you.'

'No trouble at all.' And he named Lord Peter's number.

Having rung off, he waited a moment and then called the number himself.

'Look here, Wimsey,' he said, 'I've had a call from Mrs Forrest. She wants to write to you. I wouldn't give the address, but I've given her

198

your number, so if she calls and asks for Mr Templeton, you will remember who you are, won't you?'

'Righty-ho. Wonder what the fair lady wants.'

'It's probably occurred to her that she might have told a better story, and she wants to work off a few additions and improvements on you.'

'Then she'll probably give herself away. The rough sketch is frequently so much more convincing than the worked-up canvas.'

'Quite so. I couldn't get anything out of her myself.'

'No. I expect she's thought it over and decided that it's rather unusual to employ Scotland Yard to ferret out the whereabouts of errant husbands. She fancies there's something up, and that I'm a nice soft-headed imbecile whom she can easily pump in the absence of the official Cerberus.'

'Probably. Well, you'll deal with the matter. I'm going to make a search for that solicitor.'

'Rather a vague sort of search, isn't it?'

'Well, I've got an idea which may work out. I'll let you know if I get any results.'

★ ★ ★

Mrs Forrest's call duly came through in about twenty minutes' time. Mrs Forrest had changed her mind. Would Mr Templeton come round and see her that evening — about 9 o'clock, if that was convenient? She had thought the matter over and preferred not to put her information on paper.

Mr Templeton would be very happy to come

199

round. He had no other engagement. It was no inconvenience at all. He begged Mrs Forrest not to mention it.

Would Mr Templeton be so very good as not to tell anybody about his visit? Mr Forrest and his sleuths were continually on the watch to get Mrs Forrest into trouble, and the decree absolute was due to come up in a month's time. Any trouble with the King's Proctor would be positively disastrous. It would be better if Mr Templeton would come by Underground to Bond Street, and proceed to the flats on foot, so as not to leave a car standing outside the door or put a taxi-driver into a position to give testimony against Mrs Forrest.

Mr Templeton chivalrously promised to obey these directions.

Mrs Forrest was greatly obliged, and would expect him at nine o'clock.

'Bunter!'

'My lord.'

'I am going out tonight. I've been asked not to say where, so I won't. On the other hand, I've got a kind of feelin' that it's unwise to disappear from mortal ken, so to speak. So I'm going to leave the address in a sealed envelope. If I don't turn up before tomorrow mornin', I shall consider myself absolved from all promises, what?'

'Very good, my lord.'

'And if I'm not to be found at that address, there wouldn't be any harm in tryin' — say Epping Forest, or Wimbledon Common.'

'Quite so, my lord.'

'By the way, you made the photographs of

those fingerprints I brought you some time ago?'

'Oh, yes, my lord.'

'Because possibly Mr Parker may be wanting them presently for some inquiries he will be making.'

'I quite understand, my lord.'

'Nothing whatever to do with my excursion tonight, you understand.'

'Certainly not, my lord.'

'And now you might bring me Christie's catalogue. I shall be attending a sale there and lunching at the club.'

And, detaching his mind from crime, Lord Peter bent his intellectual and financial powers to outbidding and breaking a ring of dealers, an exercise very congenial to his mischievous spirit.

★ ★ ★

Lord Peter duly fulfilled the conditions imposed upon him, and arrived on foot at the block of flats in South Audley Street. Mrs Forrest, as before, opened the door to him herself. It was surprising, he considered, that, situated as she was, she appeared to have neither maid nor companion. But then, he supposed, a chaperon, however disarming of suspicion in the eyes of the world, might prove venal. On the whole, Mrs Forrest's principle was a sound one: no accomplices. Many transgressors, he reflected, had

'died because they never knew
These simple little rules and few.'

Mrs Forrest apologised prettily for the inconvenience to which she was putting Mr Templeton.

'But I never know when I am not spied upon,' she said. 'It is sheer spite, you know. Considering how my husband has behaved to me, I think it is monstrous — don't you?'

Her guest agreed that Mr Forrest must be a monster, Jesuitically, however, reserving the opinion that the monster might be a fabulous one.

'And now you will be wondering why I have brought you here,' went on the lady. 'Do come and sit on the sofa. Will you have whisky or coffee?'

'Coffee, please.'

'The fact is,' said Mrs Forrest, 'that I've had an idea since I saw you. I — you know, having been much in the same position myself' (with a slight laugh) 'I felt *so much* for your friend's wife.'

'Sylvia,' put in Lord Peter with commendable promptitude. 'Oh, yes. Shocking temper and so on, but possibly some provocation. Yes, yes, quite. Poor woman. Feels things — extra sensitive — highly-strung and all that, don't you know.'

'Quite so.' Mrs Forrest nodded her fantastically turbanned head. Swathed to the eyebrows in gold tissue, with only two flat crescents of yellow hair plastered over her cheekbones, she looked, in an exotic smoking-suit of embroidered tissue, like a young prince out of the Arabian Nights. Her heavily ringed hands busied themselves with the coffee-cups.

'Well — I felt that your inquiries were really serious, you know, and though, as I told you, it had nothing to do with me, I was interested and mentioned the matter in a letter to — to my friend, you see, who was with me that night.'

'Just so,' said Wimsey, taking the cup from her, 'yes — er — that was very — er — it was kind of you to be interested.'

'He — my friend — is abroad at the moment. My letter had to follow him, and I only got his reply today.'

Mrs Forrest took a sip or two of coffee as though to clear her recollection.

'His letter rather surprised me. He reminded me that after dinner he had felt the room rather close, and had opened the sitting-room window — that window, there — which overlooks South Audley Street. He noticed a car standing there — a small closed one, black or dark blue or some such colour. And while he was looking idly at it — the way one does, you know — he saw a man and woman come out of this block of flats — not this door, but one or two along to the left — and get in and drive off. The man was in evening dress and he thought it might have been your friend.'

Lord Peter, with his coffee-cup at his lips, paused and listened with great attention.

'Was the girl in evening dress, too?'

'No — that struck my friend particularly. She was in just a plain little dark suit, with a hat on.'

Lord Peter recalled to mind as nearly as possible Bertha Gotobed's costume. Was this going to be real evidence at last?

'Th — that's very interesting,' he stammered. 'I suppose your friend couldn't give any more

203

exact details of the dress?'

'No,' replied Mrs Forrest, regretfully, 'but he said the man's arm was round the girl as though she was feeling tired or unwell, and he heard him say, 'That's right — the fresh air will do you good.' But you're not drinking your coffee.'

'I beg your pardon — ' Wimsey recalled himself with a start. 'I was dreamin' — putting two and two together — the artful beggar. Oh, the coffee. D'you mind if I put this away and have some without sugar?'

'I'm so sorry. Men always seem to take sugar in black coffee. Give it to me — I'll empty it away.'

'Allow me.' There was no slop-basin on the little table, but Wimsey quickly got up and poured the coffee into the window-box outside. 'That's all right. How about another cup for you?'

'Thank you — I oughtn't to take it really, it keeps me awake.'

'Just a drop.'

'Oh, well, if you like.' She filled both cups and sat sipping quietly. 'Well — that's all, really, but I thought perhaps I ought to let you know.'

'It was very good of you,' said Wimsey.

They sat talking a little longer — about plays in Town ('I go out very little, you know; it's better to keep oneself out of the limelight on these occasions'), and books ('I adore Michael Arlen'). Had she read *Young Men in Love* yet? No — she had ordered it from the library. Wouldn't Mr Templeton have something to eat or drink? Really? A brandy? A liqueur?

No, thank you. And Mr Templeton felt he really ought to be slippin' along now.

'No — don't go yet — I get so lonely, these long evenings.' There was a desperate kind of appeal in her voice. Lord Peter sat down again.

She began a rambling and rather confused story about her 'friend'. She had given up so much for the friend. And now that her divorce was really coming off, she had a terrible feeling that perhaps the friend was not as affectionate as he used to be. It was very difficult for a woman, and life was very hard.

And so on.

As the minutes passed, Lord Peter became uncomfortably aware that she was watching him. The words tumbled out — hurriedly, yet lifelessly, like a set task, but her eyes were the eyes of a person who expects something. Something alarming, he decided, yet something she was determined to have. It reminded him of a man waiting for an operation — keyed up to it — knowing that it will do him good — yet shrinking from it with all his senses.

He kept up his end of the fatuous conversation. Behind a barrage of small-talk, his mind ran quickly to and fro, analysing the position, getting the range . . .

Suddenly he became aware that she was trying — clumsily, stupidly, as though in spite of herself — to get him to make love to her.

The fact itself did not strike Wimsey as odd. He was rich enough, well-bred enough, attractive enough and man of the world enough to have received similar invitations fairly often in his thirty-seven years of life. And not always from experienced women. There had been those who sought experience as well as those qualified to bestow it. But so awkward an approach by a woman who admitted to already possessing a husband and a lover was a phenomenon ouside his previous knowledge.

Moreover, he felt that the thing would be a nuisance. Mrs Forrest was handsome enough, but she had not a particle of attraction for him. For all her make-up and her somewhat outspoken costume, she struck him as spinster-ish — even epicene. That was the thing which puzzled him during their previous interview. Parker — a young man of rigid virtue and limited worldly knowledge — was not sensitive to these emanations. But Wimsey had felt her as something essentially sexless, even then. And he felt it even more strongly now. Never had he met a woman in whom 'the great It', eloquently hymned by Mrs Elinor Glyn, was so completely lacking.

Her bare shoulder was against him now, marking his broad-cloth with white patches of powder.

Blackmail was the first explanation that occurred to him. The next move would be for the fabulous Mr Forrest, or someone representing him, to appear suddenly in the doorway, aglow with virtuous wrath and outraged sensibilities.

'A very pretty little trap,' thought Wimsey, adding aloud, 'Well, I really must be getting along.'

She caught him by the arm.

'Don't go.'

There was no caress in the touch — only a kind of desperation. He thought, 'If she really made a practice of this, she would do it better.'

'Truly,' he said, 'I oughtn't to stay longer. It wouldn't be safe for you.'

'I'll risk it,' she said.

A passionate woman might have said it passionately. Or with a brave gaiety. Or challengingly. Or alluringly. Or mysteriously.

She said it grimly. Her fingers dug at his arm.

'Well, damn it all, *I'll* risk it,' thought Wimsey. 'I must and will know what it's all about.'

'Poor little woman.' He coaxed into his voice the throaty, fatuous tone of the man who is preparing to make an amorous fool of himself.

He felt her body stiffen as he slipped his arm round her, but she gave a little sigh of relief.

He pulled her suddenly and violently to him, and kissed her mouth with a practised exaggeration of passion.

He knew then. No one who has ever encountered it can ever again mistake that awful shrinking, that uncontrollable revulsion of the flesh against a caress that is nauseous. He thought for a moment that she was going to be actually sick.

He released her gently, and stood up — his mind in a whirl, but somehow triumphant. His first instinct had been right, after all.

'That was very naughty of me,' he said, lightly. 'You made me forget myself. You will forgive me, won't you?'

She nodded, shaken.

'And I really must toddle. It's gettin' frightfully late and all that. Where's my hat? Ah, yes, in the hall. Now, goodbye, Mrs Forrest, an' take care of yourself. An' thank you ever so much for telling me about what your friend saw.'

'You are really going?'

She spoke as though she had lost all hope.

'In God's name,' thought Wimsey, 'what does she want? Does she suspect that Mr Templeton is not everything that he seems? Does she want me to stay the night so that she can get a look at the laundry-mark on my shirt? Should I suddenly save the situation for her by offering her Lord Peter Wimsey's visiting-card?'

His brain toyed freakishly with the thought as he dabbled his way to the door. She let him go without further words.

As he stepped into the hall he turned and looked at her. She stood in the middle of the room, watching him, and on her face was such a fury of fear and rage as turned his blood to water.

16

A Cast-Iron Alibi

'Oh, Sammy, Sammy, why vorn't there an
alleybi?'

Pickwick Papers

Miss Whittaker and the youngest Miss Findlater
had returned from their expedition. Miss
Climpson, most faithful of sleuths, and carrying
Lord Peter's letter of instructions in the pocket
of her skirt like a talisman, had asked the
youngest Miss Findlater to tea.

As a matter of fact, Miss Climpson had
become genuinely interested in the girl. Silly
affectation and gush, and a parrot-repetition of
the shibboleths of the modern school were
symptoms that the experienced spinster well
understood. They indicated, she thought, a real
unhappiness, a real dissatisfaction with the
narrowness of life in a country town. And
besides this, Miss Climpson felt sure that Vera
Findlater was being 'preyed upon', as she
expressed it to herself, by the handsome Mary
Whittaker. 'It would be a mercy for the girl,'
thought Miss Climpson, 'if she could form a
genuine attachment to a young man. It is natural
for a schoolgirl to be *schwärmerisch* — in a
young woman of twenty-two it is thoroughly
undesirable. That Whittaker woman encourages

it — she would, of course. She likes to have someone to admire her and run her errands. And she prefers it to be a stupid person, who will not compete with her. If Mary Whittaker were to marry, she would marry a rabbit.' (Miss Climpson's active mind quickly conjured up a picture of the rabbit — fair-haired and a little paunchy, with a habit of saying, 'I'll ask the wife.' Miss Climpson wondered why Providence saw fit to create such men. For Miss Climpson, men were intended to be masterful, even though wicked or foolish. She was a spinster made and not born — a perfectly womanly woman.)

'But,' thought Miss Climpson, 'Mary Whittaker is not of the marrying sort. She is a professional woman by nature. She has a profession, by the way, but she does not intend to go back to it. Probably nursing demands too much sympathy — and one is under the authority of the doctors. Mary Whittaker prefers to control the lives of chickens. 'Better to reign in hell than serve in heaven.' Dear me! I wonder! if it is uncharitable to compare a fellow-being to Satan. Only in poetry, of course — I daresay that makes it not so bad. At any rate, I am certain that Mary Whittaker is doing Vera Findlater no good.'

Miss Climpson's guest was very ready to tell about their month in the country. They had toured round at first for a few days, and then they had heard of a delightful poultry farm which was for sale, near Orpington in Kent. So they had gone down to have a look at it, and found that it was to be sold in about a fortnight's time. It wouldn't have been wise, of course, to take it over without some inquiries, and by the greatest good fortune they found a dear little cottage to let, furnished, quite close by. So they had taken it for a few weeks, while Miss Whittaker 'looked round' and found out about the state of the poultry business in that district, and so on. They *had* enjoyed it so, and it was delightful keeping house together, right away from all the silly people at home.

'Of course, I don't mean you, Miss Climpson. You come from London and are so much more broadminded. But I simply can't stick the Leahampton lot, nor can Mary.'

'It is very delightful,' said Miss Climpson, 'to be *free* from the conventions, I'm sure — especially if one is in company with a *kindred spirit.*'

'Yes — of course Mary and I are tremendous friends, though she is so much cleverer than I am. It's absolutely settled that we're to take the farm and run it together. Won't it be wonderful?'

'Won't you find it rather dull and lonely — just you two girls together? You mustn't forget that you've been accustomed to see quite a lot of young people in Leahampton. Shan't you miss the tennis parties, and the young men, and so on?'

'Oh no! If you only knew what a stupid lot they are! Anyway, I've no use for men!' Miss Findlater tossed her head. 'They haven't got any ideas. And they always look on women as sort of pets or playthings. As if a woman like Mary wasn't worth fifty of them! You should have heard that Markham man the other day — talking politics to Mr Tredgold, so that

211

nobody could get a word in edgeways, and then saying, 'I'm afraid this is a very dull subject of conversation for you, Miss Whittaker,' in his condescending way. Mary said in that quiet way of hers, 'Oh, I think the *subject* is anything but dull, Mr Markham.' But he was so stupid, he couldn't even grasp that and said, 'One doesn't expect ladies to be interested in politics, you know. But perhaps you are one of the modern young ladies who want the flapper's vote.' Ladies, indeed! Why are men so insufferable when they talk about ladies?'

'I think men are apt to be *jealous* of women,' replied Miss Climpson, thoughtfully, 'and jealousy *does* make people rather *peevish* and *ill-mannered*. I suppose that when one would *like* to despise a set of people and yet has a horrid suspicion that one *can't* genuinely despise them, it makes one *exaggerate* one's contempt for them in conversation. That is why, my dear, I am always *very* careful not to speak sneeringly about men — even though they *often deserve* it, you know. But if I did, everybody would think I was an *envious old maid*, wouldn't they?'

'Well, I mean to be an old maid, anyhow,' retorted Miss Findlater, 'Mary and I have quite decided that. We're interested in things, not in men.'

'You've made a good start at finding out how it's going to work,' said Miss Climpson. 'Living with a person for a month is an *excellent* test. I suppose you had somebody to do the housework for you?'

'Not a soul. We did every bit of it, and it was

great fun. I'm ever so good at scrubbing floors and laying fires and things, and Mary's a simply marvellous cook. It was such a change from having the servants always bothering round like they do at home. Of course, it was quite a modern, labour-saving cottage — it belongs to some theatrical people, I think.'

'And what did you do when you weren't inquiring into the poultry business?'

'Oh, we ran round in the car and saw places and attended markets. Markets are frightfully amusing, with all the funny old farmers and people. Of course, I'd often been to markets before, but Mary made it all so interesting — and then, too, we were picking up hints all the time for our own marketing later on.'

'Did you run up to Town at all?'

'No.'

'I should have thought you'd have taken the opportunity for a little jaunt.'

'Mary hates Town.'

'I thought *you* rather enjoyed a run up now and then.'

'I'm not keen. Not now. I used to think I was, but I expect that was only the sort of spiritual restlessness one gets when one hasn't an object in life. There's nothing in it.'

Miss Findlater spoke with the air of a disillusioned rake, who has sucked life's orange and found it dead sea fruit. Miss Climpson did not smile. She was accustomed to the role of confidante.

'So you were together — just you two — all the time?'

'Every minute of it. And we weren't bored with one another a bit.'

'I hope your experiment will prove very successful,' said Miss Climpson. 'But when you really start on your life together, don't you think it would be wise to arrange for a few *breaks* in it? A little *change of companionship* is good for *everybody*. I've known so many *happy friendships* spoilt by people seeing *too much* of one another.'

'They couldn't have been *real friendships*, then,' asserted the girl, dogmatically. 'Mary and I are *absolutely* happy together.'

'Still,' said Miss Climpson, 'if you don't mind an *old woman* giving you a word of warning, I should be inclined not to keep the bow *always* bent. Suppose Miss Whittaker, for instance, wanted to go off and have a day in Town on her own, say — or to go to stay with friends — you would have to learn not to mind that.'

'Of course, I shouldn't mind. Why — ' she checked herself. 'I mean, I'm quite sure that Mary would be every bit as loyal to me as I am to her.'

'That's right,' said Miss Climpson. 'The longer I live, my dear, the more *certain* I become that *jealousy* is the most *fatal* of feelings. The Bible calls it 'cruel as the grave' and I'm sure that is so. *Absolute* loyalty, without jealousy, is the essential thing.'

'Yes. Though naturally one would hate to think that the person one was really friends with was putting another person in one's place . . . Miss Climpson, you do believe, don't you, that a

214

friendship ought to be 'fifty-fifty'?'

'That is the ideal friendship, I suppose,' said Miss Climpson, thoughtfully, 'but I think it is a *very rare thing*. Among women, that is. I doubt very much if I've ever seen an example of it. *Men*, I believe, find it easier to give and take in that way — probably because they have so many outside interests.'

'Men's friendships — oh, yes! I know one hears a lot about them. But half the time, I don't believe they're *real* friendships at all. Men can go off for years and forget all about their friends. And they don't really confide in one another. Mary and I tell each other all our thoughts and feelings. Men seem just content to think each other good sorts without ever bothering about their inmost selves.'

'Probably that's why their friendships last so well,' replied Miss Climpson. 'They don't make such demands on one another.'

'But a great friendship does make demands,' cried Miss Findlater eagerly. 'It's got to be just everything to one. It's wonderful the way it seems to colour all one's thoughts. Instead of being centred in oneself, one's centred in the other person. That's what Christian love means — one's ready to die for the other person.'

'Well, I don't know,' said Miss Climpson. 'I once heard a sermon about that from a most *splendid* priest — and he said that that kind of love might become *idolatry* if one wasn't very careful. He said that Milton's remark about Eve — you know, 'he for God only, she for God in him' — was not congruous with Catholic

215

doctrine. One must get the *proportions* right, and it was *out of proportion* to see everything through the eyes of another fellow-creature.'

'One must put God first, of course,' said Miss Findlater, a little formally. 'But if the friendship is mutual — that was the point — quite unselfish on both sides, it *must* be a good thing.'

'Love is always good, when it's the *right kind*,' agreed Miss Climpson, 'but I don't think it ought to be *too* possessive. One has to *train* oneself — ' she hesitated, and went on courageously — 'and in any case, my dear, I cannot help feeling that it is more natural — more proper, in a sense — for a man and woman to be all in all to one another than for two persons of the same sex. Er — after all, it is a — a *fruitful* affection,' said Miss Climpson, boggling a trifle at this idea, 'and — and all that, you know, and I am sure that when the *right* MAN comes along for you — '

'Bother the right man!' cried Miss Findlater, crossly. 'I do hate that kind of talk. It makes one feel dreadful — like a prize cow or something. Surely, we have got beyond that point of view these days.'

Miss Climpson perceived that she had let her honest zeal outrun her detective discretion. She had lost the Goodwill of her informant, and it was better to change the conversation. However, she could assure Lord Peter now of one thing. Whoever the woman was that Mrs Cropper had seen at Liverpool, it was not Miss Whittaker. The attached Miss Findlater, who had never left her friend's side, was sufficient guarantee of that.

216

17

The Country Lawyer's Story

'And he that gives us in these days new lords
may give us new laws.'
WITHER: *Contented Man's Morrice*

*Letter from Mr Probyn, retired Solicitor, of Villa
Bianca, Fiesole, to Mr Murbles, Solicitor, of
Staple Inn.*

'*Private and confidential.*
'DEAR SIR,
'I was much interested in your letter relative to
the death of Miss Agatha Dawson, late of
Leahampton, and will do my best to answer your
inquiries as briefly as possible, always, of course,
on the understanding that all information as to
the affairs of my late client will be treated as
strictly confidential. I make an exception, of
course, in favour of the police officer you
mention in connection with the matter.
'You wish to know (1) whether Miss Agatha
Dawson was aware that it might possibly prove
necessary, under the provisions of the new Act,
for her to make a testamentary disposition, in
order to ensure that her great-niece, Miss Mary
Whittaker, should inherit her personal property.
(2) Whether I ever urged her to make this
testamentary disposition and what her reply was.

217

(3) Whether I had made Miss Mary Whittaker aware of the situation in which she might be placed, supposing her great-aunt to die intestate later than December 31, 1925.

'In the course of the spring of 1925, my attention was called by a learned friend to the ambiguity of the wording of certain clauses in the Act, especially in respect of the failure to define the precise interpretation to be placed on the word 'Issue'. I immediately passed in review the affairs of my various clients, with a view to satisfying myself that the proper dispositions had been made in each case to avoid misunderstanding and litigation in case of intestacy. I at once realised that Miss Whittaker's inheritance of Miss Dawson's property entirely dependent on the interpretation given to the clause in question. I was aware that Miss Dawson was extremely averse from making a will, owing to that superstitious dread of decease which we meet with so frequently in our profession. However, I thought it my duty to make her understand the question and to do my utmost to get a will signed. Accordingly, I went down to Leahampton and laid the matter before her. This was on March the 14th, or thereabouts — I am not certain to the precise day.

'Unhappily, I encountered Miss Dawson at a moment when her opposition to the obnoxious idea of making a will was at its strongest. Her doctor had informed her that a further operation would become necessary in the course of the next few weeks, and I could have selected no more unfortunate occasion for intruding the

218

subject of death upon her mind. She resented any such suggestion — there was a conspiracy, she declared, to frighten her into dying under the operation. It appears that that very tactless practitioner of hers had frightened her with a similar suggestion before her previous operation. But she had come through that and she meant to come through this, if only people would not anger and alarm her.

'Of course, if she *had* died under the operation, the whole question would have settled itself and there would have been no need of any will. I pointed out that the very reason why I was anxious for the will to be made was that I fully expected her to live on into the following year, and I explained the provisions of the Act once more, as clearly as I could. She retorted that in that case I had no business to come and trouble her about the question at all. It would be time enough when the Act was passed.

'Naturally, the fool of a doctor had insisted that she was not to be told what her disease was — they always do — and she was convinced that the next operation would make all right and that she would live for years. When I ventured to insist — giving as my reason that we men of law always preferred to be on the safe and cautious side, she became exceedingly angry with me, and practically ordered me out of the house. A few days afterwards I received a letter from her, complaining of my impertinence, and saying that she could no longer feel any confidence in a person who treated her with such inconsiderate rudeness. At her request, I forwarded all her private papers in my possession to Mr Hodgson, of Leahampton, and I have not held any communication with any member of the family since that date.

'This answers your first and second questions. With regard to the third: I certainly did not think it proper to inform Miss Whittaker that her inheritance might depend upon her great-aunt's either making a will or dying before December 31, 1925. While I know nothing to the young lady's disadvantage, I have always held it inadvisable that persons should know too exactly how much they stand to gain by the unexpected decease of other persons. In case of any unforseen accident, their heirs may find themselves in an equivocal position, where the fact of their possessing such knowledge might — if made public — be highly prejudicial to their interests. The most that I thought it proper to say was that if at any time Miss Dawson should express a wish to see me, I should like to be sent for without delay. Of course, the withdrawal of Miss Dawson's affairs from my hands put it out of my power to interfere any further.

'In October, 1925, feeling that my health was not what it had been, I retired from business and came to Italy. In this country the English papers do not always arrive regularly, and I missed the announcement of Miss Dawson's death. That it should have occurred so suddenly and under circumstances somewhat mysterious, is certainly interesting.

'You say further that you would be glad of my opinion on Miss Agatha Dawson's mental condition at the same time when I last saw her. It was perfectly clear and competent — in so far as she was ever competent to deal with business. She was in no way gifted to grapple with legal problems, and I had extreme difficulty in getting her to understand what the trouble was with regard to the new Property Act. Having been brought up all her life to the idea that property went of right to the next of kin, she found it inconceivable that this state of things should ever alter. She assured me that the law would never permit the Government to pass such an Act. When I had reluctantly persuaded her that it would, she was quite sure that no court would be wicked enough to interpret the Act so as to give the money to anybody but Miss Whittaker, when she was clearly the proper person to have it. 'Why should the Duchy of Lancaster have any right to it?' she kept on saying. 'I don't even know the Duke of Lancaster.' She was not a particularly sensible woman, and in the end I was not at all sure that I had made her comprehend the situation — quite apart from the dislike she had of pursuing the subject. However, there is no doubt that she was then quite *compos mentis*. My reason for urging her to make the will before her final operation was, of course, that I feared she might subsequently lose the use of her faculties, or — which comes to the same thing from a business point of view — might have to be kept continually under the influence of opiates.

'Trusting that you will find here the information you require,

'I remain,
'Yours faithfully,
'THOS. PROBYN.'

Mr Murbles read this letter through twice, very thoughtfully. To even his cautious mind, the thing began to look like the makings of a case. In his neat, elderly hand, he wrote a little note to Detective-Inspector Parker, begging him to call at Staple Inn at his earliest convenience.

Mr Parker, however, was expecting nothing at that moment but inconvenience. He had been calling on solicitors for two whole days, and his soul sickened at the sight of a brass plate. He glanced at the long list in his hand, and distastefully counted up the scores of names that still remained unticked.

Parker was one of those methodical, painstaking people whom the world could so ill spare. When he worked with Wimsey on a case, it was an understood thing that anything lengthy, intricate, tedious and soul-destroying was done by Parker. He sometimes felt that it was irritating of Wimsey to take this so much for granted. He felt so now. It was a hot day. The pavements were dusty. Pieces of paper blew about the streets. Buses were grilling outside and stuffy inside. The Express Dairy, where Parker was eating a hurried lunch, seemed full of the odours of fried plaice and boiling tea-urns. Wimsey, he knew, was lunching at his club, before running down with Freddy Arbuthnot to see the New Zealanders at somewhere or other. He had seen him — a vision of exquisite pale grey, ambling gently along Pall

Mall. Damn Wimsey! Why couldn't he have let Miss Dawson rest quietly in her grave? There she was, doing no harm to anybody — and Wimsey must insist on prying into her affairs and bringing the inquiry to such a point that Parker simply had to take official notice of it. Oh well! he supposed he must go on with these infernal solicitors.

He was proceeding on a system of his own, which might or might not prove fruitful. He had reviewed the subject of the new Property Act, and decided that if and when Miss Whittaker had become aware of its possible effect on her own expectations, she would at once consider taking legal advice.

Her first thought would no doubt be to consult a solicitor in Leahampton, and unless she already had the idea of foul play in her mind, there was nothing to deter her from doing so. Accordingly, Parker's first move had been to run down to Leahampton and interview the three firms of solicitors there. All three were able to reply quite positively that they had never received such an inquiry from Miss Whittaker, or from anybody, during the year 1925. One solicitor, indeed — the senior partner of Hodgson & Hodgson, to whom Miss Dawson had entrusted her affairs after her quarrel with Mr Probyn — looked a little oddly at Parker when he heard the question.

'I assure you, Inspector,' he said, 'that if the point had been brought to my notice in such a way, I should certainly have remembered it, in the light of subsequent events.'

'The matter never crossed your mind, I suppose,' said Parker, 'when the question arose of winding up the estate and proving Miss Whittaker's claim to inherit?'

'I can't say it did. Had there been any question of searching for next-of-kin it might — I don't say it would — have occurred to me. But I had a very clear history of the family connections from Mr Probyn; the death took place nearly two months before the Act came into force, and the formalities all went through more or less automatically. In fact I never thought about the Act one way or another in that connection.'

Parker said he was surprised to hear it, and favoured Mr Hodgson with Mr Towkington's learned opinion on the subject, which interested Mr Hodgson very much. And that was all he got at Leahampton, except that he flattered Miss Climpson very much by calling upon her and hearing all about her interview with Vera Findlater. Miss Climpson walked to the station with him, in the hope that they might meet Miss Whittaker — 'I am sure you would be *interested* to *see* her' — but they were unlucky. On the whole, thought Parker, it might be just as well. After all, though he would like to see Miss Whittaker, he was not particularly keen on her seeing him, especially in Miss Climpson's company. 'By the way,' he said to Miss Climpson, 'you had better explain me in some way to Mrs Budge, or she may be a bit inquisitive.'

'But I *have*,' replied Miss Climpson, with an engaging giggle, 'when Mrs Budge said there was

224

a Mr Parker to see me, of course I realised at once that she mustn't know *who* you were, so I said, quite quickly, 'Mr Parker! Oh, that must be my nephew Adolphus.' You don't mind being Adolphus, do you? It's funny, but that was the *only* name that came into my mind at the moment. I can't *think* why, for I've never known an Adolphus.'

'Miss Climpson,' said Parker, solemnly, 'you are a marvellous woman, and I wouldn't mind even if you'd called me Marmaduke.'

So here he was, working out his second line of inquiry. If Miss Whittaker did not go to a Leahampton solicitor, to whom would she go? There was Mr Probyn, of course, but he did not think she would have selected him. She would not have known him at Crofton, of course — she had never actually lived with her great-aunts. She had met him the day he came down to Leahampton to see Miss Dawson. He had not then taken her into his confidence about the object of his visit, but she must have known from what her aunt said that it had to do with the making of a will. In the light of her new knowledge, she would guess that Mr Probyn had then had the Act in his mind, and had not thought fit to trust her with the facts. If she asked him now, he would probably reply that Miss Dawson's affairs were no longer in his hands, and refer her to Mr Hodgson. And besides, if she asked the question and anything were to happen — Mr Probyn might remember it. No, she would not have approached Mr Probyn.

What then?

To the person who has anything to conceal — to the person who wants to lose his identity as one leaf among the leaves of a forest — to the person who asks no more than to pass by and be forgotten, there is one name above others which promises a haven of safety and oblivion. London. Where no one knows his neighbour. Where shops do not know their customers. Where physicians are suddenly called to unknown patients whom they never see again. Where you may lie dead in your house for months together unmissed and unnoticed till the gas inspector comes to look at the meter. Where strangers are friendly and friends are casual. London, whose rather untidy and grubby bosom is the repository of so many odd secrets. Discreet, incurious and all-enfolding London.

Not that Parker put it that way to himself. He merely thought, 'Ten to one she'd try London. They mostly think they're safer there.'

Miss Whittaker knew London, of course. She had trained at the Royal Free. That meant she would know Bloomsbury better than any other district. For nobody knew better than Parker how rarely Londoners move out of their own particular little orbit. Unless, of course, she had at some time during her time at the hospital been recommended to a solicitor in another quarter, the chances were that she would have gone to a solicitor in the Bloomsbury or Holborn district.

Unfortunately for Parker, this is a quarter which swarms with solicitors. Gray's Inn Road,

226

Gray's Inn itself, Bedford Row, Holborn, Lincoln's Inn — the brass plates grow all about as thick as blackberries.

Which was why Parker was feeling so hot, tired and fed-up that June afternoon.

With an impatient grunt he pushed away his eggy plate, paid-at-the-desk-please, and crossed the road towards Bedford Row, which he had marked down as his portion for the afternoon.

He started at the first solicitor's he came to, which happened to be the office of one J. F. Trigg. He was lucky. The youth in the outer office informed him that Mr Trigg had just returned from lunch, was disengaged, and would see him. Would he walk in?

Mr Trigg was a pleasant, fresh-faced man in his early forties. He begged Mr Parker to be seated and asked what he could do for him.

For the thirty-seventh time, Parker started on the opening gambit which he had devised to suit his purpose.

'I am only temporarily in London, Mr Trigg, and finding I needed legal advice I was recommended to you by a man I met in a restaurant. He did give me his name, but it has escaped me, and anyway, it's of no great importance, is it? The point is this. My wife and I have come up to Town to see her great-aunt, who is in a very bad way. In fact, she isn't expected to live.

'Well, now, the old lady has always been very fond of my wife, don't you see, and it has always been an understood thing that Mrs Parker was to come into her money when she died. It's quite a tidy bit, and we have been — I won't say looking forward to it, but in a kind of mild way counting on it as something for us to retire upon later on. You understand. There aren't any other relations at all, so though the old lady has often talked about making a will, we didn't worry much, one way or the other, because we took it for granted my wife would come in for anything there was. But we were talking about it to a friend yesterday, and he took us rather aback by saying that there was a new law or something, and that if my wife's great-aunt hadn't made a will we shouldn't get anything at all. I think he said it would all go to the Crown. I didn't think that could be right and told him so, but my wife is a bit nervous — there are the children to be considered, you see — and she urged me to get legal advice, because her great-aunt may go off at any minute, and we don't know whether there is a will or not. Now, how does a great-niece stand under the new arrangements?'

'The point has not been made very clear,' said Mr Trigg, 'but my advice to you is, to find out whether a will has been made and if not, to get one made without delay if the testatrix is capable of making one. Otherwise I think there is a very real danger of your wife's losing her inheritance.'

'You seem quite familiar with the question,' said Parker, with a smile, 'I suppose you are always being asked it since this new Act came in?'

'I wouldn't say 'always'. It is comparatively rare for a great-niece to be left as sole next-of-kin.'

228

'Is it? Well, yes, I should think it must be. Do you remember being asked that question in the summer of 1925, Mr Trigg?'

A most curious expression came over the solicitor's face — it looked almost like alarm.

'What makes you ask that?'

'You need have no hesitation in answering,' said Parker, taking out his official card. 'I am a police officer and have a good reason for asking. I put the legal point to you first as a problem of my own, because I was anxious to have your professional opinion first.'

'I see. Well, Inspector, in that case, I suppose I am justified in telling you all about it. I *was* asked that question in June, 1925.'

'Do you remember the circumstances?'

'Clearly. I am not likely to forget them — or rather, the sequel to them.'

'That sounds interesting. Will you tell the story in your own way and with all the details you can remember?'

'Certainly. Just a moment.' Mr Trigg put his head out into the outer office. 'Badcock, I am engaged with Mr Parker and can't see anybody. Now, Mr Parker, I am at your service. Won't you smoke?'

Parker accepted the invitation and lit up his well-worn briar, while Mr Trigg, rapidly smoking cigarette after cigarette, unfolded his remarkable story.

18

The London Lawyer's Story

'I who am given to novel-reading, how often have I gone out with the doctor when the stranger has summoned him to visit the unknown patient in the lonely house . . . This Strange Adventure may lead, in a later chapter, to the revealing of a mysterious crime.'

The Londoner

'I think,' said Mr Trigg, 'that it was on the 15th, or 16th June, 1925, that a lady called to ask almost exactly the same question that you have done — only that she represented herself as inquiring on behalf of a friend whose name she did not mention. Yes — I think I can describe her pretty well. She was tall and handsome, with a very clear skin, dark hair and blue eyes — an attractive girl. I remember that she had very fine brows, rather straight, and not much colour in her face, and she was dressed in something summery but very neat. I should think it would be called an embroidered linen dress — I am not an expert on those things — and a shady white hat of panama straw.'

'Your recollection seems very clear,' said Parker.

'It is; I have rather a good memory; besides, I saw her on other occasions, as you shall hear.

'At this first visit she told me — much as you did — that she was only temporarily in Town, and had been casually recommended to me. I told her that I should not like to answer her question offhand. The Act, you may remember, had only recently passed its Final Reading, and I was by no means up in it. Beside, from just skimming through it, I had convinced myself that various important questions were bound to crop up.

'I told the lady — Miss Grant was the name she gave, by the way — that I should like to take counsel's opinion before giving her any advice, and asked if she could call again the following day. She said she could, rose and thanked me, offering me her hand. In taking it, I happened to notice rather an odd scar, running across the backs of all the fingers — rather as though a chisel or something had slipped at some time. I noticed it quite idly, of course, but it was lucky for me I did.

'Miss Grant duly turned up the next day. I had looked up a very learned friend in the interval, and gave her the same opinion that I gave you just now. She looked rather concerned about it — in fact, almost more annoyed than concerned.

'"It seems rather unfair,' she said, 'that people's family money should go away to the Crown like that. After all, a great-niece is quite a near relation, really.'

'I replied that, provided the great-niece could call witnesses to prove that the deceased had always had the intention of leaving her the money, the Crown would, in all probability, allot the estate, or a suitable proportion of it, in accordance with the wishes of the deceased. It would, however, lie entirely within the discretion of the court to do so or not, and, of course, if there had been any quarrel or dispute about the matter at any time, the judge might take an unfavourable view of the great-niece's application.

'"In any case,' I added, 'I don't *know* that the great-niece is excluded under the Act — I only understand that she *may* be. In any case, there are still six months before the Act comes into force, and many things may happen before then.'

'"You mean that Auntie may die,' she said, 'but she's not really dangerously ill — only mental, as Nurse calls it.'

'Anyhow, she went away then after paying my fee, and I noticed that the 'friend's great-aunt' had suddenly become 'Auntie', and decided that my client felt a certain personal interest in the matter.'

'I fancy she had,' said Parker. 'When did you see her again?'

'Oddly enough, I ran across her in the following December. I was having a quick and early dinner in Soho, before going on to a show. The little place I usually patronise was very full, and I had to sit at a table where a woman was already seated. As I muttered the usual formula about 'Was anybody sitting there', she looked up, and I promptly recognised my client.

'"Why, how do you do, Miss Grant?' I said.

'"I beg your pardon,' she replied rather stiffly. 'I think you are mistaken.'

' 'I beg your pardon,' said I stiffer still, 'my name is Trigg, and you came to consult me in Bedford Row last June. But if I am intruding, I apologise and withdraw.'

'She smiled then, and said, 'I'm sorry, I did not recognise you for the moment.'

'I obtained permission to sit at her table.

'By way of starting a conversation, I asked whether she had taken any further advice in the matter of the inheritance. She said no, she had been quite content with what I had told her. Still to make conversation, I inquired whether the great-aunt had made a will after all. She replied, rather briefly, that it had not been necessary; the old lady had died. I noticed that she was dressed in black, and was confirmed in my opinion that she herself was the great-niece concerned.

'We talked for some time, Inspector, and I will not conceal from you that I found Miss Grant a very interesting personality. She had an almost masculine understanding. I may say I am not the sort of man who prefers women to be brainless. No, I am rather modern in that respect. If ever I was to take a wife, Inspector, I should wish her to be an intelligent companion.'

Parker said Mr Trigg's attitude did him great credit. He also made the mental observation that Mr Trigg would probably not object to marrying a young woman who had inherited money and was unencumbered with relations.

'It is rare,' went on Mr Trigg, 'to find a woman with a legal mind. Miss Grant was unusual in that respect. She took a great interest in some case or other that was prominent in the newspapers at the time — I forget now what it was — and asked me some remarkably sensible and intelligent questions. I must say that I quite enjoyed our conversation. Before dinner was over, we had got on to more personal topics, in the course of which I happened to mention that I lived in Golders Green.'

'Did she give you her own address?'

'She said she was staying at the Peveril Hotel in Bloomsbury, and that she was looking for a house in Town. I said that I might possibly hear of something out Hampstead way, and offered my professional services in case she should require them. After dinner I accompanied her back to her hotel, and bade her good-bye in the lounge.'

'She was really staying there, then?'

'Apparently. However, about a fortnight later, I happened to hear of a house in Golders Green that had fallen vacant suddenly. It belonged, as a matter of fact, to a client of mine. In pursuance of my promise, I wrote to Miss Grant at the Peveril. Receiving no reply, I made inquiries there, and found that she had left the hotel the day after our meeting, leaving no address. In the hotel register, she had merely given her address as Manchester. I was somewhat disappointed, but thought no more about the matter.

'About a month later — on January 26th, to be exact, I was sitting at home reading a book, preparatory to retiring to bed. I should say that I occupy a flat, or rather maisonette, in a small house which has been divided to make two establishments. The people on the ground floor

234

were away at that time, so that I was quite alone in the house. My housekeeper only comes in by the day. The telephone rang — I noticed the time. It was a quarter to eleven. I answered it, and a woman's voice spoke, begging me to come instantly to a certain house on Hampstead Heath, to make a will for someone who was at the point of death.'

'Did you recognise the voice?'

'No. It sounded like a servant's voice. At any rate, it had a strong cockney accent. I asked whether tomorrow would not be time enough, but the voice urged me to hurry or it might be too late. Rather annoyed, I put my things on and went out. It was a most unpleasant night, cold and foggy. I was lucky enough to find a taxi on the nearest rank. We drove to the address, which we had great difficulty in finding, as everything was pitch-black. It turned out to be a small house in a very isolated position on the Heath — in fact, there was no proper approach to it. I left the taxi on the road, about a couple of hundred yards off, and asked the man to wait for me, as I was very doubtful of ever finding another taxi in that spot at that time of night. He grumbled a good deal, but consented to wait if I promised not to be very long.

'I made my way to the house. At first I thought it was quite dark, but presently I saw a faint glimmer in a ground-floor room. I rang the bell. No answer, though I could hear it trilling loudly. I rang again and knocked. Still no answer. It was bitterly cold. I struck a match to be sure I had come to the right house, and then I noticed that the front door was ajar.

'I thought that perhaps the servant who had called me was so much occupied with her sick mistress as to be unable to leave her to come to the door. Thinking that in that case I might be of assistance to her, I pushed the door open and went in. The hall was perfectly dark, and I bumped against an umbrella-stand in entering. I thought I heard a faint voice calling or moaning, and when my eyes had become accustomed to the darkness, I stumbled forward, and saw a dim light coming from a door on the left.'

'Was that the room which you had seen to be illuminated from outside?'

'I think so. I called out, 'May I come in?' and a very low, weak voice replied, 'Yes, please.' I pushed the door open and entered a room furnished as a sitting-room. In one corner there was a couch, on which some bedclothes appeared to have been hurriedly thrown to enable it to be used as a bed. On the couch lay a woman, all alone.

'I could only dimly make her out. There was no light in the room except a small oil-lamp, with a green shade so tilted as to keep the light from the sick woman's eyes. There was a fire in the grate, but it had burnt low. I could see, however, that the woman's head and face were swathed in white bandages. I put out my hand and felt for the electric switch, but she called out:

''No light, please — it hurts me.''

'How did she see you put your hand to the switch?'

'Well,' said Mr Trigg, 'that was an odd thing. She didn't speak, as a matter of fact, till I had actually clicked the switch down. But nothing happened. The light didn't come on.'

'Really?'

'No. I supposed that the bulb had been taken away or had gone phut. However, I said nothing, and came up to the bed. She said in a sort of half-whisper, 'Is that the lawyer?'

'I said, 'Yes,' and asked what I could do for her.

'She said, 'I have had a terrible accident. I can't live. I want to make my will quickly.' I asked whether there was nobody with her. 'Yes, yes,' she said in a hurried way, 'my servant will be back in a moment. She has gone to look for a doctor.' 'But,' I said, 'couldn't she have rung up? You are not fit to be left alone.' 'We couldn't get through to one,' she replied, 'it's all right. She will be here soon. Don't waste time. I must make my will.' She spoke in a dreadful, gasping way, and I felt the best thing would be to do what she wanted, for fear of agitating her. I drew a chair to the table where the lamp was, got out my fountain pen and a printed will-form which I had provided myself, and expressed myself ready to receive her instructions.

'Before beginning, she asked me to give her a little brandy and water from a decanter which stood on the table. I did so, and she took a small sip, which seemed to revive her. I placed the glass near her hand, and at her suggestion mixed another glass for myself. I was very glad of it, for as I said, it was a beast of a night, and the room was cold. I looked round for some extra coals to put on the fire, but could see none.'

'That,' said Parker, 'is extremely interesting and suggestive.'

'I thought it queer at the time. But the whole thing was queer. Anyway, I then said I was ready to begin. She said, 'You may think I am a little mad, because my head has been so hurt. But I am quite sane. But he shan't have a penny of the money.' I asked her if someone had attacked her. She replied, 'My husband. He thinks he has killed me. But I am going to live long enough to will the money away.' She then said that her name was Mrs Marion Mead, and proceeded to make a will, leaving her estate, which amounted to about £10,000, among various legatees, including a daughter and three or four sisters. It was rather a complicated will, as it included various devices for tying up the daughter's money in a trust, so as to prevent her from ever handing over any of it to her father.'

'Did you make a note of the names and addresses of the people involved?'

'I did, but, as you will see later on, I could make no use of them. The testatrix was certainly clear-headed enough about the provisions of the will, though she seemed terribly weak, and her voice never rose above a whisper after that one time when she had called to me not to turn on the light.

'At length I finished my notes of the will, and started to draft it out on to the proper form. There were no signs of the servant's return, and I began to be really anxious. Also the extreme

238

cold — or something else — added to the fact that it was now long past my bed-time, was making me apallingly sleepy. I poured out another stiff little dose of the brandy to warm me up, and went on writing out the will.

'When I had finished I said:

' 'How about signing this? We need another witness to make it legal.'

'She said, 'My servant must be here in a minute or two. I can't think what has happened to her.'

' 'I expect she has missed her way in the fog,' I said. 'However, I will wait a little longer. I can't go and leave you like this.'

'She thanked me feebly, and we sat for some time in silence. As time went on, I began to feel the situation to be increasingly uncanny. The sick woman breathed heavily, and moaned from time to time. The desire for sleep overpowered me more and more. I could not understand it.

'Presently it occurred to me, stupefied though I felt, that the most sensible thing would be to get the taxi-man — if he was still there — to come in and witness the will with me, and then to go myself to find a doctor. I sat, sleepily revolving this in my mind, and trying to summon energy to speak. I felt as though a great weight of inertia was pressing down upon me. Exertion of any kind seemed almost beyond my powers.

'Suddenly something happened which brought me back to myself. Mrs Mead turned a little over upon the couch and peered at me intently, as it seemed, in the lamplight. To support herself, she put both her hands on the edge of the table. I

239

noticed, with a vague sense of something unexpected, that the left hand bore no wedding ring. And then I noticed something else.

'Across the back of the fingers of the right hand went a curious scar — as though a chisel or some such thing had slipped and cut them.'

Parker sat upright in his chair.

'Yes,' said Mr Trigg, 'that interests you. It startled me. Or rather, startled isn't quite the word. In my oppressed state, it affected me like some kind of nightmare. I struggled upright in my chair, and the woman sank back upon her pillows.

'At that moment there came a violent ring at the bell.'

'The servant?'

'No — thank Heaven it was my taxi-driver, who had become tired of waiting. I thought — I don't quite know what I thought — but I was alarmed. I gave some kind of shout or groan, and the man came straight in. Happily, I had left the door open as I had found it.

'I pulled myself together sufficiently to ask him to witness the will. I must have looked queer and spoken in a strange way, for I remember how he looked from me to the brandy bottle. However, he signed the paper after Mrs Mead, who wrote her name in a weak, straggling hand as she lay on her back.

' "Wot next, guv'nor?" asked the man, when this was done.

'I was feeling dreadfully ill by now. I could only say, 'Take me home.'

'He looked at Mrs Mead and then at me, and

said, 'Ain't there nobody to see to the lady, sir?'

'I said, 'Fetch a doctor. But take me home first.'

'I stumbled out of the house on his arm. I heard him muttering something about its being a rum start. I don't remember the drive home. When I came back to life, I was in my own bed, and one of the local doctors standing over me.

'I'm afraid this story is getting very long and tedious. To cut matters short, it seems the taxi-driver, who was a very decent, intelligent fellow, had found me completely insensible at the end of the drive. He didn't know who I was, but he hunted in my pocket and found my visiting-card and my latch-key. He took me home, got me upstairs and, deciding that if I was drunk, I was a worse drunk than he had ever encountered in his experience, humanely went round and fetched a doctor.

'The doctor's opinion was that I had been heavily drugged with veronal or something of that kind. Fortunately, if the idea was to murder me, the dose had been very much underestimated. We went into the matter thoroughly, and the upshot was that I must have taken about 30 grains of the stuff. It appears that it is a difficult drug to trace by analysis, but that was the conclusion the doctor came to, looking at the matter all round. Undoubtedly the brandy had been doped.

'Of course, we went round to look at the house next day. It was all shut up, and the local milkman informed us that the occupiers had been away for a week and were not expected

241

home for another ten days. We got into communication with them, but they appeared to be perfectly genuine, ordinary people, and they declared they knew nothing whatever about it. They were accustomed to go away every so often, just shutting the house and not bothering about a caretaker or anything. The man came along at once, naturally, to investigate matters, but couldn't find anything had been stolen or disturbed, except that a pair of sheets and some pillows showed signs of use, and a scuttle of coal had been used in the sitting-room. The coal cellar, which also contained the electric meter, had been left locked and the meter turned off before the family left — they apparently had a few grains of sense — which accounts for the chill darkness of the house when I entered it. The visitor had apparently slipped back the catch of the pantry window — one of the usual gimcrack affairs — with a knife or something, and had brought her own lamp, siphon and brandy. Daring, but not really difficult.

'No Mrs Mead or Grant was to be heard of anywhere, as I needn't tell you. The tenants of the house were not keen to start expensive inquiries — after all, they'd lost nothing but a shilling's worth of coals — and on consideration, and seeing that I hadn't actually been murdered or anything, I thought it best to let the matter slide. It was a most unpleasant adventure.'

'I'm sure it was. Did you ever hear from Miss Grant again?'

'Why, yes. She rang me up twice — once, after three months, and again only a fortnight ago, asking for an appointment. You may think me cowardly, Mr Parker, but each time I put her off. I didn't quite know what might happen. As a matter of fact, the opinion I formed in my own mind was that I had been entrapped into that house with the idea of making me spend the night there and afterwards blackmailing me. That was the only explanation I could think of which would account for the sleeping-draught. I thought discretion was the better part of valour, and gave my clerks and my housekeeper instructions that if Miss Grant should call at any time I was out and not expected back.'

'H'm. Do you suppose she knew you had recognised the scar on her hand?'

'I'm sure she didn't. Otherwise she would hardly have made advances to me in her own name again.'

'No. I think you are right. Well, Mr Trigg, I am much obliged to you for this information, which may turn out to be very valuable. And if Miss Grant should ring you up again — where did she call from, by the way?'

'From call-boxes, each time. I know that, because the operator always tells one when the call is from a public box. I didn't have the calls traced.'

'No, of course not. Well, if she does it again, will you please make an appointment with her, and then let me know about it at once? A call to Scotland Yard will always find me.'

Mr Trigg promised that he would do this, and Parker took his leave.

'And now we know,' thought Parker as he

returned home, 'that somebody — an odd unscrupulous somebody — was making inquiries about great-nieces in 1925. A word to Miss Climpson, I fancy, is indicated — just to find out whether Mary Whittaker has a scar on her right hand, or whether I've got to hunt up any more solicitors.'

The hot streets seemed less oppressively oven-like than before. In fact, Parker was so cheered by his interview that he actually bestowed a cigarette-card upon the next urchin who accosted him.

Part Three

THE MEDICO-LEGAL PROBLEM

'There's not a crime
But takes its proper change out still in crime
If once rung on the counter of the world.'
E. B. BROWNING: *Aurora Leigh*

19

Gone Away

'There is nothing good or evil save in the will.'
EPICTETUS

'You will not, I imagine, deny,' observed Lord Peter, 'that very odd things seem to happen to the people who are in a position to give information about the last days of Agatha Dawson. Bertha Gotobed dies suddenly, under suspicious circumstances; her sister thinks she sees Miss Whittaker lying in wait for her at Liverpool docks; Mr Trigg is inveigled into a house of mystery and is semi-poisoned. I wonder what would have happened to Mr Probyn, if he had been careless enough to remain in England.'

'I deny nothing,' replied Parker. 'I will only point out to you that during the month in which these disasters occurred to the Gotobed family, the object of your suspicions was in Kent with Miss Vera Findlater, who never left her side.'

'As against that undoubted snag,' rejoined Wimsey, 'I bring forward a letter from Miss Climpson in which — amid a lot of rigmarole with which I will not trouble you — she informs me that upon Miss Whittaker's right hand there is a scar, precisely similar to the one which Mr Trigg describes.'

'Is there? That does seem to connect Miss

247

Whittaker pretty definitely with the Trigg business. But is it your theory that she is trying to polish off all the people who know anything about Miss Dawson? Rather a big job, don't you think, for a single-handed female? And if so, why is Dr Carr spared? and Nurse Philliter? and Nurse Forbes? And the other doctor chappie? And the rest of the population of Leahampton, if it comes to that?'

'That's an interesting point which had already occurred to me. I think I know why. Up to the present, the Dawson case has presented two different problems, one legal and one medical — the motive and the means, if you like that better. As far as opportunity goes, only two people figure as possibles — Miss Whittaker and Nurse Forbes. The Forbes woman had nothing to gain by killin' a good patient, so for the moment we can wash her out.

'Well now, as to the medical problem — the means. I must say that up to now that appears completely insoluble. I am baffled, Watson (said he, his hawk-like eyes gleaming angrily from under the half-closed lids). Even I am baffled. But not for long! (he cried, with a magnificent burst of self-confidence). My Honour (capital H) is concerned to track this Human Fiend (capitals) to its hidden source, and nail the whited sepulchre to the mast even though it crush me in the attempt! Loud applause. His chin sank broodingly upon his dressing-gown, and he breathed a few guttural notes into the bass saxophone which was the cherished companion of his solitary hours in the bathroom.'

Parker ostentatiously took up the book which he had laid aside on Wimsey's entrance.

'Tell me when you've finished,' he said, caustically.

'I've hardly begun. The means, I repeat, seems insoluble — and so the criminal evidently thinks. There has been no exaggerated mortality among the doctors and nurses. On that side of the business the lady feels herself safe. No. The motive is the weak point — hence the hurry to stop the mouths of the people who knew about the legal part of the problem.'

'Yes, I see. Mrs Cropper has started back to Canada, by the way. She doesn't seem to have been molested at all.'

'No — and that's why I still think there was somebody on the watch in Liverpool. Mrs Cropper was only worth silencing so long as she had told nobody her story. That is why I was careful to meet her and accompany her ostentatiously to Town.'

'Oh, rot, Peter! Even if Miss Whittaker had been there — which we know she couldn't have been — how was she to know that you were going to ask about the Dawson business? She doesn't know you from Adam.'

'She might have found out who Murbles was. The advertisement which started the whole business was in his name, you know.'

'In that case, why hasn't she attacked Murbles or you?'

'Murbles is a wise old bird. In vain are nets spread in his sight. He is seeing no female clients, answering no invitations, and never goes out without an escort.'

'I didn't know he took it so seriously.'

'Oh, yes. Murbles is old enough to have learnt the value of his own skin. As for me — have you noticed the remarkable similarity in some ways between Mr Trigg's adventure and my own little adventurelet, as you might say, in South Audley Street?'

'What, with Mrs Forrest?'

'Yes. The secret appointment. The drink. The endeavour to get one to stay the night at all costs. I'm positive there was something in that sugar, Charles, that no sugar should contain — see Public Health (Adulteration of Food) Acts, various.'

'You think Mrs Forrest is an accomplice?'

'I do. I don't know what she has to gain by it — probably money. But I feel sure there is some connection. Partly because of Bertha Gotobed's £5 note; partly because Mrs Forrest's story was a palpable fake — I'm certain the woman's never had a lover, let alone a husband — you can't mistake real inexperience; and chiefly because of the similarity of method. Criminals always tend to repeat their effects. Look at George Joseph Smith and his brides. Look at Neill Cream. Look at Armstrong and his tea-parties.'

'Well, if there's an accomplice, all the better. Accomplices generally end by giving the show away.'

'True. And we are in a good position because up till now I don't think they know that we suspect any connection between them.'

'But I still think, you know, we ought to get

some evidence that actual crimes have been committed. Call me finicking, if you like. If you *could* suggest a means of doing away with these people so as to leave no trace, I should feel happier about it.'

'The means, eh? — Well, we do know something about it.'

'As what?'

'Well — take the two victims — '

'Alleged.'

'All right, old particular. The two alleged victims and the two (alleged) intended victims. Miss Dawson was ill and helpless; Bertha Gotobed possibly stupefied by a heavy meal and an unaccustomed quantity of wine; Trigg was given a sufficient dose of veronal to send him to sleep, and I was offered something of probably the same kind — I wish I could have kept the remains of that coffee. So we deduce from that, what?'

'I suppose that it was a means of death which could only be used on somebody more or less helpless or unconscious.'

'Exactly. As for instance, a hypodermic injection — only nothing appears to have been injected. Or a delicate operation of some kind — if we could only think of one to fit the case. Or the inhalation of something — such as chloroform — only we could find no traces of suffocation.'

'Yes. That doesn't get us very far, though.'

'It's something. Then, again, it may very well be something that a trained nurse would have learnt or heard about. Miss Whittaker was trained, you know — which, by the way, was what made it so easy for her to bandage up her own head and provide a pitiful and unrecognisable spectacle for the stupid Mr Trigg.'

'It wouldn't have to be anything very out of the way — nothing, I mean, that only a trained surgeon could do, or that required very specialised knowledge.'

'Oh, no. Probably something picked up in conversation with a doctor or the other nurses. I say, how about getting hold of Dr Carr again? Or, no — if he'd got any ideas on the subject he'd have trotted 'em out before now. I know! I'll ask Lubbock, the analyst. He'll do. I'll get in touch with him tomorrow.'

'And meanwhile,' said Parker, 'I suppose we just sit round and wait for somebody else to be murdered.'

'It's beastly, isn't it? I still feel poor Bertha Gotobed's blood on my head, so to speak. I say!'

'Yes?'

'We've practically got clear proof on the Trigg business. Couldn't you put the lady in quod on a charge of burglary while we think out the rest of the dope? It's often done. It *was* a burglary, you know. She broke into a house after dark and appropriated a scuttleful of coal to her own use. Trigg could identify her — he seems to have paid the lady particular attention on more than one occasion — and we could rake up his taxi-man for corroborative detail.'

Parker pulled at his pipe for a few minutes.

'There's something in that,' he said finally. 'I think perhaps it's worth while putting it before the authorities. But we mustn't be in too much of a hurry, you know. I wish we were farther ahead with our other proofs. There's such a thing as Habeas Corpus — you can't hold on to people indefinitely just on a charge of stealing coal — '

'There's the breaking and entering, don't forget that. It's burglary, after all. You can get penal servitude for life for burglary.'

'But it all depends on the view the law takes of the coal. It might decide that there was no original intention of stealing coal, and treat the thing as a mere misdemeanour or civil trespass. Anyhow, we don't really *want* a conviction for stealing coal. But I'll see what they think about it at our place, and meanwhile I'll get hold of Trigg again and try to find the taxi-driver. And Trigg's doctor. We might get it as an attempt to murder Trigg, or at least to inflict grievous bodily harm. But I should like some more evidence about — '

'Cuckoo! So should I. But I can't manufacture evidence out of nothing. Dash it all, be reasonable. I've built you up a case out of nothing. Isn't that handsome enough? Base ingratitude — that's what's the matter with you.'

★ ★ ★

Parker's inquiries took some time, and June lingered into its longest days.

Chamberlin and Levine flew the Atlantic, and Segrave bade farewell to Brooklands. The *Daily Yell* wrote anti-Red leaders and discovered a plot, somebody laid claim to a marquisate, and a

Czecho-Slovakian pretended to swim the Channel. Hammond out-graced Grace, there was an outburst of murder at Moscow, Foxlaw won the Gold Cup and the earth opened at Oxhey and swallowed up somebody's front garden. Oxford decided that women were dangerous, and the electric hare consented to run at the White City. England's supremacy was challenged at Wimbledon, and the House of Lords made the gesture of stooping to conquer.

Meanwhile, Lord Peter's projected *magnum opus* on a-hundred-and-one ways of causing sudden death had advanced by the accumulation of a mass of notes which flowed all over the library at the flat, and threatened to engulf Bunter, whose task it was to file and cross-reference and generally to produce order from chaos. Oriental scholars and explorers were buttonholed in clubs and strenuously pumped on the subject of abstruse native poisons; horrid experiments performed in German laboratories were communicated in unreadable documents; and the life of Sir James Lubbock, who had the misfortune to be a particular friend of Lord Peter's, was made a burden to him with daily inquiries as to the post-mortem detection of such varying substances as chloroform, curare, hydrocyanic acid gas and diethylsulphon-methylethymethane.

'But surely there must be something which kills without leaving a trace,' pleaded Lord Peter, when at length informed that the persecution must cease. 'A thing in such universal demand — surely it is not beyond the wit of scientists to invent it. It must exist. Why isn't it properly advertised? There ought to be a company to exploit it. It's simply ridiculous. Why, it's a thing one might be wantin' one's self any day.'

'You don't understand,' said Sir James Lubbock. 'Plenty of poisons leave no particular post-mortem appearances. And plenty of them — especially the vegetable ones — are difficult to find by analysis, unless you know what you are looking for. For instance, if you're testing for arsenic, that test won't tell you whether strychnine is present or not. And if you're testing for strychnine, you won't find morphia. You've got to try one test after another till you hit the right one. And of course there are certain poisons for which no recognised tests exist.'

'I know all that,' said Wimsey. 'I've tested things myself. But these poisons with no recognised test — how do you set about proving that they're there?'

'Well, of course, you'd take the symptoms into account, and so on. You would look at the history of the case.'

'Yes — but I want a poison that doesn't produce any symptoms. Except death, of course — if you call that a symptom. Isn't there a poison with no symptoms and no test? Something that just makes you go off, Pouf! like that?'

'Certainly not,' said the analyst rather annoyed — for your medical analyst lives by symptoms and tests, and nobody likes suggestions that undermine the very foundations of his profession — 'not even old age or mental decay. There are always symptoms.'

Fortunately, before the symptoms of mental

255

decay could become too pronounced in Lord Peter, Parker sounded the call to action.

'I'm going down to Leahampton with a warrant,' he said. 'I may not use it, but the chief thinks it might be worth while to make an inquiry. What with the Battersea mystery and the Daniels business, and Bertha Gotobed, there seems to be a feeling that there have been too many unexplained tragedies this year, and the Press have begun yelping again, blast them! There's an article in *John Citizen* this week, with a poster: 'Ninety-six Murderers at Large', and the *Evening Views* is starting its reports with 'Six weeks have now passed, and the police are no nearer the solution — ' you know the kind of thing. We'll simply have to get some sort of move on. Do you want to come?'

'Certainly — a breath of country air would do me good, I fancy. Blow away the cobwebs, don't you know. It might even inspire me to invent a good way of murderin' people. 'O Inspiration, solitary child, warbling thy native woodnotes wild — ' Did somebody write that, or did I invent it? It sounds reminiscent, somehow.'

Parker, who was out of temper, replied rather shortly, and intimated that the police car would be starting for Leahampton in an hour's time.

'I will be there,' said Wimsey, 'though, mind you, I hate being driven by another fellow. It feels so unsafe. Never mind. I will be bloody, bold and resolute, as Queen Victoria said to the Archbishop of Canterbury.'

★ ★ ★

They reached Leahampton without any incident to justify Lord Peter's fears. Parker had brought another officer with him, and on the way they picked up the Chief Constable of the County, who appeared very dubiously disposed towards their errand. Lord Peter, observing their array of five strong men, going out to seize upon one young woman, was reminded of the Marquise de Brinvilliers — ('What! all that water for a little person like me?') — but this led him back to the subject of poison, and he remained steeped in thought and gloom until the car drew up before the house in Wellington Avenue.

Parker got out, and went up the path with the Chief Constable. The door was opened to them by a frightened-looking maid, who gave a little shriek at the sight of them.

'Oh, sir! have you come to say something's happened to Miss Whittaker?'

'Isn't Miss Whittaker at home, then?'

'No, sir. She went out in the car with Miss Vera Findlater on Monday — that's four days back, sir, and she hasn't come back home, nor Miss Findlater neither, and I'm frightened something's happened to them. When I see you, sir, I thought you was the police come to say there had been an accident. I didn't know what to do, sir.'

'Skipped, by God!' was Parker's instant thought, but he controlled his annoyance, and asked:

'Do you know where they were going?'

'Crow's Beach, Miss Whittaker said, sir.'

'That's a good fifty miles,' said the Chief

Constable. 'Probably they've just decided to stay there a day or two.'

'More likely gone in the opposite direction,' thought Parker.

'They didn't take no things for the night, sir. They went off about ten in the morning. They said they was going to have lunch there and come home in the evening. And Miss Whittaker hasn't written nor nothing. And her always so particular. Cook and me, we didn't know what — '

'Oh, well, I expect it's all right,' said the Chief Constable. 'It's a pity, as we particularly wanted to see Miss Whittaker. When you hear from her, you might say Sir Charles Pillington called with a friend.'

'Yes, sir. But please, sir, what ought we to do, sir?'

'Nothing. Don't worry. I'll have inquiries made. I'm the Chief Constable, you know, and I can soon find out whether there's been an accident or anything. But if there had been, depend upon it we should have heard about it. Come, my girl, pull yourself together, there's nothing to cry about. We'll let you know as soon as we hear anything.'

But Sir Charles looked disturbed. Coming on top of Parker's arrival in the district, the thing had an unpleasant look about it.

Lord Peter received the news cheerfully.

'Good,' said he, 'joggle 'em up. Keep 'em moving. That's the spirit. Always like it when somethin' happens. My worst suspicions are goin' to be justified. That always makes one feel

258

so important and virtuous, don't you think? Wonder why she took the girl with her, though. By the way, we'd better look up the Findlaters. They may have heard something.'

This obvious suggestion was acted upon at once. But at the Findlaters' house they drew a blank. The family were at the seaside, with the exception of Miss Vera, who was staying in Wellington Avenue with Miss Whittaker. No anxiety was expressed by the parlour-maid and none, apparently, felt. The investigators took care not to arouse any alarm, and, leaving a trivial and polite message from Sir Charles, withdrew for a consultation.

'There's nothing for it, so far as I can see,' said Parker, 'but an all-stations call to look out for the car and the ladies. And we must put inquiries through to all the ports, of course. With four days' start, they may be anywhere by now. I wish to Heaven I'd risked a bit and started earlier, approval or no approval. What's this Findlater girl like? I'd better go back to the house and get photographs of her and the Whittaker woman. And, Wimsey, I wish you'd look in on Miss Climpson and see if she has any information.'

'And you might tell 'em at the Yard to keep an eye on Mrs Forrest's place,' said Wimsey. 'When anything sensational happens to a criminal it's a good tip to watch the accomplice.'

'I feel sure you are both quite mistaken about this,' urged Sir Charles Pillington. 'Criminal — accomplice — bless me! I have had considerable experience in the course of a long life — longer than either of yours — and I really feel convinced that Miss Whittaker, whom I know quite well, is as good and nice a girl as you could wish to find. But there has undoubtedly been an accident of some kind, and it is our duty to make the fullest investigation. I will get on to Crow's Beach police immediately, as soon as I know the description of the car.'

'It's an Austin Seven and the number is XX9917,' said Wimsey, much to the Chief Constable's surprise. 'But I doubt very much whether you'll find it at Crow's Beach, or anywhere near it.'

'Well, we'd better get a move on,' snapped Parker. 'We'd better separate. How about a spot of lunch in an hour's time at the George?'

Wimsey was unlucky. Miss Climpson was not to be found. She had had her lunch early and gone out, saying she felt that a long country walk would do her good. Mrs Budge was rather afraid she had had some bad news — she had seemed so upset and worried since yesterday evening.

'But indeed, sir,' she added, 'if you was quick, you might find her up at the church. She often drops in there to say her prayers like. Not a respectful way to approach a place of worship to my mind, do you think so yourself, sir? Popping in and out on a week-day, the same as if it was a friend's house. And coming home from Communion as cheerful as anything and ready to laugh and make jokes. I don't see as how we was meant to make an ordinary thing of religion that way — so disrespectful and nothing uplifting to the 'art about it. But there! we all 'as our failings, and Miss Climpson is a nice lady and that I must say, even if she is a Roaming Catholic or next-door to one.'

Lord Peter thought that Roaming Catholic was rather an appropriate name for the more ultramontane section of the High Church party. At the moment, however, he felt he could not afford time for religious discussion, and set off for the church in quest of Miss Climpson.

The doors of S Onesimus were hospitably open, and the red Sanctuary lamp made a little spot of welcoming brightness in the rather dark building. Coming in from the June sunshine, Wimsey blinked a little before he could distinguish anything else. Presently he was able to make out a dark, bowed figure kneeling before the lamp. For a moment he hoped it was Miss Climpson, but presently saw to his disappointment that it was merely a Sister in a black habit, presumably taking her turn to watch before the Host. The only other occupant of the church was a priest in a cassock, who was busy with the ornaments on the High Altar. It was the Feast of S John, Wimsey remembered suddenly. He walked up the aisle, hoping to find his quarry hidden in some obscure corner. His shoes squeaked. This annoyed him. It was a thing which Bunter never permitted. He was seized with a fancy that the squeak was produced by diabolic possession — a protest against a religious atmosphere on the part of his own particular besetting devil. Pleased with this thought, he moved forward more confidently.

The priest's attention was attracted by the squeak. He turned and came down towards the intruder. No doubt, thought Wimsey, to offer his professional services to exorcise the evil spirit.

'Were you looking for anybody?' inquired the priest, courteously.

'Well, I was looking for a lady,' began Wimsey. Then it struck him that this sounded a little odd under the circumstances, and he hastened to explain more fully, in the stifled tones considered appropriate to consecrated surroundings.

'Oh, yes,' said the priest, quite unperturbed, 'Miss Climpson was here a little time ago, but I fancy she has gone. Not that I usually keep tabs on my flock,' he added, with a laugh, 'but she spoke to me before she went. Was it urgent? What a pity you should have missed her. Can I give any kind of message or help you in any way?'

'No, thanks,' said Wimsey. 'Sorry to bother you. Unseemly to come and try to haul people out of church, but — yes, it was rather important. I'll leave a message at the house. Thanks frightfully.'

He turned away; then stopped and came back.

'I say,' he said, 'you give advice on moral problems and all that sort of thing, don't you?'

'Well, we're supposed to try,' said the priest. 'Is anything bothering you in particular?'

'Ye-es,' said Wimsey, 'nothing religious, I don't mean — nothing about infallibility or the Virgin Mary or anything of that sort. Just something I'm not comfortable about.'

The priest — who was, in fact, the vicar, Mr Tredgold — indicated that he was quite at Lord Peter's service.

'It's very good of you. Could we come somewhere where I didn't have to whisper so much. I never can explain things in a whisper. Sort of paralyzes one, don't you know.'

'Let's go outside,' said Mr Tredgold.

So they went out and sat on a flat tombstone.

'It's like this,' said Wimsey. 'Hypothetical case, you see, and so on. S'posin' one knows somebody who's very, very ill and can't last long anyhow. And they're in awful pain and all that, and kept under morphia — pratically dead to the world, you know. And suppose that by dyin' straight away they could make something happen which they really wanted to happen and which couldn't happen if they lived on a little longer. (I can't explain exactly how, because I don't want to give personal details and so on) — you get the idea? Well, supposin' somebody who knew all that was just to give 'em a little push off so to speak — hurry matters on — why should that be a very dreadful crime?'

'The law — ' began Mr Tredgold.

'Oh, the law says it's a crime, fast enough,' said Wimsey.

'But do you honestly think it's very bad? I know you'd call it a sin, of course, but why is it so very dreadful? It doesn't do the person any harm, does it?'

'We can't answer that,' said Mr Tredgold, 'without knowing the ways of God with the soul. In those last weeks or hours of pain and unconsciousness, the soul may be undergoing some necessary part of its pilgrimage on earth. It isn't our business to cut it short. Who are we to

263

take life and death into our hands?'

'Well, we do it all day, one way and another. Juries — soldiers — doctors — all that. And yet I do feel, somehow, that it isn't a right thing in this case. And yet, by interfering — finding things out and so on — one may do far worse harm. Start all kinds of things.'

'I think,' said Mr Tredgold, 'that the sin — I won't use that word — the damage to Society, the wrongness of the thing lies much more in the harm it does the killer than in anything it can do to the person who is killed. Especially, of course, if the killing is to the killer's own advantage. The consequence you mention — this thing which the sick person wants done — does the other person stand to benefit by it, may I ask?'

'Yes. That's just it. He — she — they do.'

'That puts it at once on a different plane from just hastening a person's death out of pity. Sin is in the intention, not the deed. That is the difference between divine law and human law. It is bad for a human being to get to feel that he has any right whatever to dispose of another person's life to his own advantage. It leads him on to think himself above all laws — Society is never safe from the man who has deliberately committed murder with impunity. That is why — or one reason why — God forbids private vengeance.'

'You mean that one murder leads to another.'

'Very often. In any case it leads to readiness to commit others.'

'It has. That's the trouble. But it wouldn't have if I hadn't started trying to find things out.

264

Ought I to have left it alone?'

'I see. That is very difficult. Terrible, too, for you. You feel responsible!'

'Yes.'

'You yourself are not serving a private vengeance?'

'Oh, no. Nothing really to do with me. Started in like a fool to help somebody who'd got into trouble about the thing through having suspicions himself. And my beastly interference started the crimes all over again.'

'I shouldn't be too troubled. Probably the murderer's own guilty fears would have led him into fresh crimes even without your interference.'

'That's true,' said Wimsey, remembering Mr Trigg.

'My advice to you is to do what you think is right, according to the laws which we have been brought up to respect. Leave the consequences to God. And try to think charitably, even of wicked people. You know what I mean. Bring the offender to justice, but remember that if we all got justice, you and I wouldn't escape either.'

'I know. Knock the man down but don't dance on the body. Quite. Forgive my troublin' you — and excuse my bargin' off, because I've got a date with a friend. Thanks so much. I don't feel quite so rotten about it now. But I was gettin' worried.'

Mr Tredgold watched him as he trotted away between the graves. 'Dear, dear,' he said, 'how nice they are. So kindly and scrupulous and so vague outside their public-school code. And much more nervous and sensitive than people

265

think. A very difficult class to reach. I must make a special intention for him at Mass tomorrow.'

Being a practical man, Mr Tredgold made a knot in his handkerchief to remind himself of this pious resolve.

'The problem — to interfere or not to interfere — God's law and Caesar's. Policemen, now — it's no problem to them. But for the ordinary man — how hard to disentangle his own motives. I wonder what brought him here. Could it possibly be — No!' said the vicar, checking himself, 'I have no right to speculate! He drew out his handkerchief again and made another mnemonic knot as a reminder against his next confession that he had fallen into the sin of inquisitiveness.

20

Murder

SIEGFRIED: 'What does this mean?'
ISERAND: 'A pretty piece of kidnapping, that's all.'

BEDDOES: *Death's Jest-Book*

Parker, too, had spent a disappointing half-hour. It appeared that Miss Whittaker not only disliked having her photograph taken, but had actually destroyed all the existing portraits she could lay hands on, shortly after Miss Dawson's death. Of course, many of Miss Whittaker's friends might be in possession of one — notably, of course, Miss Findlater. But Parker was not sure that he wanted to start a local hue-and-cry at the moment. Miss Climpson might be able to get one, of course. He went round to Nelson Avenue. Miss Climpson was out; there had been another gentleman asking for her. Mrs Budge's eyes were beginning to bulge with curiosity — evidently she was becoming dubious about Miss Climpson's 'nephew' and his friends. Parker then went to the local photographers. There were five. From two of them he extracted a number of local groups, containing unrecognisable portraits of Miss Whittaker at church bazaars and private theatricals. She had never had a studio portrait made in Leahampton.

Of Miss Findlater, on the other hand, he got several excellent likenesses — a slight, fair girl, with a rather sentimental look — plump and prettyish. All these he despatched to Town, with directions that they should be broadcast to the police, together with a description of the girl's dress when last seen.

The only really cheerful members of the party at the George were the second policeman, who had been having a pleasant gossip with various garage proprietors and publicans, with a view to picking up information, and the Chief Constable, who was vindicated and triumphant. He had been telephoning to various country police stations, and had discovered that XX9917 had actually been observed on the previous Monday by an AA scout on the road to Crow's Beach. Having maintained all along that the Crow's Beach excursion was a genuine one, he was inclined to exult over the Scotland Yard man. Wimsey and Parker dispiritedly agreed that they had better go down and make inquiries at Crow's Beach.

Meanwhile, one of the photographers, whose cousin was on the staff of the *Leahampton Mercury*, had put a call through to the office of that up-to-date paper, which was just going to press. A stop-press announcement was followed by a special edition; somebody rang up the London *Evening Views* which burst out into a front-page scoop; the fat was in the fire, and the *Daily Yell, Daily Views, Daily Wire* and *Daily Tidings*, who were all suffering from lack of excitement, came brightly out next morning with bold headlines about disappearing young women.

Crow's Beach, indeed, that pleasant and respectable watering-place, knew nothing of Miss Whittaker, Miss Findlater, or car XX9917. No hotel had received them; no garage had refuelled or repaired them; no policeman had observed them. The Chief Constable held to his theory of an accident, and scouting parties were sent out. Wires arrived at Scotland Yard from all over the place. They had been seen at Dover, at Newcastle, at Sheffield, at Winchester, at Rugby. Two young women had had tea in a suspicious manner at Folkestone; a car had passed noisily through Dorchester at a late hour on Monday night; a dark-haired girl in an 'agitated condition' had entered a public house in New Alresford just before closing time and asked the way to Hazelmere. Among all these reports, Parker selected that of a Boy Scout, who reported on the Saturday morning that he had noticed two ladies with a car having a picnic on the downs on the previous Monday, not far from Shelly Head. The car was an Austin Seven — he knew that, because he was keen on motors (an unanswerable reason for accuracy in a boy of his age), and he had noticed that it was a London number though he couldn't say positively what the number was.

Shelly Head lies about ten miles along the coast from Crow's Beach, and is curiously lonely, considering how near it lies to the watering-place. Under the cliffs is a long stretch of clear sandy beach, never visited, and overlooked by no houses. The cliffs themselves are chalk, and covered with short turf, running back into a wide

269

expanse of downs, covered with gorse and heather. Then comes a belt of pine trees, beyond which is a steep, narrow and rutty road, leading at length into the tarmac high-road between Ramborough and Ryders Heath. The downs are by no means frequented, though there are plenty of rough tracks which a car can follow, if you are not particular about comfort or fussy over your springs.

Under the leadership of the Boy Scout, the police car bumped uncomfortably over these disagreeable roads. It was hopeless to look for any previous car tracks, for the chalk was dry and hard, and the grass and heath retained no marks. Everywhere, little dells and hollows presented themselves — all exactly alike, and many of them capable of hiding a small car, not to speak of the mere signs and remains of a recent picnic. Having arrived at what their guide thought to be approximately the right place, they pulled up and got out. Parker quartered the ground between the five of them and they set off.

Wimsey took a dislike to gorse-bushes that day. There were so many of them and so thick. Any of them might hold a cigarette package or a sandwich paper or a scrap of cloth or a clue of some kind. He trudged along unhappily, back bent and eyes on the ground, over one ridge and down into the hollow — then circling to right and to left, taking his bearings by the police car; over the next ridge and down into the next hollow; over the next ridge —

Yes. There was something in the hollow.

He saw it first sticking out round the edge of a

gorse-bush. It was light in colour, and pointed, rather like a foot.

He felt a little sick.

'Somebody has gone to sleep here,' he said, aloud.

Then he thought:

'Funny it's always the feet they leave showing.'

He scrambled down among the bushes, slipping on the short turf and nearly rolling to the bottom. He swore irritably.

The person was sleeping oddly. The flies must be a nuisance all over her head like that.

It occurred to him that it was rather early in the year for flies. There had been an advertising rhyme in the papers. Something about 'Each fly you swat now means, remember, Three hundred fewer next September.' Or was it a thousand fewer? He couldn't get the metre quite right.

Then he pulled himself together and went forward. The flies rose up in a little cloud.

It must have been a pretty heavy blow, he thought, to smash the back of the skull in like that. The shingled hair was blonde. The face lay between the bare arms.

He turned the body on its back.

Of course, without the photograph, he could not — he need not — be certain that this was Vera Findlater.

All this had taken him perhaps thirty seconds.

He scrambled up to the rim of the hollow and shouted.

A small black figure at some distance stopped and turned. He saw its face as a white spot with no expression on it. He shouted again, and waved his arms in wide gestures of explanation. The figure came running; it lurched slowly and awkwardly over the heathy ground. It was the policeman — a heavy man, not built for running in the heat. Wimsey shouted again, and the policeman shouted too. Wimsey saw the others closing in upon him. The grotesque figure of the Boy Scout topped a ridge, waving its staff — then disappeared again. The policeman was quite near now. His bowler hat was thrust back on his head, and there was something on his watch-chain that glinted in the sun as he ran. Wimsey found himself running to meet him and calling — explaining at great length. It was too far off to make himself heard but he explained wordily, with emphasis, pointing, indicating. He was quite breathless when the policeman and he came together. They were both breathless. They wagged their heads and gasped. It was ludicrous. He started running again, with the man at his heels. Presently they were all there, pointing, measuring, taking notes, grubbing under the gorse-bushes. Wimsey sat down. He was dreadfully tired.

'Peter,' said Parker's voice, 'come and look at this.'

He got up wearily.

There were the remains of a picnic lunch a little farther down the hollow. The policeman had a little bag in his hand — he had taken it from under the body, and was now turning over the trifles it contained. On the ground, close to the dead girl's head, was a thick, heavy spanner — unpleasantly discoloured and with a few fair

272

hairs sticking to its jaws. But what Parker was calling his attention to was none of these, but a man's mauve-grey cap.

'Where did you find that?' asked Wimsey.

'Alf here picked it up at the top of the hollow,' said Parker.

'Tumbled off into the gorse it was,' corroborated the scout, 'just up here, lying upside-down just as if it had fallen off somebody's head.'

'Any footmarks?'

'Not likely. But there's a place where the bushes are all trodden and broken. Looks as if there'd been some sort of struggle. What's become of the Austin? Hi! don't touch that spanner, my lad. There may be fingerprints on it. This looks like an attack by some gang or other. Any money in that purse? Ten-shilling note, sixpence and a few coppers — oh! Well, the other woman may have had more on her. She's very well off, you know. Held up for ransom, I shouldn't wonder.' Parker bent down and very gingerly enfolded the spanner in a silk handkerchief, carrying it slung by the four comers. 'Well, we'd better spread about and have a look for the car. Better try that belt of trees over there. Looks a likely spot. And, Hopkins — I think you'd better run back with our car to Crow's Beach and let 'em know at the station, and come back with a photographer. And take this wire and send it to the Chief Commissioner at Scotland Yard, and find a doctor and bring him along with you. And you'd better hire another car while you're about it, in case we don't find the Austin — we shall be too many to get away in this one. Take Alf back with you if you're not sure of finding the place again. Oh! and Hopkins, fetch us along something to eat and drink, will you? we may be at it a long time. Here's some money — that enough?'

'Yes, thank you sir.'

The constable went off, taking Alf, who was torn between a desire to stay and do some more detecting, and the pride and glory of being first back with the news. Parker gave a few words of praise for his valuable assistance which filled him with delight, and then turned to the Chief Constable.

'They obviously went off in this direction. Would you bear away to the left, sir, and enter the trees from that end, and Peter, will you bear to the right and work through from the other end, while I go straight up the middle?'

The Chief Constable, who seemed a good deal shaken by the discovery of the body, obeyed without a word. Wimsey caught Parker by the arm.

'I say,' he said, 'have you looked at the wound? Something funny, isn't there? There ought to be more mess, somehow. What do you think?'

'I'm not thinking anything for the moment,' said Parker, a little grimly. 'We'll wait for the doctor's report. Come on, Steve! We want to dig out that car.'

'Let's have a look at the cap. H'm. Sold by a gentleman of the Jewish persuasion, resident in Stepney. Almost new. Smells strongly of Californian Poppy — rather a swell sort of gangsman, apparently. Quite one of the lads of the village.'

274

'Yes — we ought to be able to trace that. Thank Heaven, they always overlook something. Well, we'd better get along.'

The search for the car presented no difficulties. Parker stumbled upon it almost as soon as he got in under the trees. There was a clearing, with a little rivulet of water running through it, beside which stood the missing Austin. There were other trees here, mingled with the pines, and the water made an elbow and spread into a shallow pool, with a kind of muddy beach.

The hood of the car was up, and Parker approached with an uncomfortable feeling that there might be something disagreeable inside, but it was empty. He tried the gears. They were in neutral and the handbrake was on. On the seat was a handkerchief, very grubby and with no initials or laundry-mark. Parker grunted a little over the criminal's careless habit of strewing his belongings about. He came round in front of the car and received immediate further proof of carelessness. For on the mud there were footmarks — two men's and a woman's, it seemed.

The woman had got out of the car first — he could see where the left heel had sunk heavily in as she extricated herself from the low seat. Then the right foot — less heavily — then she had staggered a little and started to run. But one of the men had been there to catch her. He had stepped out of the bracken in shoes with new rubbers on them, and there were some scuffling marks as though he had held her and she had tried to break away. Finally, the second man, who seemed to possess rather narrow feet and to wear the long-toed boots affected by Jew boys of the louder sort — had come after her from the car — the marks of his feet were clear, crossing and half-obliterating hers. All three had stood together for a little. Then the tracks moved away, with those of the woman in the middle, and led up to where the mark of a Michelin balloon tyre showed clearly. The tyres on the Austin were ordinary Dunlops — besides, this was obviously a bigger car. It had apparently stood there for some little time, for a little pool of engine-oil had dripped from the crank-case. Then the bigger car moved off, down a sort of ride that led away through the trees. Parker followed it for a little distance, but the tracks soon became lost in a thick carpet of pine-needles. Still, there was no other road for a car to take. He turned to the Austin to investigate further. Presently shouts told him that the other two were converging upon the centre of the wood. He called back and before long Wimsey and Sir Charles Pillington came crashing towards him through the bracken which fringed the pines.

'Well,' said Wimsey, 'I imagine we may put down this elegant bit of purple headgear to the gentleman in the slim boots. Bright yellow, I fancy, with buttons. He must be lamenting his beautiful cap. The woman's footprints belong to Mary Whittaker, I take it.'

'I suppose so. I don't see how they can be the Findlater girl's. This woman went or was taken off in the car.'

'They are certainly not Vera Findlater's — there was no mud on her shoes when we found her.'

'Oh! you were taking notice, then. I thought you were feeling a bit dead to the world.'

'So I was, old dear, but I can't help noticin' things, though moribund. Hullo! What's this?'

He put his hand down behind the cushions of the car and pulled out an American magazine — that monthly collection of mystery and sensational fiction published under the name of *The Black Mask*.

'Light reading for the masses,' said Parker.

'Brought by the gentleman in the yellow boots, perhaps,' suggested the Chief Constable.

'More likely by Miss Findlater,' said Wimsey.

'Hardly a lady's choice,' said Sir Charles, in a pained tone.

'Oh, I dunno. From all I hear, Miss Whittaker was dead against sentimentality and roses round the porch, and the other poor girl copied her in everything. They might have a boyish taste in fiction.'

'Well, it's not very important,' said Parker.

'Wait a bit. Look at this. Somebody's been making marks on it.'

Wimsey held out the cover for inspection. A thick pencil-mark had been drawn under the first two words of the title.

'Do you think it's some sort of message? Perhaps the book was on the seat, and she contrived to make the marks unnoticed and shove it away here before they transferred her to the other car.'

'Ingenious,' said Sir Charles, 'but what does it mean? The Black. It makes no sense.'

'Perhaps the long-toed gentleman was a nigger,' suggested Parker. 'Nigger taste runs rather to boots and hair-oil. Or possibly a Hindu or Parsee of sorts.'

'God bless my soul,' said Sir Charles, horrified, 'an English girl in the hands of a nigger. How abominable!'

'Well, we'll hope it isn't so. Shall we follow the road out or wait for the doctor to arrive?'

'Better go back to the body, I think,' said Parker. 'They've got a long start on us, and half an hour more or less in following them up won't make much odds.'

They turned from the translucent cool greenness of the little wood back over to the downs. The streamlet clacked merrily away over the pebbles, running out to the south-west on its way to the river and the sea.

'It's all very well your chattering,' said Wimsey to the water. 'Why can't you say what you've seen?'

21

By What Means?

'Death hath so many doors to let out life.'
BEAUMONT AND FLETCHER: *Custom of the Country*

The doctor turned out to be a plumpish, fussy man — and what Wimsey impatiently called a 'Tutster'. He tutted over the mangled head of poor Vera Findlater as though it was an attack of measles after a party or a self-provoked fit of the gout.

'Tst, tst, tst. A terrible blow. How did we come by that. I wonder? Tst, tst. Life extinct? Oh, for several days, you know. Tst, tst — which makes it so much more painful, of course. Dear me, how shocking for her poor parents. And her sisters. They are very agreeable girls; you know them, of course, Sir Charles. Yes. Tst, tst.'

'There is no doubt, I suppose,' said Parker, 'that it is Miss Findlater?'

'None whatever,' said Sir Charles.

'Well, as you can identify her, it may be possible to spare the relatives the shock of seeing her like this. Just a moment, doctor — the photographer wants to record the position of the body before you move anything. Now, Mr — Andrews? — yes — have you ever done any photographs of this kind before? No? — well, you mustn't be upset by it! I know it's rather unpleasant. One from here, please, to show the position of the body — now from the top of the bank — that's right — now one of the wound itself — a close-up view, please. Yes. Thank you. Now, doctor, you can turn her over, please — I'm sorry, Mr Andrews — I know exactly how you are feeling, but these things have to be done. Hullo! look how her arms are all scratched about. Looks as if she'd put up a bit of a fight. The right wrist and left elbow — as though someone had been trying to hold her down. We must have a photograph of the marks, Mr Andrews — they may be important. I say, doctor, what do you make of this on the face?'

The doctor looked as though he would have preferred not to make so much as an examination of the face. However, with many tuts he worked himself up to giving an opinion.

'As far as one can tell, with all these post-mortem changes,' he ventured, 'it looks as though the face had been roughened or burnt about the nose and lips. Yet there is no appearance of the kind on the bridge of the nose, neck or forehead. Tst, tst — otherwise I should have put it down to severe sunburn.'

'How about chloroform burns?' suggested Parker.

'Tst, tst,' said the doctor, annoyed at not having thought of this himself — 'I wish you gentlemen of the police force would not be quite so abrupt. You want everything decided in too great a hurry. I was about to remark — if you had not anticipated me — that since I could *not* put the appearance down to sunburn, there remains some such possibility as you suggest. I can't possibly say that it is the result of chloroform — medical pronouncements of that kind cannot be hastily made without cautious investigation — but I was about to remark that it *might* be.'

'In that case,' put in Wimsey, 'could she have died from the effects of the chloroform? Supposing she was given too much or that her heart was weak?'

'My good sir,' said the doctor, deeply offended this time, 'look at that blow upon the head, and ask yourself whether it is necessary to suggest any other cause of death. Moreover, if she had died of the chloroform, where would be the necessity for the blow?'

'That is exactly what I was wondering,' said Wimsey.

'I suppose,' went on the doctor, 'you will hardly dispute my medical knowledge?'

'Certainly not,' said Wimsey, 'but as you say, it is unwise to make any medical pronouncement without cautious investigation.'

'And this is not the place for it,' put in Parker, hastily. 'I think we have done all there is to do here. Will you go with the body to the mortuary, doctor? Mr Andrews, I shall be obliged if you will come and take a few photographs of some footmarks and so on up in the wood. The light is bad, I'm afraid, but we must do our best.'

He took Wimsey by the arm.

'The man is a fool, of course,' he said, 'but we can get a second opinion. In the meantime, we

281

had better let it be supposed that we accept the surface explanation of all this.'

'What is the difficulty?' asked Sir Charles, curiously.

'Oh, nothing much,' replied Parker. 'All the appearances are in favour of the girls having been attacked by a couple of ruffians, who have carried Miss Whittaker off with a view to ransom, after brutally knocking Miss Findlater on the head when she offered resistance. Probably that is the true explanation. Any minor discrepancies will doubtless clear themselves up in time. We shall know better when we have had a proper medical examination.'

They returned to the wood, where photographs were taken and careful measurements made of the footprints. The Chief Constable followed these activities with intense interest, looking over Parker's shoulder as he entered the particulars in his notebook.

'I say,' he said, suddenly, 'isn't it rather odd — '

'Here's somebody coming,' broke in Parker.

The sound of a motor-cycle being urged in second gear over the rough ground proved to be the herald of a young man armed with a camera.

'Oh, God!' groaned Parker. 'The damned Press already.'

He received the journalist courteously enough, showing him the wheel-tracks and footprints, and outlining the kidnapping theory as they walked back to the place where the body was found.

'Can you give us any idea, Inspector, of the

appearance of the two wanted men?'

'Well,' said Parker, 'one of them appears to be something of a dandy; he wears a loathsome mauve cap and narrow-pointed shoes, and, if those marks on the magazine cover mean anything, one or other of the men may possibly be a coloured man of some kind. Of the second man, all we can definitely say is that he wears number 10 shoes, with rubber heels.'

'I was going to say,' said Pillington, 'that, à propos de bottes, it is rather remarkable — '

'And this is where we found the body of Miss Findlater,' went on Parker, ruthlessly. He described the injuries and the position of the body, and the journalist gratefully occupied himself with taking photographs, including a group of Wimsey, Parker and the Chief Constable standing among the gorse-bushes, while the latter majestically indicated the fatal spot with his walking-stick.

'And now you've got what you want, old son,' said Parker, benevolently, 'buzz off, won't you, and tell the rest of the boys. You've got all we can tell you, and we've got other things to do beyond granting special interviews.'

The reporter asked no better. This was tantamount to making his information exclusive, and no Victorian matron could have a more delicate appreciation of the virtues of exclusiveness than a modern newspaper man.

'Well now, Sir Charles,' said Parker, when the man had happily chugged and popped himself away, 'what were you about to say in the matter of the footprints?'

But Sir Charles was offended. The Scotland Yard man had snubbed him and thrown doubt on his discretion.

'Nothing,' he replied. 'I feel sure that my conclusion would appear very elementary to you.'

And he preserved a dignified silence throughout the return journey.

*   *   *

The Whittaker case had begun almost imperceptibly, in the overhearing of a casual remark dropped in a Soho restaurant; it ended amid a roar of publicity that shook England from end to end and crowded even Wimbledon into the second place. The bare facts of the murder and kidnapping appeared exclusively that night in a Late Extra edition of the *Evening Views*. Next morning it sprawled over the Sunday papers with photographs and full details, actual and imaginary. The idea of two English girls — the one brutally killed, the other carried off for some end unthinkably sinister, by a black man — aroused all the passion of horror and indignation of which the English temperament is capable. Reporters swarmed down upon Crow's Beach like locusts — the downs near Shelly Head were like a fair with motors, bicycles and parties on foot, rushing out to spend a happy week-end amid surroundings of mystery and bloodshed. Parker, who with Wimsey had taken rooms at the Green Lion, sat answering the telephone and receiving the letters and wires which descended upon him from all sides, with a stalwart policeman posted at the end of the passage to keep out all intruders.

Wimsey fidgeted about the room, smoking cigarette after cigarette in his excitement.

'This time we've got them,' he said. 'They've overreached themselves, thank God!'

'Yes. But have a little patience, old man. We can't lose them — but we must have all the facts first.'

'You're sure those fellows have got Mrs Forrest safe?'

'Oh, yes. She came back to the flat on Monday night — or so the garage man says. Our men are shadowing her continually and will let us know the moment anybody comes to the flat.'

'Monday night!'

'Yes. But that's no proof in itself. Monday night is quite a usual time for week-enders to return to Town. Besides I don't want to frighten her till we know whether she's the principal or merely the accomplice. Look here, Peter, I've had a message from another of our men. He's been looking into the finances of Miss Whittaker and Mrs Forrest. Miss Whittaker has been drawing out big sums, ever since December last year in cheques to Self, and these correspond almost exactly, amount for amount, with sums which Mrs Forrest has been paying into her own account. That woman has had a big hold over Miss Whittaker, ever since old Miss Dawson died. She's in it up to the neck, Peter.'

'I knew it. She's been doing the jobs while the Whittaker woman held down her alibi in Kent.

For God's sake, Charles, make no mistake. Nobody's life is safe for a second while either of them is at large.'

'When a woman is wicked and unscrupulous,' said Parker, sententiously, 'she is the most ruthless criminal in the world — fifty times worse than a man, because she is always so much more single-minded about it.'

'They're not troubled with sentimentality, that's why,' said Wimsey, 'and we poor mutts of men stuff ourselves up with the idea that they're romantic and emotional. All punk, my son. Damn that phone!'

Parker snatched up the receiver.

'Yes — yes — speaking. Good God, you don't say so. All right. Yes. Yes, of course you must detain him. I think myself it's a plant, but he must be held and questioned. And see that all the papers have it. Tell 'em you're sure he's the man. See? Soak it well into 'em that that's the official view. And — wait a moment — I want photographs of the cheque and of any fingerprints on it. Send 'em down immediately by a special messenger. It's genuine, I suppose? The Bank people say it is? Good! What's his story? . . . Oh! . . . any envelope? — Destroyed? — Silly devil. Right. Right Good-bye.'

He turned to Wimsey with some excitement.

'Hallelujah Dawson walked into Lloyds Bank in Stepney yesterday morning and presented Mary Whittaker's cheque for £10,000, drawn on their Leahampton branch to Bearer, and dated Friday 24th. As the sum was such a large one and the story of the disappearance was in Friday night's paper, they asked him to call again. Meanwhile, they communicated with Leahampton. When the news of the murder came out yesterday evening, the Leahampton manager remembered about it and phoned the Yard, with the result that they sent round this morning and had Hallelujah up for a few inquiries. His story is that the cheque arrived on Saturday morning, all by itself in an envelope, without a word of explanation. Of course the old juggins chucked the envelope away, so that we can't verify his tale or get a line on the post-mark. Our people thought the whole thing looked a bit fishy, so Hallelujah is detained pending investigation — in other words, arrested for murder and conspiracy!'

'Poor old Hallelujah! Charles, this is simply devilish! That innocent decent old creature, who couldn't harm a fly.'

'I know. Well, he's in for it and will have to go through with it. It's all the better for us. Hell's bells, there's somebody at the door. Come in.'

'It's Dr Faulkner to see you, sir,' said the constable, putting his head in.

'Oh, good. Come in, doctor. Have you made your examination?'

'I have, Inspector. Very interesting. You were quite right. I'll tell you that much straight away.'

'I'm glad to hear that. Sit down and tell us all about it.'

'I'll be as brief as possible,' said the doctor. He was a London man, sent down by Scotland Yard, and accustomed to police work — a lean, grey badger of a man, businesslike and keen-eyed, the

287

direct opposite of the 'tutster' who had annoyed Parker the evening before.

'Well, first of all, the blow on the head had, of course, nothing whatever to do with the death. You saw yourself that there had been next to no bleeding. The wound was inflicted some time after death — no doubt to create the impression of an attack by a gang. Similarly with the cuts and scratches on the arms. They are the merest camouflage.'

'Exactly. Your colleague — '

'My colleague, as you call him, is a fool,' snorted the doctor. 'If that's a specimen of his diagnosis, I should think there would be a high death-rate in Crow's Beach. That's by the way. You want the cause of death?'

'Chloroform?'

'Possibly. I opened the body but found no special symptoms suggestive of poisoning or anything. I have removed the necessary organs and sent them to Sir James Lubbock for analysis at your suggestion, but candidly I expect nothing from that. There was no odour of chloroform on opening the thorax. Either the time elapsed since the death was too long, as is very possible, seeing how volatile the stuff is, or the dose was too small. I found no indication of any heart weakness, so that, to produce death in a healthy young girl, chloroform would have had to be administered over a considerable time.'

'Do you think it was administered at all?'

'Yes, I think it was. The burns on the face certainly suggest it.'

'That would also account for the handkerchief

found in the car,' said Wimsey.

'I suppose,' pursued Parker, 'that it would require considerable strength and determination to administer chloroform to a strong young woman. She would probably resist strenuously.'

'She would,' said the doctor, grimly, 'but the odd thing is, she didn't. As I said before, all the marks of violence were inflicted post-mortem.'

'Suppose she had been asleep at the time,' suggested Wimsey, 'couldn't it have been done quietly then?'

'Oh, yes — easily. After a few long breaths of the stuff she would become semi-conscious, and then could be more firmly dealt with. It is quite possible, I suppose, that she fell asleep in the sunshine, while her companion wandered off and was kidnapped, and that the kidnappers then came along and got rid of Miss Findlater.'

'That seems a little unnecessary,' said Parker. 'Why come back to her at all?'

'Do you suggest that they both fell asleep and were both set on and chloroformed at the same time? It sounds rather unlikely.'

'I don't. Listen, doctor — only keep this to yourself.'

He outlined the history of their suspicions about Mary Whittaker, to which the doctor listened in horrified amazement.

'What happened,' said Parker, 'as we think, is this. We think that for some reason Miss Whittaker had determined to get rid of this poor girl who was so devoted to her. She arranged that they should go off for a picnic and that it should be known where they were going to. Then when Vera Findlater was dozing in the sunshine, our theory is that she murdered her — either with chloroform or — more likely, I fancy — by the same method that she used upon her other victims, whatever that was. Then she struck her on the head and produced the other appearances suggestive of a struggle, and left on the bushes a cap which she had previously purchased and stained with brilliantine. I am, of course, having the cap traced. Miss Whittaker is a tall, powerful woman — I don't think it would be beyond her strength to inflict that blow on an unresisting body.'

'But how about these footmarks in the wood?'

'I'm coming to that. There are one or two very odd things about them. To begin with, if this was the work of a secret gang, why should they go out of their way to pick out the one damp, muddy spot in twenty miles of country to leave their footprints in, when almost anywhere else they could have come and gone without leaving any recognisable traces at all?'

'Good point,' said the doctor. 'And I add to that, that they must have noticed they'd left a cap behind. Why not come back and remove it?'

'Exactly. Then again. Both pairs of shoes left prints entirely free from the marks left by wear and tear. I mean that there were no signs of the heels or soles being worn at all, while the rubbers on the larger pair were obviously just out of the shop. We shall have the photographs here in a moment, and you will see. Of course, it's not impossible that both men should be wearing brand new shoes, but on the whole it's unlikely.'

'It is,' agreed the doctor.

'And now we come to the most suggestive thing of all. One of the supposed men had very much bigger feet than the other, from which you would expect a taller and possibly heavier man with a longer stride. But on measuring the footprints, what do we find? In all three cases — the big man, the little man and the woman — we have exactly the same length of stride. Not only that, but the footprints have sunk into the ground to precisely the same depth, indicating that all three people were of the same weight. Now, the other discrepancies might pass, but that is absolutely beyond the reach of coincidence.'

Dr Faulkner considered this for a moment.

'You've proved your point,' he said at length. 'I consider that absolutely convincing.'

'It struck even Sir Charles Pillington, who is none too bright,' said Parker. 'I had the greatest difficulty in preventing him from blurting out the extraordinary agreement of the measurements to that *Evening Views* man.'

'You think, then, that Miss Whittaker had come provided with these shoes and produced the tracks herself.'

'Yes, returning each time through the bracken. Cleverly done. She had made no mistake about superimposing the footprints. It was all worked out to a nicety — each set over and under the two others; to produce the impression that three people had been there at the same time. Intensive study of the works of Mr Austin Freeman, I should say.'

'And what next?'

'Well, I think we shall find that this Mrs Forrest, who we think has been her accomplice all along, had brought her car down — the big car, that is — and was waiting there for her. Possibly she did the making of the footprints while Mary Whittaker was staging the assault. Anyhow, she probably arrived there after Mary Whittaker and Vera Findlater had left the Austin and departed to the hollow on the down. When Mary Whittaker had finished her part of the job, they put the handkerchief and the magazines called *The Black Mask* into the Austin and drove off in Mrs Forrest's car. I'm having the movements of the car investigated, naturally. It's a dark blue Renault four-seater, with Michelin balloon-tyres, and the number is XO4247. We know that it returned to Mrs Forrest's garage on the Monday night with Mrs Forrest in it.'

'But where is Miss Whittaker?'

'In hiding somewhere. We shall get her all right. She can't get money from her own bank — they're warned. If Mrs Forrest tries to get money for her, she will be followed. So if the worst comes to the worst, we can starve her out in time with any luck. But we've got another clue. There has been a most determined attempt to throw suspicion on an unfortunate relative of Miss Whittaker's — a black Nonconformist parson, with the remarkable name of Hallelujah Dawson. He has certain pecuniary claims on Miss Whittaker — not legal claims, but claims which any decent and humane person should have respected. She didn't respect them, and the poor old man might very well have been expected to nurse a grudge against her. Yesterday morning he tried to cash a Bearer cheque of hers for £10,000, with a lame-sounding story to the effect that it had arrived by the first post, without explanation, in an envelope. So, of course, he's had to be detained as one of the kidnappers.'

'But that is very clumsy, surely. He's almost certain to have an alibi.'

'I fancy the story will be that he hired some gangsters to do the job for him. He belongs to a Mission in Stepney — where that mauve cap came from — and no doubt there are plenty of tough lads in his neighbourhood. Of course we shall make close inquiries and publish details in all the papers.'

'And then?'

'Well then, I fancy, the idea is that Miss Whittaker will turn up somewhere in an agitated condition with a story of assault and holding to ransom made to fit the case. If Cousin Hallelujah has not produced a satisfactory alibi, we shall learn that he was on the spot, directing the murders. If he has definitely shown that he wasn't there, his name will have been mentioned, or he will have turned up at some time which the poor dear girl couldn't exactly ascertain, in some dreadful den to which she was taken in a place which she won't be able to identify.'

'What a devilish plot.'

'Yes. Miss Whittaker is a charming young woman. If there's anything she'd stop at, I don't know what it is. And the amiable Mrs Forrest appears to be another of the same kidney. Of course, doctor, we're taking you into our confidence. You understand that our catching Mary Whittaker depends on her believing that we've swallowed all these false clues of hers.'

'I'm not a talker,' said the doctor. 'Gang you call it, and gang it is, as far as I'm concerned. And Miss Findlater was hit on the head and died of it. I only hope my colleague and the Chief Constable will be equally discreet. I warned them, naturally, after what you said last night.'

'It's all very well,' said Wimsey, 'but what positive evidence have we, after all, against this woman? A clever defending counsel would tear the whole thing to rags. The only thing we can absolutely *prove* her to have done is the burgling of that house on Hampstead Heath and stealing the coal. The other deaths were returned natural deaths at the inquest. And as for Miss Findlater — even if we show it to be chloroform — well, chloroform isn't difficult stuff to get hold of — it's not arsenic or cyanide. And even if there were fingerprints on the spanner — '

'There were not,' said Parker, gloomily. 'This girl knows what she's about.'

'What did she want to kill Vera Findlater for, anyway?' asked the doctor, suddenly. 'According to you, the girl was the most valuable bit of evidence she had. She was the one witness who could prove that Miss Whittaker had an alibi for the other crimes — if they were crimes.'

'She may have found out too much about the connection between Miss Whittaker and Mrs Forrest. My impression is that she had served her turn and become dangerous. What we're

294

hoping to surprise now is some communication between Forrest and Whittaker. Once we've got that — '

'Humph!' said Dr Faulkner. He had strolled to the window. 'I don't want to worry you unduly, but I perceive Sir Charles Pillington in conference with the Special Correspondent of the *Wire*. The *Yell* came out with the gang story all over the front page this morning, and a patriotic leader about the danger of encouraging coloured aliens. I needn't remind you that the *Wire* would be ready to corrupt the Archangel Gabriel in order to kill the *Yell's* story.'

'Oh, hell!' said Parker, rushing to the window.

'Too late,' said the doctor. 'The *Wire* man has vanished into the post office. Of course, you can phone up and try to stop it.'

Parker did so, and was courteously assured by the editor of the *Wire* that the story had not reached him, and that if it did, he would bear Inspector Parker's instructions in mind.

The editor of the *Wire* was speaking the exact truth. The story had been received by the editor of the *Evening Banner*, sister paper to the *Wire*. In times of crisis, it is sometimes convenient that the left hand should not know what the right hand does. After all, it was an exclusive story.

22

A Case of Conscience

'I know thou art religious,
And hast a thing within thee called conscience,
With twenty popish tricks and ceremonies
Which I have seen thee careful to observe.'

Titus Andronicus

Thursday, June 23rd, was the Eve of S John. The
sober green workaday dress in which the church
settles down to her daily duties after the bridal
raptures of Pentecost, had been put away, and
the altar was white and shining once again.
Vespers were over in the Lady Chapel at S
Onesimus — a faint reek of incense hung
cloudily under the dim beams of the roof. A very
short acolyte with a very long brass extinguisher
snuffed out the candles, adding the faintly unpleasant yet sanctified odour of hot wax. The small
congregation of elderly ladies rose up lingeringly
from their devotions and slipped away in a series
of deep genuflections. Miss Climpson gathered
up a quantity of little manuals, and groped for
her gloves. In doing so, she dropped her office-
book. It fell, annoyingly, behind the long kneeler,
scattering as it went a small Pentecostal shower
of Easter cards, book-markers, sacred pictures,
dried palms and Ave Marias into the dark corner
behind the confessional.

Miss Climpson gave a little exclamation of wrath as she dived after them — and immediately repented this improper outburst of anger in a sacred place. 'Discipline,' she murmured, retrieving the last lost sheep from under a hassock, 'discipline. I must learn self-control.' She crammed the papers back into the office-book, grasped her gloves and handbag, bowed to the Sanctuary, dropped her bag, picked it up this time in a kind of glow of martyrdom, bustled down the aisle and across the church to the south door, where the sacristan stood, key in hand, waiting to let her out. As she went, she glanced up at the High Altar, unlit and lonely, with the tall candles like faint ghosts in the twilight of the apse. It had a grim and awful look she thought, suddenly.

'Good-night, Mr Stanniforth,' she said, quickly.

'Good-night, Miss Climpson, good-night.'

She was glad to come out of the shadowy porch into the green glow of the June evening. She had felt a menace. Was it the thought of the stern Baptist with his call to repentance? the prayer for grace to speak the truth and boldly rebuke vice? Miss Climpson decided that she would hurry home and read the Epistle and Gospel — curiously tender and comfortable for the festival of that harsh and uncompromising Saint. 'And I can tidy up these cards at the same time,' she thought.

Mrs Budge's first-floor front seemed stuffy after the scented loveliness of the walk home. Miss Climpson flung the window open and sat down by it to rearrange her sanctified oddments. The card of the Last Supper went in at the

297

Prayer of Consecration; the Fra Angelico Annunciation had strayed out of the office for March 25th and was wandering among the Sundays after Trinity; the Sacred Heart with its French text belonged to Corpus Christi; the . . . 'Dear me!' said Miss Climpson, 'I must have picked this up in church.'

Certainly the little sheet of paper was not in her writing. Somebody must have dropped it. It was natural to look and see whether it was anything of importance.

Miss Climpson was one of those people who say: 'I am not the kind of person who reads other people's postcards.' This is clear notice to all and sundry that they are, precisely, that kind of person. They are not untruthful; the delusion is real to them. It is merely that Providence has provided them with a warning rattle, like that of the rattlesnake. After that, if you are so foolish as to leave your correspondence in their way, it is your own affair.

Miss Climpson perused the paper.

In the manuals for self-examination issued to the Catholic-minded, there is often included an unwise little paragraph which speaks volumes for the innocent unworldliness of the compilers. You are advised, when preparing for confession, to make a little list of your misdeeds, lest one or two peccadilloes should slip your mind. It is true that you are cautioned against writing down the names of other people or showing your list to your friends, or leaving it about. But accidents may happen — and it may be that this recording of sins is contrary to the mind of the church, who bids you whisper them with fleeting breath into the ear of a priest and bids him, in the same moment that he absolves, forget them as though they had never been spoken.

At any rate, somebody had been recently shriven of the sins set forth upon the paper — probably the previous Saturday and the document had fluttered down unnoticed between the confession-box and the hassock, escaping the eye of the cleaner. And here it was — the tale that should have been told to none but God — lying open upon Mrs Budge's round mahogany table under the eye of a fellow-mortal.

To do Miss Climpson justice, she would probably have destroyed it instantly unread, if one sentence had not caught her eye:

'The lies I told for M. W.'s sake.'

At the same moment she realised that this was Vera Findlater's handwriting, and it 'came over her like a flash' — as she explained afterwards — exactly what the implication of the words was.

For a full half-hour Miss Climpson sat alone, struggling with her conscience. Her natural inquisitiveness said, 'Read'; her religious training said, 'You must not read'; her sense of duty to Wimsey, who employed her, said, 'Find out'; her own sense of decency said, 'Do no such thing'; a dreadful, harsh voice muttered gratingly, 'Murder is the question. Are you going to be the accomplice of Murder?' She felt like Lancelot Gobbo between conscience and the fiend — but which was the fiend and which was conscience?

'To speak the truth and boldly rebuke vice.'

Murder.

There was a real possibility now.

But *was* it a possibility? Perhaps she had read into the sentence more than it would bear.

In that case, was it not — almost — a duty to read further and free her mind from this horrible suspicion?

She would have liked to go to Mr Tredgold and ask his advice. Probably he would tell her to burn the paper promptly and drive suspicion out of her mind with prayer and fasting.

She got up and began searching for the matchbox. It would be better to get rid of the thing quickly.

What, exactly, was she about to do? — To destroy the clue to the discovery of a Murder?

Whenever she thought of the word, it wrote itself upon her brain in large capitals, heavily underlined. MURDER — like a police-bill.

Then she had an idea. Parker was a policeman — and probably also he had no particular feelings about the sacred secrecy of the Confessional. He had a Protestant appearance — or possibly he thought nothing of religion one way or the other. In any case, he would put his professional duty before everything. Why not send him the paper without reading it, briefly explaining how she had come upon it? Then the responsibility would be his.

On consideration, however, Miss Climpson's innate honesty scouted this scheme as Jesuitical. Secrecy was violated by this open publication as much as if she had read the thing — or more so. The old Adam, too, raised his head at this point, suggesting that if anybody was going to see the confession, she might just as well satisfy her own reasonable curiosity. Besides — suppose she was quite mistaken. After all, the 'lies' might have nothing whatever to do with Mary Whittaker's alibi. In that case, she would have betrayed another person's secret wantonly, and to no purpose. If she *did* decide to show it, she was bound to read it first — in justice to all parties concerned.

Perhaps — if she just glanced at another word or two, she would see that it had nothing to do with — MURDER — and then she could destroy it and forget it. She knew that if she destroyed it unread she never would forget it, to the end of her life. She would always carry with her that grim suspicion. She would think of Mary Whittaker as — perhaps — a Murderess. When she looked into those hard blue eyes, she would be wondering what sort of expression they had when the soul behind them was plotting — MURDER. Of course, the suspicions had been there before, planted by Wimsey, but now they were her own suspicions. They crystallised — became real to her.

'What shall I do?'

She gave a quick, shamefaced glance at the paper again, This time she saw the word 'London'.

Miss Climpson gave a kind of little gasp, like a person stepping under a cold shower-bath.

'Well,' said Miss Climpson, 'if this is a sin I am going to do it, and may I be forgiven.'

With a red flush creeping over her cheeks as though she were stripping something naked, she turned her attention to the paper.

The jottings were brief and ambiguous. Parker might not have made much of them, but to Miss Climpson, trained in this kind of devotional shorthand, the story was clear as print.

'Jealousy' — the word was written large and underlined. Then there was a reference to a quarrel, to wicked accusations and angry words and to a pre-occupation coming between the penitent's soul and God. 'Idol' — and a long dash.

From these few fossil bones, Miss Climpson had little difficulty in reconstructing one of those hateful and passionate 'scenes' of slighted jealousy with which a woman-ridden life had made her only too familiar. 'I do everything for you — you don't care a bit for me — you treat me cruelly — you're simply sick of me, that's what it is!' And, 'Don't be so ridiculous. Really, I can't stand this. Oh, stop it, Vera! I hate being slobbered over.' Humiliating, degrading, exhausting, beastly scenes. Girls' school, boarding-house, Bloomsbury-flat scenes. Damnable selfishness wearying of its victim. Silly *schwärmerei* swamping all decent self-respect. Barren quarrels ending in shame and hatred.

'Beastly, blood-sucking woman,' said Miss Climpson, viciously. 'It's too bad. She's only making use of the girl.'

But the self-examiner was now troubled with a more difficult problem. Piecing the hints together, Miss Climpson sorted it out with practised ease. Lies had been told — that was wrong, even though done to help a friend. Bad confessions

302

had been made, suppressing those lies. This ought to be confessed and put right. But (the girl asked herself) had she come to this conclusion out of hatred of the lies or out of spite against the friend? Difficult, this searching of the heart. And ought she, not content with confessing the lies to the priest, also to tell the truth to the world?

Miss Climpson had here no doubt what the priest's ruling would be. 'You need not go out of your way to betray your friend's confidence. Keep silent if you can, but if you speak you must speak the truth. You must tell your friend that she is not to expect any more lying from you. She is entitled to ask for secrecy — no more.'

So far, so good. But there was a further problem.

'Ought I to connive at her doing what is wrong?' — and then a sort of explanatory aside — 'the man in South Audley Street.'

This was a little mysterious . . . No! — on the contrary, it explained the whole mystery, jealousy, quarrel and all.

In those weeks of April and May, when Mary Whittaker had been supposed to be all the time in Kent with Vera Findlater, she had been going up to London. And Vera had promised to say that Mary was with her the whole time. And the visits to London had to do with a man in South Audley Street, and there was something sinful about it. That probably meant a love-affair. Miss Climpson pursed her lips virtuously, but she was more surprised than shocked. Mary Whittaker! she would never have suspected it of her, somehow. But it so explained the jealousy and the quarrel — the sense of desertion. But how had Vera found out? Had Mary Whittaker confided in her? — No; that sentence again, under the heading 'Jealousy' — what was it — 'following M. W. to London.' She had followed then, and seen. And then, at some moment, she had burst out with her knowledge — reproached her friend. Yet this expedition to London must have happened before her own conversation with Vera Findlater, and the girl had then seemed so sure of Mary's affection. Or had it been that she was trying to persuade herself, with determined self-deception, that there was 'nothing in' this business about the man? Probably. And probably some brutality of Mary's had brought all the miserable suspicions boiling to the surface, vocal, reproachful and furious. And so they had gone on to the row and the break.

'Queer,' thought Miss Climpson, 'that Vera has never come and told me about her trouble. But perhaps she is ashamed, poor child. I haven't seen her for nearly a week. I think I'll call and see her and perhaps she'll tell me all about it. In which case' — cried Miss Climpson's conscience, suddenly emerging with a bright and beaming smile from under the buffets of the enemy — 'in which case I shall know the whole history of it legitimately and can *quite honourably* tell Lord Peter about it.'

The next day — which was the Friday — she awoke, however, with an unpleasant ache in the conscience. The paper — still tucked into the office-book — worried her. She went round early to Vera Findlater's house, only to hear that she was staying with Miss Whittaker. 'Then I suppose they've made it up,' she said. She did not want to see Mary Whittaker, whether her secret was murder or mere immorality; but she was tormented by the desire to clear up the matter of the alibi for Lord Peter.

In Wellington Avenue she was told that the two girls had gone away on the Monday and had not yet returned. She tried to reassure the maid, but her own heart misgave her. Without any real reason, she was uneasy. She went round to the church and said her prayers, but her mind was not on what she was saying. On an impulse, she caught Mr Tredgold as he pottered in and out of the Sacristy, and asked if she might come the next evening to lay a case of conscience before him. So far, so good, and she felt that a 'good walk' might help to clear the cobwebs from her brain.

So she started off, missing Lord Peter by a quarter of an hour, and took the train to Guildford and then walked and had lunch in a wayside teashop and walked back into Guildford and so came home, where she learnt that 'Mr Parker and ever so many gentlemen had been asking for her all day, and what a dreadful thing, miss, here was Miss Whittaker and Miss Findlater disappeared and the police out looking for them, and the motor cars was such dangerous things, miss, wasn't they? It was to be hoped there wasn't an accident.'

And into Miss Climpson's mind there came, like an inspiration, the words, 'South Audley Street'.

Miss Climpson did not, of course, know that Wimsey was at Crow's Beach. She hoped to find him in Town. For she was seized with a desire, which she could hardly have explained even to herself, to go and look at South Audley Street. What she was to do when she got there she did not know, but go there she must. It was the old reluctance to make open use of that confession paper. Vera Findlater's story at first hand — that was the idea to which she obscurely clung. So she took the first train to Waterloo, leaving behind her, in case Wimsey or Parker, should call again, a letter so obscure and mysterious and so lavishly underlined and interlined that it was perhaps fortunate for their reason that they were never faced with it.

In Piccadilly she saw Bunter, and learned that his lordship was at Crow's Beach with Mr Parker, where he, Bunter, was just off to join him. Miss Climpson promptly charged him with a message to his employer slightly more involved and mysterious than her letter, and departed for South Audley Street. It was only when she was walking up it that she realised how vague her quest was and how little investigation one can do by merely walking along a street. Also, it suddenly occurred to her that if Miss Whittaker was carrying on anything of a secret nature in South Audley Street, the sight of an acquaintance patrolling the pavement would put her on her guard. Much struck by this reflection, Miss Climpson plunged abruptly into a chemist's shop and bought a toothbrush by way of concealing her movements and gaining time.

One can while away many minutes comparing shapes, sizes and bristles of toothbrushes, and sometimes chemists will be nice and gossipy.

Looking round the shop for inspiration, Miss Climpson observed a tin of nasal snuff labelled with the chemist's own name.

'I will take a tin of that, too, please,' she said. 'What *excellent* stuff it is — quite *wonderful*. I have used it for *years* and am really *delighted* with it. I recommend it to all my friends, particularly for *hay fever*. In fact, there's a friend of mine who often passes your shop, who told me only *yesterday* what a *martyr* she was to that complaint. 'My dear,' I said to her, 'you have only to get a tin of this *splendid* stuff and you will be *quite* all right *all summer*.' She was so *grateful* to me for telling her about it. Has she been in for it yet?' And she described Mary Whittaker closely.

It will be noticed, by the way, that in the struggle between Miss Climpson's conscience and what Wilkie Collins calls 'detective fever', conscience was getting the worst of it and was winking at an amount of deliberate untruth which a little time earlier would have staggered it.

The chemist, however, had seen nothing of Miss Climpson's friend. Nothing, therefore, was to be done but to retire from the field and think what was next to be done. Miss Climpson left, but before leaving she neatly dropped her latch-key into a large basket full of sponges standing at her elbow. She felt she might like to have an excuse to visit South Audley Street again.

Conscience sighed deeply, and her guardian

307

angel dropped a tear among the sponges.

Retiring into the nearest teashop she came to, Miss Climpson ordered a cup of coffee and started to think out a plan for honey-combing South Audley Street. She needed an excuse — and a disguise. An adventurous spirit was welling up in her elderly bosom, and her first dozen or so ideas were more lurid than practical.

At length a really brilliant notice occurred to her. She was (she did not attempt to hide it from herself) precisely the type and build of person one associates with the collection of subscriptions. Moreover, she had a perfectly good and genuine cause ready to hand. The church which she attended in London ran a slum mission, which was badly in need of funds, and she possessed a number of collecting cards, bearing full authority to receive subscriptions on its behalf. What more natural than that she should try a little house-to-house visiting in a wealthy quarter?

The question of disguise, also, was less formidable than it might appear. Miss Whittaker had only known her well-dressed and affluent in appearance, Ugly, clumping shoes, a hat of virtuous ugliness, a shapeless coat and a pair of tinted glasses would disguise her sufficiently at a distance. At close quarters, it would not matter if she was recognised, for if once she got to close quarters with Mary Whittaker, her job was done and she had found the house she wanted.

Miss Climpson rose from the table, paid her bill and hurried out to buy the glasses, remembering that it was a Saturday. Having secured a pair which hid her eyes effectively without looking exaggeratedly mysterious, she made for her rooms in St George's Square, to choose suitable clothing for her adventure. She realised, of course, that she could hardly start work till Monday — Saturday afternoon and Sunday are hopeless from the collector's point off view.

The choice of clothes and accessories occupied her for the better part of the afternoon. When she was at last satisfied she went downstairs to ask her landlady for some tea.

'Certainly, miss,' said the good woman. 'Ain't it awful, miss, about this murder?'

'What murder?' asked Miss Climpson, vaguely.

She took the *Evening Views* from her landlady's hand, and read the story of Vera Findlater's death.

★ ★ ★

Sunday was the most awful day Miss Climpson had ever spent. An active woman, she was condemned to inactivity, and she had time to brood over the tragedy. Not having Wimsey's or Parker's inside knowledge, she took the kidnapping story at its face value. In a sense, she found it comforting, for she was able to acquit Mary Whittaker of any share in this or the previous murders. She put them down — except, of course, in the case of Miss Dawson, and that might never have been a murder after all — to the mysterious man in South Audley Street. She formed a nightmare image of him in her mind

309

— blood-boltered, sinister, and — most horrible of all — an associate and employer of debauched and brutal black assassins. To Miss Climpson's credit be it said that she never for one moment faltered in her determination to track the monster to his lurking-place.

She wrote a long letter to Lord Peter, detailing her plans. Bunter, she knew, had left 110A Piccadilly, so after considerable thought, she addressed it to Lord Peter Wimsey, c/o Inspector Parker, the Police Station, Crow's Beach. There was, of course, no Sunday post from Town. However, it would go with the midnight collection.

On the Monday morning she see out early, in her old clothes and her spectacles, for South Audley Street. Never had her natural inquisitiveness and her hard training in third-rate boarding houses stood her in better stead. She had learned to ask questions without heeding rebuffs — to be persistent, insensitive, and observant. In every flat she visited she acted her natural self, with so much sincerity and such limpet-like obstinacy that she seldom came away without a subscription and almost never without some information about the flat and its inmates.

By tea time, she had done one side of the street and nearly half the other, without result. She was thinking of going to get some food, when she caught sight of a woman about a hundred yards ahead walking briskly in the same direction as herself.

Now it is easy to be mistaken in faces, but almost impossible not to recognise a back. Miss

310

Climpson's heart gave a bound. 'Mary Whittaker!' she said to herself, and started to follow.

The woman stopped to look into a shop window. Miss Climpson hesitated to come closer. If Mary Whittaker was at large, then — why then the kidnapping had been done with her own consent. Puzzled, Miss Climpson determined to play a waiting game. The woman went into the shop. The friendly chemist's was almost opposite. Miss Climpson decided that this was the moment to reclaim her latchkey. She went in and asked for it. It had been put aside for her and the assistant produced it at once. The woman was still in the shop over the way. Miss Climpson embarked upon a long string of apologies and circumstantial details about her carelessness. The woman came out. Miss Climpson gave her a longish start, brought the conversation to a close and fussed out again, replacing the glasses which she had removed for the chemist's benefit.

The woman walked on without stopping, but she looked into the shop windows from time to time. A man with a fruiterer's barrow removed his cap as she passed and scratched his head. Almost at once, the woman turned quickly and came back. The fruiterer picked up the handles of his barrow and trundled it away into a side street. The woman came straight on, and Miss Climpson was obliged to dive into a doorway and pretend to be tying a bootlace, to avoid a face to face encounter.

Apparently the woman had only forgotten to buy cigarettes. She went into a tobacconist's and emerged again in a minute or two, passing Miss Climpson again. That lady had dropped her bag and was agitatedly sorting its contents. The woman passed her without a glance and went on. Miss Climpson, flushed from stooping, followed again. The woman turned in at the entrance to a block of flats next door to a florist's. Miss Climpson was hard on her heels now, for she was afraid of losing her.

Mary Whittaker — if it was Mary Whittaker — went straight through the hall to the lift, which was one of the kind worked by the passenger. She stepped in and shot up. Miss Climpson — gazing at the orchids and roses in the florist's window — watched the lift out of sight. Then, with her subscription card prominently in her hand, she too entered the flats.

There was a porter on duty in a little glass case. He at once spotted Miss Climpson as a stranger and asked politely if he could do anything for her. Miss Climpson, selecting a name at random from the list of occupants in the entrance, asked which was Mrs Forrest's flat. The man replied that it was on the fourth floor, and stepped forward to bring the lift down for her. A man, to whom he had been chatting, moved quietly from the glass case and took up a position in the doorway. As the lift ascended, Miss Climpson noticed that the fruiterer had returned. His barrow now stood just outside.

The porter had come up with her, and pointed out the door of Mrs Forrest's flat. His presence was reassuring. She wished he would stay within call till she had concluded her search of the building. However, having asked for Mrs Forrest, she must begin there. She pressed the bell.

At first she thought the flat was empty, but after ringing a second time she heard footsteps. The door opened, and a heavily overdressed and peroxided lady made her appearance, whom Lord Peter would at once — and embarrassingly — have recognised.

'I have come,' said Miss Climpson, wedging herself briskly in at the doorway with the skill of the practised canvasser, 'to try if I can enlist your help for our Mission Settlement. May I come in? I am sure you — '

'No thanks,' said Mrs Forrest, shortly, and in a hurried, breathless tone, as if there was somebody behind her who she was anxious should not overhear her, 'I'm not interested in Missions.'

She tried to shut the door. But Miss Climpson had seen and heard enough.

'Good gracious!' she cried, staring, 'why, it's — '

'Come in.' Mrs Forrest caught her by the arm almost roughly and pulled her over the threshold, slamming the door behind them.

'How extraordinary!' said Miss Climpson; 'I hardly recognised you, Miss Whittaker, with your hair like that.'

'You!' said Mary Whittaker. 'You — of all people!' They sat facing one another in the sitting-room with its tawdry pink silk cushions. 'I knew you were a meddler. How did you get here? Is there anyone with you?'

'No — yes — I just happened,' began Miss

Climpson vaguely. One thought was uppermost in her mind. 'How did you get free? What happened? Who killed Vera?' She knew she was asking her questions crudely and stupidly. 'Why are you disguised like that?'

'Who sent you?' reiterated Mary Whittaker.

'Who is the man with you?' pursued Miss Climpson. 'Is he here? Did he do the murder?'

'What man?'

'The man Vera saw leaving your flat. Did he — '

'So that's it. Vera told you. The liar. I thought I had been quick enough.'

Suddenly, something which had been troubling Miss Climpson for weeks crystallised and became plain to her. The expression in Mary Whittaker's eyes. A long time ago, Miss Climpson had assisted a relative to run a boarding-house, and there had been a young man who paid his bill by cheque. She had had to make a certain amount of unpleasantness about the bill, and he had written the cheque unwillingly, sitting, with her eye upon him, at the little plush-covered table in the drawing-room. Then he had gone away — slinking out with his bag when no one was about. And the cheque had come back, like the bad penny that it was. A forgery. Miss Climpson had had to give evidence. She remembered now the odd, defiant look with which the young man had taken up his pen for his first plunge into crime. And today she was seeing it again — an unattractive mingling of recklessness and calculation. It was the look which had once warned Wimsey and should have

314

warned her. She breathed more quickly.

'Who was the man?'

'The man?' Mary Whittaker laughed suddenly. 'A man called Templeton — no friend of mine. It's really funny that you should think he was a friend of mine. I would have killed him if I could.'

'But where is he? What are you doing? Don't you know that everybody is looking for you? Why don't you — ?'

'That's why!'

Mary Whittaker flung her ten o'clock edition of the *Evening Banner*, which was lying on the sofa. Miss Climpson read the glaring headlines:

'AMAZING NEW DEVELOPMENTS
IN CROW'S BEACH CRIME

'WOUNDS ON BODY INFLICTED
AFTER DEATH

'FAKED FOOTPRINTS'

Miss Climpson gasped with amazement, and bent over the smaller type. 'How extraordinary!' she said, looking up quickly.

Not quite quickly enough. The heavy brass lamp missed her head indeed, but fell numbingly on her shoulder. She sprang to her feet with a loud shriek, just as Mary Whittaker's strong white hands closed upon her throat.

23

— And Smote Him, Thus

''Tis not so deep as a well, nor so wide as a
church door; but 'tis enough, 'twill serve.'
Romeo and Juliet

Lord Peter missed both Miss Climpson's
communications. Absorbed in the police inquiry,
he never thought to go back to Leahampton.
Bunter had duly arrived with 'Mrs Merdle' on
the Saturday evening. Immense police activity
was displayed in the neighbourhood of the
downs, and at Southampton and Portsmouth, in
order to foster the idea that the authorities
supposed the 'gang' to be lurking in those
districts. Nothing, as a matter of fact, was farther
from Parker's thoughts. 'Let her think she is
safe,' he said, 'and she'll come back. It's the
cat-and-mouse act for us, old man.' Wimsey
fretted. He wanted the analysis of the body to be
complete and loathed the thought of the long
days he had to wait. And he had small hope of
the result.

'It's all very well sitting round with your large
disguised policeman outside Mrs Forrest's flat,'
he said irritably, over the bacon and eggs on
Monday morning, 'but you do realise, don't you,
that we've still got no proof of murder. Not in
one single case.'

'That's so,' replied Parker, placidly.

'Well, doesn't it make your blood boil?' said Wimsey.

'Hardly,' said Parker. 'This kind of thing happens too often. If my blood boiled every time there was a delay in getting evidence, I should be in a perpetual fever. Why worry? It may be that perfect crime you're so fond of talking about — the one that leaves no trace. You ought to be charmed with it.'

'Oh, I daresay. O Turpitude, where are the charms that sages have seen in thy face? Time's called at the Criminals' Arms, and there isn't a drink in the place. Wimsey's Standard Poets, with emendations by Thingummy. As a matter of fact, I'm not at all sure that Miss Dawson's death *wasn't* the perfect crime — if only the Whittaker girl had stopped at that and not tried to cover it up. If you notice, the deaths are becoming more and more violent, elaborate and unlikely in appearance. Telephone again. If the Post Office accounts don't show a handsome profit on telephones this year it won't be your fault.'

'It's the cap and shoes,' said Parker, mildly. 'They've traced them. They were ordered from an outfitter's in Stepney, to be sent to the Rev H. Dawson, Peveril Hotel, Bloomsbury, to await arrival.'

'The Peveril again!'

'Yes. I recognise the hand of Mr Trigg's mysterious charmer. The Rev Hallelujah Dawson's card, with message 'Please give parcel to bearer', was presented by a District Messenger

317

next day, with a verbal explanation that the gentleman found he could not get up to Town after all. The messenger, obeying instructions received by telephone, took the parcel to a lady in a nurse's dress on the platform at Charing Cross. Asked to describe the lady, he said she was tall and wore blue glasses and the usual cloak and bonnet. So that's that.'

'How were the goods paid for?'

'Postal order, purchased at the West Central office at the busiest moment of the day.'

'And when did all this happen?'

'That's the most interesting part of the business. Last month, shortly before Miss Whittaker and Miss Findlater returned from Kent. This plot was well thought out beforehand.'

'Yes. Well, that's something more for you to pin on to Mrs Forrest. It looks like proof of conspiracy, but whether it's proof of murder — '

'It's *meant* to look like a conspiracy of Cousin Hallelujah's, I suppose. Oh, well, we shall have to trace the letters and the typewriter that wrote them and interrogate all these people, I suppose. God! What a grind! Hullo! Come in! Oh, it's you, doctor?'

'Excuse my interrupting your breakfast,' said Dr Faulkner, 'but early this morning, while lying awake, I was visited with a bright idea. So I had to come and work it off on you while it was fresh. About the blow on the head and the marks on the arms, you know. Do you suppose they served a double purpose? Besides making it look like the work of a gang, could they be hiding some other, smaller mark? Poison, for instance,

318

could be injected, and the mark covered up by scratches and cuts inflicted after death.'

'Frankly,' said Parker, 'I wish I could think it. It's a very sound idea and may be the right one. Our trouble is, that in the two previous deaths which we have been investigating, and which we are inclined to think form a part of the same series as this one, there have been no signs or traces of poison discoverable in the bodies at all by any examination or analysis that skill can devise. In fact, not only no proof of poison, but no proof of anything but natural death.'

And he related the cases in fuller detail.

'Odd,' said the doctor. 'And you think this may turn out the same way. Still, in this case the death can't very well have been natural — or why these elaborate efforts to cover up?'

'It wasn't,' said Parker; 'the proof being that — as we now know — the plot was laid nearly two months ago.'

'But the method!' cried Wimsey, 'the method! Hang it all — here are all we people with our brilliant brains and our professional reputations — and this half-trained girl out of a hospital can beat the lot of us. How was it done?'

'It's probably something so simple and obvious that it's never occurred to us,' said Parker. 'The sort of principle you learn when you're in the fourth form and never apply to anything. Rudimentary. Like that motor-cycling imbecile we met up at Crofton, who sat in the rain and prayed for help because he'd never heard of an air-lock in his feed. Now I daresay that boy had learnt — What's the matter with you?'

319

'My God!' cried Wimsey. He smashed his hand down among the breakfast things, upsetting his cup. 'My God! But that's it! You've got it — you've done it — Obvious? God Almighty — it doesn't need a doctor. A garage hand could have told you. People die of it every day. Of course, it was an air-lock in the feed.'

'Bear up, doctor,' said Parker, 'he's always like this when he gets an idea. It wears off in time. D'you mind explaining yourself, old thing?'

Wimsey's pallid face was flushed. He turned on the doctor.

'Look here,' he said, 'the body's a pumping engine, isn't it? The jolly old heart pumps the blood round the arteries and back through the veins and so on, doesn't it? That's what keeps things working, what? Round and home again in two minutes — that sort of thing?'

'Certainly.'

'Little valve to let the blood out; 'nother little valve to let it in — just like an internal combustion engine, which it is?'

'Of course.'

'And s'posin' that stops?'

'You die.'

'Yes. Now, look here. S'posin' you take a good big hypodermic, empty, and dig it into one of the big arteries and push the handle — what would happen? What would happen, doctor? You'd be pumpin' a big air bubble into your engine feed, wouldn't you? What would become of your circulation then?'

'It would stop it,' said the doctor, without hesitation. 'That is why nurses have to be

320

particular to fill the syringe properly, especially when doing an intravenous injection.'

'I *knew* it was the kind of thing you learnt in the fourth form. Well, go on. Your circulation would stop — it would be like an embolism in its effect, wouldn't it?'

'Only if it was in a main artery, of course. In a small vein the blood would find away round. That is why' (this seemed to be the doctor's favourite opening) 'that is why it is so important that embolisms — blood clots — should be dispersed as soon as possible and not left to wander about the system.'

'Yes — yes — but the air bubble, doctor — in a main artery — say the femoral or the big vein in the bend of the elbow — that would stop the circulation, wouldn't it? How soon?'

'Why, at once. The heart would stop beating.'

'And then?'

'You would die.'

'With what symptoms?'

'None to speak of. Just a gasp or two. The lungs would make a desperate effort to keep things going. Then you'd just stop. Like heart failure. It would *be* heart failure.'

'How well I know it . . . That sneeze in the carburettor — a gasping, as you say. And what would be the post-mortem symptoms?'

'None. Just the appearances of heart failure. And, of course, the little mark of the needle, if you happened to be looking for it.'

'You're sure of all this, doctor?' said Parker.

'Well, it's simple, isn't it? A plain problem in

mechanics. Of course that would happen. It must happen.'

'Could it be proved?' insisted Parker.

'That's more difficult.'

'We must try,' said Parker. 'It's ingenious, and it explains a lot of things. Doctor, will you go down to the mortuary again, and see if you can find any puncture mark on the body. I really think you've got the explanation of the whole thing, Peter. Oh, dear! Who's on the phone now? . . . What? *what?* — oh, hell! — Well, that's torn it. She'll never come back now. Warn all the ports — send out an all-stations call — watch the railways and go through Bloomsbury with a toothcomb — that's the part she knows best. I'm coming straight up to Town now — yes, immediately. Right you are.' He hung up the receiver with a few brief, choice expressions.

'That adjectival imbecile, Pillington, has let out all he knows. The whole story is in the early editions of the *Banner*. We're doing no good here. Mary Whittaker will know the game's up, and she'll be out of the country in two twos, if she isn't already. Coming back to Town, Wimsey?'

'Naturally. Take you up in the car. Lose no time. Ring the bell for Bunter, would you? Oh, Bunter, we're going up to Town. How soon can we start?'

'At once, my lord. I have been holding your lordship's and Mr Parker's things ready packed from hour to hour, in case a hurried adjournment should be necessary.'

'Good man.'

'And there is a letter for you, Mr Parker, sir.'

'Oh, thanks. Ah, yes. The finger-prints off the cheque. H'm. Two sets only — besides those of the cashier, of course — Cousin Hallelujah's and a female set, presumably those of Mary Whittaker. Yes, obviously — here are the four fingers of the left hand, just as one would place them to hold the cheque flat while signing.'

'Pardon me, sir — but might I look at that photograph?'

'Certainly. Take a copy for yourself. I know it interests you as a photographer. Well, cheerio, doctor. See you in Town some time. Come on, Peter.'

Lord Peter came on. And that, as Dr Faulkner would say, was why Miss Climpson's second letter was brought up from the police-station too late to catch him.

⋆ ⋆ ⋆

They reached Town at twelve — owing to Wimsey's brisk work at the wheel — and went straight to Scotland Yard, dropping Bunter, at his own request, as he was anxious to return to the flat. They found the Chief Commissioner in rather a brusque mood — angry with the *Banner* and annoyed with Parker for having failed to muzzle Pillington.

'God knows where she will be found next. She's probably got a disguise and a get-away all ready.'

'Probably gone already,' said Wimsey. 'She could easily have left England on the Monday or Tuesday and nobody a penny the wiser. If the

323

coast had seemed clear, she'll have come back and taken possession of her goods again. Now she'll stay abroad. That's all.'

'I'm very much afraid you're right,' agreed Parker, gloomily.

'Meanwhile, what is Mrs Forrest doing?'

'Behaving quite normally. She's been carefully shadowed, of course, but not interfered with in any way. We've got three men out there now — one as a coster — one as a dear friend of the hall-porter's who drops in every so often with racing tips, and an odd job man doing a spot of work in the backyard. They report that she has been in and out, shopping and so on, but mostly having her meals at home. No one has called. The men deputed to shadow her away from the flat have watched carefully to see if she speaks to anyone or slips money to anyone. We're pretty sure the two haven't met yet.'

'Excuse me, sir. An officer put his head in at the door. 'Here's Lord Peter Wimsey's man, sir, with an urgent message.'

Bunter entered, trimly correct in bearing, but with a glitter in his eye. He laid down two photographs on the table.

'Excuse me, my lord and gentlemen, but would you be so good as to cast your eyes on these two photographs?'

'Finger-prints?' said the Chief, interrogatively.

'One of them is our own official photograph of the prints on the £10,000 cheque,' said Parker. 'The other — where did you get this Bunter? It looks like the same set of prints, but it's not one of ours.'

'They appeared similar, sir, to my unin-
structed eye. I thought it better to place the
matter before you.'

'Send Dewsby here,' said the Chief Commissioner.

Dewsby was the head of the finger-print
department, and he had no hesitation at all.

'They are undoubtedly the same prints,' he
said.

A light was slowly breaking in on Wimsey.

'Bunter — did these come off that wine glass?'

'Yes, my lord!'

'But they are Mrs Forrest's!'

'So I understood you to say, my lord, and I
have filed them under that name.'

'Then, if the signature on the cheque is
genuine — '

'We haven't far to look for our bird,' said
Parker, brutally. 'A double identity, damn the
woman, she's made us waste a lot of time. Well, I
think we shall get her now, on the Findlater
murder at least, and possibly on the Gotobed
business.'

'But I understand there was an alibi for that,'
said the Chief.

'There was,' said Parker, grimly, 'but the
witness was the girl that's just been murdered.
Looks as though she had made up her mind to
split and was got rid of.'

'Looks as though several people had had a
near squeak of it,' said Wimsey.

'Including you. That yellow hair was a wig,
then.'

'Probably. It never looked natural, you know.

When I was there that night she had on one of those close turban affairs — she might have been bald for all one could see.'

'Did you notice the scar on the fingers of the right hand?'

'I did not — for the very good reason that her fingers were stiff with rings to the knuckles. There was pretty good sense behind her ugly bad taste. I suppose I was to be drugged — or, failing that, caressed into slumber and then — shall we say, put out of circulation! Highly distressin' incident, Amorous clubman dies in a flat. Relations very anxious to hush matter up. I was selected, I suppose, because I was seen with Evelyn Cropper at Liverpool. Bertha Gotobed got the same sort of dose, too, I take it. Met by old employer, accidentally, on leaving work — £5 note and nice little dinner — lashings of champagne — poor kid as drunk as a blind fiddler bundled into the car — finished off there and trundled out to Epping in company with a ham sandwich and a bottle of Bass. Easy, ain't it — when you know how?'

'That being so,' said the Chief Commissioner, 'the sooner we get hold of her the better. You'd better go at once, Inspector; take a warrant for Whittaker or Forrest — and any help you may require.'

'May I come?' asked Wimsey, when they were outside the building.

'Why not? You may be useful. With the men we've got there already we shan't need any extra help.'

The car whizzed swiftly through Pall Mall, up

St. James's Street and along Piccadilly. Half way up South Audley Street they passed the fruit seller, with whom Parker had exchanged an almost imperceptible signal. A few doors below the entrance to the flats they got out and were almost immediately joined by the hall-porter's sporting friend.

'I was just going to call you up,' said the latter. 'She's arrived.'

'What, the Whittaker woman?'

'Yes. Went up about two minutes ago.'

'Is Forrest there too?'

'Yes. She came in just before the other woman.'

'Queer,' said Parker. 'Another good theory gone west. Are you sure it's Whittaker?'

'Well, she's made up with old-fashioned clothes and greyish hair and so on. But she's the right height and general appearance. And she's running the old blue-spectacle stunt again. I think it's the right one — though of course I didn't get close to her, remembering your instructions.'

'Well, we'll have a look, anyhow. Come along.'

The coster had joined them now, and they all entered together.

'Did the old girl go up to Forrest's flat all right?' asked the third detective of the porter.

'That's right. Went straight to the door and started something about a subscription. Then Mrs Forrest pulled her in quick and slammed the door. Nobody's come down since.'

'Right. We'll take ourselves up — and mind you don't let anybody give us the slip by the

327

staircase. Now then, Wimsey, she knows you as Templeton, but she may still not know for certain that you're working with us. Ring the bell, and when the door's opened, stick your foot inside. We'll stand just round the corner here and be ready to rush.'

This manoeuvre was executed. They heard the bell trill loudly.

Nobody came to answer it, however. Wimsey rang again, and then bent his ear to the door.

'Charles,' he cried suddenly, 'there's something going on here.' His face was white. 'Be quick! I couldn't stand *another* — '

Parker hastened up and listened. Then he caught Peter's stick and hammered on the door, so that the hollow liftshaft echoed with the clamour.

'Come on there — open the door — this is the police.'

And all the time, a horrid, stealthy thumping and gurgling sounded inside — dragging of something heavy and a scuffling noise. Then a loud crash, as though a piece of furniture had been flung to the floor — and then a loud hoarse scream, cut brutally off in the middle.

'Break in the door,' said Wimsey, the sweat pouring down his face.

Parker signalled to the heavier of the two policemen. He came along, shoulder first, lunging. The door shook and cracked. Parker added his weight, thrusting Wimsey's slight body into the corner. They stamped and panted in the narrow space.

The door gave way, and they tumbled into the

hall. Everything was ominously quiet.

'Oh, quick!' sobbed Peter.

A door on the right stood open. A glance assured them that there was nothing there. They sprang to the sitting-room door and pushed it. It opened about a foot. Something bulky impeded its progress. They shoved violently and the obstacle gave. Wimsey leapt over it — it was a tall cabinet, fallen, with broken china strewing the floor. The room bore signs of a violent struggle — tables flung down, a broken chair, a smashed lamp. He dashed for the bedroom, with Parker hard at his heels.

The body of a woman lay limply on the bed. Her long, grizzled hair hung in a dank rope over the pillow and blood was on her head and throat. But the blood was running freely, and Wimsey could have shouted for joy at the sight. Dead men do not bleed.

Parker gave only one glance at the injured woman. He made promptly for the dressing-room beyond. A shot sang past his head — there was a snarl and a shriek — and the episode was over. The constable stood shaking his bitten hand, while Parker put the come-along-o'-me grip on the quarry. He recognised her readily, though the peroxide wig had fallen awry and the blue eyes were bleared with terror and fury.

'That'll do,' said Parker, quietly, 'the game's up. It's not a bit of use. Come, be reasonable. You don't want us to put the bracelets on, do you? Mary Whittaker, alias Forrest, I arrest you on the charge — ' he hesitated for a moment and she saw it.

'On what charge? What have you got against me?'

'Of attempting to murder this lady, for a start,' said Parker.

'The old fool!' she said, contemptuously; 'she forced her way in here and attacked me. Is that all?'

'Very probably not,' said Parker; 'I warn you that anything you say may be taken down and used in evidence at your trial.'

Indeed, the third officer had already produced a notebook and was imperturbably writing down: 'When told the charge, the prisoner said: 'Is that all?'' The remark evidently struck him as an injudicious one, for he licked his pencil with an air of satisfaction.

'Is the lady all right — who is it?' asked Parker, coming back to a survey of the situation.

'It's Miss Climpson — God knows how she got here. I think she's all right, but she's had a rough time.'

He was anxiously sponging her head as he spoke, and at that moment her eyes opened.

'Help!' said Miss Climpson, confusedly, 'The syringe — you shan't — oh!' She struggled feebly, and then recognised Wimsey's anxious face. 'Oh, dear!' she exclaimed, 'Lord Peter, such an upset. Did you get my letter? Is it all right? . . . Oh, dear! What a state I'm in. I — that woman — '

'Now, don't worry, Miss Climpson,' said Wimsey, much relieved, 'everything's quite all right and you mustn't talk. You must tell us about it later.'

'What was that about a syringe?' said Parker, intent on his case.

'She'd got a syringe in her hand,' panted Miss Climpson, trying to sit up, and fumbling with her hands over the bed. 'I fainted, I think — such a struggle — and something hit me on the head. And I saw her coming at me with the thing. And I knocked it out of her hand and I can't remember what happened afterwards. But I have *remarkable* vitality,' said Miss Climpson, cheerfully. 'My dear father always used to say 'Climpsons take a lot of killing'!'

Parker was groping on the floor.

'Here you are,' said he. In his hand was a hypodermic syringe.

'She's mental, that's what she is,' said the prisoner. 'That's only the hypodermic I use for my injections when I get neuralgia. There's nothing in that.'

'That's quite correct,' said Parker, with a significant nod at Wimsey. 'There is — nothing in it.'

★ ★ ★

On the Tuesday night, when the prisoner had been committed for trial on the charges of murdering Bertha Gotobed and Vera Findlater, and attempting to murder Alexandra Climpson, Wimsey dined with Parker. The former was depressed and nervous.

'The whole thing's been beastly,' he grumbled. They had sat up discussing the case into the small hours.

331

'Interesting,' said Parker, 'interesting. I owe you seven and six, by the way. We ought to have seen through that Forrest business earlier, but there seemed no real reason to suspect the Findlater girl's word as to the alibi. These mistaken loyalties make a lot of trouble.

'I think the thing that put us off was that it all started so early. There seemed no reason for it, but looking back on Trigg's story it's as plain as a pike-staff. She took a big risk with that empty house, and she couldn't always expect to find empty houses handy to do away with people in. The idea was, I suppose, to build up a double identity, so that, if Mary Whittaker was ever suspected of anything, she could quietly disappear and become the frail but otherwise innocent Mrs Forrest. The real slip-up was forgetting to take back that £5 note from Bertha Gotobed. If it hadn't been for that, we might never have known anything about Mrs Forrest. It must have rattled her horribly when we turned up there. After that, she was known to the police in both her characters. The Findlater business was a desperate attempt to cover up her tracks — and it was bound to fail, because it was so complicated.'

'Yes. But the Dawson murder was beautiful in its ease and simplicity.'

'If she had stuck to that and left well alone, we could never have proved anything. We can't prove it now, which is why I left it off the charge-sheet. I don't think I've ever met a more greedy and heartless murderer. She probably thought that anyone who inconvenienced her had no right to exist.'

'Greedy and malicious. Fancy tryin' to shove the blame on poor old Hallelujah. I suppose he'd committed the unforgivable sin of askin' her for money.'

'Well, he'll get it, that's one good thing. The pit digged for Cousin Hallelujah has turned into a gold mine. That £10,000 cheque has been honoured. I saw to that first thing, before Whittaker could remember and try to stop it. Probably she couldn't have stopped it anyway, as it was duly presented last Saturday.'

'Is the money legally hers?'

'Of course it is. We know it was gained by a crime, but we haven't charged her with the crime, so that legally no such crime was committed. I've not said anything to Cousin Hallelujah, of course, or he mightn't like to take it. He thinks it was sent him in a burst of contrition, poor old dear.'

'So Cousin Hallelujah and all the little Hallelujahs will be rich. That's splendid. How about the rest of the money? Will the Crown get it after all?'

'No. Unless she wills it to someone, it will go to the Whittaker next-of-kin — a first cousin, I believe, called Allock. A very decent fellow, living in Birmingham. That is,' he added, assailed by sudden doubt, 'if first cousins *do* inherit under this confounded Act.'

'Oh, I think first cousins are safe,' said Wimsey, 'though nothing seems safe nowadays. Still, dash it all, some relation must still be allowed a look-in, or what becomes of the sanctity of family life? If so, that's the most cheering thing about the beastly business. Do you know, when I rang up that man Carr and told him all about it, he wasn't a bit interested or grateful. Said he'd always suspected something like that, and he hoped we weren't going to rake it all up again, because he'd come into that money he told us about and was setting up for himself in Harley Street, so he didn't want any more scandals.'

'I never did like that man. I'm sorry for Nurse Philliter.'

'You needn't be. I put my foot in it again over that. Carr's too grand to marry a nurse now — at least, I fancy that's what it is. Anyway, the engagement's off. And I was so pleased at the idea of playing Providence to two deserving young people,' added Wimsey, pathetically.

'Dear, dear! Well, the girl's well out of it. Hullo! there's the phone. Who on earth — ? Some damned thing at the Yard, I suppose. At three ack emma! Who'd be a policeman? — Yes? — Oh! — right, I'll come round. The case has gone west, Peter.'

'How?'

'Suicide. Strangled herself with a sheet. I'd better go round, I suppose.'

'I'll come with you.'

'An evil woman, if ever there was one,' said Parker, softly, as they looked at the rigid body, with its swollen face and the deep, red ring about the throat.

Wimsey said nothing. He felt cold and sick. While Parker and the Governor of the prison made the necessary arrangements and discussed the case, he sat hunched unhappily upon his chair. Their voices went on and on interminably. Six o'clock had struck some time before they rose to go. It reminded him of the eight strokes of the clock which announce the running-up of the black and hideous flag.

As the gate clanged open to let them out, they stepped into a wan and awful darkness. The June day had risen long ago, but only a pale and yellowish gleam lit the half-deserted streets. And it was bitterly cold and raining.

'What is the matter with the day?' said Wimsey. 'Is the world coming to an end?'

'No,' said Parker, 'it is the eclipse.'

Biographical Note
Communicated by Paul Austin Delagardie

I am asked by Miss Sayers to fill up certain lacunae and correct a few trifling errors of fact in her account of my nephew Peter's career. I shall do so with pleasure. To appear publicly in print is every man's ambition, and by acting as a kind of running footman to my nephew's triumph I shall only be showing a modesty suitable to my advanced age.

The Wimsey family is an ancient one — too ancient, if you ask me. The only sensible thing Peter's father ever did was to ally his exhausted stock with the vigorous French-English strain of the Delagardies. Even so, my nephew Gerald (the present Duke of Denver) is nothing but a beef-witted English squire, and my niece Mary was flighty and foolish enough till she married a policeman and settled down. Peter, I am glad to say, takes after his mother and me. True, he is all nerves and nose — but that is better than being all brawn and no brains like his father and brother, or a bundle of emotions, like Gerald's boy, Saint-George. He has at least inherited the Delagardie brains, by way of safeguard to the unfortunate Wimsey temperament.

Peter was born in 1890. His mother was being very much worried at the time by her husband's behaviour (Denver was always tiresome, though the big scandal did not break out till the Jubilee year), and her anxieties may have affected the boy. He was a colourless shrimp of a child, very restless and mischievous, and always much too sharp for his age. He had nothing of Gerald's robust physical beauty, but he developed what I can best call a kind of bodily cleverness, more skill than strength. He had a quick eye for a ball and beautiful hands for a horse. He had the devil's own pluck, too: the intelligent sort of pluck that sees the risk before it takes it. He suffered badly from nightmares as a child. To his father's consternation he grew up with a passion for books and music.

His early school days were not happy. He was a fastidious child, and I suppose it was natural that his school-fellows should call him 'Flimsy' and treat him as a kind of comic turn. And he might, in sheer self-protection, have accepted the position and degenerated into a mere licensed buffoon, if some games-master at Eton had not discovered that he was a brilliant natural cricketer. After that, of course, all his eccentricities were accepted as wit, and Gerald underwent the salutary shock of seeing his despised younger brother become a bigger personality than himself. By the time he reached the Sixth Form, Peter had contrived to become the fashion — athlete, scholar, *arbiter elegantiarum* — *nec pluribus impar*. Cricket had a great deal to do with it — plenty of Eton men will remember the 'Great Flim' and his performance against Harrow — but I take credit to myself for introducing him to a good tailor, showing him the way about Town, and teaching him to distinguish good wine from bad. Denver bothered little about him — he had too many entanglements of his own and in addition was taken up with Gerald, who by this time was making a prize fool of himself at Oxford. As a matter of fact Peter never got on with his father, he was a ruthless young critic of the paternal misdemeanours, and his sympathy for his mother had a destructive effect upon his sense of humour.

Denver, needless to say, was the last person to tolerate his own failings in his offspring. It cost him a good deal of money to extricate Gerald from the Oxford affair, and he was willing enough to turn his other son over to me. Indeed, at the age of seventeen, Peter came to me of his own accord. He was old for his age and exceedingly reasonable, and I treated him as a man of the world. I established him in trustworthy hands in Paris, instructing him to keep his affairs upon a sound business footing and to see that they terminated with goodwill on both sides and generosity on his. He fully justified my confidence. I believe that no woman has ever found cause to complain of Peter's treatment; and two at least of them have since married royalty (rather obscure royalties, I admit, but royalty of a sort). Here again, I insist upon my due share of the credit; however good the material one has to work upon it is ridiculous to leave any young man's social education to chance.

The Peter of this period was really charming, very frank, modest and well-mannered, with a pretty, lively wit. In 1909 he went up with a scholarship to read History at Balliol, and here, I must confess, he became rather intolerable. The world was at his feet, and he began to give himself airs. He acquired affectations, an exaggerated Oxford manner and a monocle, and aired his opinions a good deal, both in and out of the Union, though I will do him the justice to say that he never attempted to patronise his mother or me. He was in his second year when Denver broke his neck out hunting and Gerald succeeded to the title. Gerald showed more sense of responsibility than I had expected in dealing with the estate; his worst mistake was to marry his cousin Helen, a scrawny, over-bred prude, all county from head to heel. She and Peter loathed each other cordially; but he could always take refuge with his mother at the Dower House.

And then, in his last year at Oxford, Peter fell in love with a child of seventeen and instantly forgot everything he had ever been taught. He treated that girl as if she was made of gossamer, and me as a hardened old monster of depravity who had made him unfit to touch her delicate purity. I won't deny that they made an exquisite pair — all white and gold — a prince and princess of moonlight, people said. Moonshine would have been nearer the mark. What Peter was to do in twenty years' time with a wife who had neither brains nor character nobody but his mother and myself ever troubled to ask, and he, of course, was completely besotted. Happily, Barbara's parents decided that she was too young to marry; so Peter went in for his final Schools in the temper of a Sir Eglamore achieving his first dragon; laid his First-Class Honours at his lady's feet like the dragon's head, and settled down to a period of virtuous probation.

Then came the War. Of course the young idiot was mad to get married before he went. But his own honourable scruples made him mere wax in other people's hands. It was pointed out to him that if he came back mutilated it would be very unfair to the girl. He hadn't thought of that, and rushed off in a frenzy of self-abnegation to release her from the engagement. I had no hand in that; I was glad enough of the result, but I couldn't stomach the means.

He did very well in France; he made a good officer and the men liked him. And then, if you please, he came back on leave with his captaincy in '16, to find the girl married — to a hardbitten rake of a Major Somebody, whom she had nursed in the V.A.D, hospital, and whose motto with women was catch 'em quick and treat 'em rough. It was pretty brutal; for the girl hadn't had the nerve to tell Peter beforehand. They got married in a hurry when they heard he was coming home, and all he got on landing was a letter, announcing the *fait accompli* and reminding him that he had set her free himself.

I will say for Peter that he came straight to me and admitted that he had been a fool. 'All right,' said I, 'you've had your lesson. Don't go and make a fool of yourself in the other direction.' So he went back to his job with (I am sure) the fixed intention of getting killed; but all he got was his majority and his D.S.O. for some recklessly good intelligence work behind the German front. In 1918 he was blown up and buried in a shell-hole near Caudry, and that left him with a bad nervous breakdown, lasting, on and off, for two years. After that, he set himself up in a flat in Piccadilly, with the man Bunter (who had been his sergeant and was, and is, devoted to him), and started out to put himself together again.

I don't mind saying that I was prepared for almost anything. He had lost all his beautiful frankness, he shut everybody out of his confidence, including his mother and me, adopted an impenetrable frivolity of manner and a dilettante pose, and became, in fact, the complete comedian. He was wealthy and could do as he chose, and it gave me a certain amount of sardonic entertainment to watch the efforts of post-war feminine London to capture him. 'It can't,' said one solicitous matron, 'be good for poor Peter to live like a hermit.' 'Madam,' said I, 'if he did, it wouldn't be.' No; from that point of view he gave me no anxiety. But I could not but think it dangerous that a man of his ability should have no job to occupy his mind, and I told him so.

In 1921 came the business of the Attenbury Emeralds. That affair has never been written up, but it made a good deal of noise, even at that noisiest of periods. But the trial of the thief was a series of red-hot sensations, and the biggest sensation of the bunch was when Lord Peter Wimsey walked into the witness-box as chief witness for the prosecution.

That was notoriety with a vengeance. Actually, to an experienced intelligence officer, I don't suppose the investigation had offered any great difficulties; but a 'noble sleuth' was something new in thrills. Denver was furious; personally, I didn't mind what Peter did, provided he did something. I thought he seemed happier for the work, and I liked the Scotland Yard man he had picked up during the run of the case. Charles Parker is a quiet, sensible, well-bred fellow, and has been a good friend and brother-in-law to Peter. He has the valuable quality of being fond of people without wanting to turn them inside out.

The only trouble about Peter's new hobby was that it had to be more than a hobby, if it was to be any hobby for a gentleman. You cannot get murderers hanged for your private entertainment. Peter's intellect pulled him one way and his nerves another, till I began to be afraid they would pull him to pieces. At the end of every case we had the old nightmares and shell-shock over again. And then Denver, of all people — Denver, the crashing great booby, in the middle of his fulminations against Peter's degrading and notorious police activities, must needs get himself indicated on a murder charge and stand his trial in the House of Lords, amid a blaze of publicity which made all Peter's efforts in that direction look like damp squibs.

Peter pulled his brother out of that mess, and,

to my relief, was human enough to get drunk on the strength of it. He now admits that his 'hobby' is his legitimate work for society, and has developed sufficient interest in public affairs to undertake small diplomatic jobs from time to time under the Foreign Office, Of late he has become a little more ready to show his feelings, and a little less terrified of having to show.

His latest eccentricity had been to fall in love with that girl whom he cleared of the charge of poisoning her lover. She refused to marry him, as any woman of character would. Gratitude and a humiliating inferiority complex are no foundation for matrimony; the position was false from the start. Peter had the sense, this time, to take my advice. 'My boy,' I said, 'what was wrong for you twenty years back is right now. It's not the innocent young things that need gentle handling — it's the ones that have been frightened and hurt. Begin again from the beginning — but I warn you that you will need all the self-discipline you have ever learnt.'

Well, he has tried. I don't think I have ever seen such patience. The girl has brains and character and honesty; but he has got to teach her how to take, which is far more difficult than learning to give. I think they will find one another, if they can keep their passions from running ahead of their wills. He does realise, I know, that in this case there can be no consent but free consent.

Peter is forty-five now, it is really time he was settled. As you will see, I have been one of the important formative influences in his career, and, on the whole, I feel he does me credit. He is a true Delagardie, with little of the Wimseys about him except (I must be fair) that underlying sense of social responsibility which prevents the English landed gentry from being a total loss, spiritually speaking. Detective or no detective, he is a scholar and a gentleman; it will amuse me to see what sort of shot he makes at being a husband and father. I am getting an old man, and have no son of my own (that I know of); I should be glad to see Peter happy. But as his mother says, 'Peter has always had everything except the things he really wanted,' and I suppose he is luckier than most.

PAUL AUSTIN DELAGARDIE

WIMSEY, PETER DEATH BREDON, D.S.O.; *born* 1890, *2nd son* of Mortimer Gerald Bredon Wimsey, 15th Duke of Denver, and of Honoria Lucasta, *daughter of* Francis Delagardie of Bellingham Manor, Hants.

Educated: Eton College and Balliol College, Oxford (1st class honours, Sch. of Mod. Hist. 1912); served with H.M. Forces 1914/18 (Major, Rifle Brigade). *Author of:* 'Notes on the Collecting of Incunabula', 'The Murderer's Vade-Mecum', etc. *Recreations:* Criminology; bibliophily; music; cricket.

Clubs: Marlborough; Egotists'. *Residences:* 110A Piccadilly, W.; Bredon Hall, Duke's Denver, Norfolk.

Arms: Sable, 3 mice courant, argent; crest, a domestic cat crouched as to spring, proper; motto: As my Whimsy takes me.

We do hope that you have enjoyed reading this large print book.

Did you know that all of our titles are available for purchase?

We publish a wide range of high quality large print books including:

Romances, Mysteries, Classics
General Fiction
Non Fiction and Westerns

Special interest titles available in large print are:

The Little Oxford Dictionary
Music Book
Song Book
Hymn Book
Service Book

Also available from us courtesy of Oxford University Press:

Young Readers' Dictionary
(large print edition)
Young Readers' Thesaurus
(large print edition)

For further information or a free brochure, please contact us at:

Ulverscroft Large Print Books Ltd.,
The Green, Bradgate Road, Anstey,
Leicester, LE7 7FU, England.
Tel: (00 44) 0116 236 4325
Fax: (00 44) 0116 234 0205